POP STAR

FAMOUS BOOK 1

EDEN FINLEY

POP STAR

CHAPTER 1
HARLEY

WHAT HAPPENS when the most successful boy band on the planet breaks up?

How about twenty thousand screaming fans yelling my name.

Only my name.

The atmosphere of a stadium show is indescribable. I've never gotten used to it. Not while in a group, and definitely not as the focus of everyone's attention. No matter how much previous fame I had, no matter how many dollars line my pockets, and no matter how many Grammys I have on my mantel.

The awards wouldn't mean shit if not for the people in this audience tonight.

Constant flashes go off from cell phone cameras, the people at the front try to push their way closer by pressing themselves against the barricades, and the whole stadium is buzzing with a high that's more addictive than any drug.

The pulse of the crowd beats through my veins. I can taste it in the sweat on my top lip.

It's the part of the set toward the end where I slow things down and have a chance to take it all in. I sing a slew of ballads from my backlog of mostly peppy, teenybopper songs.

I'm on my last show of a short tour, so I need to take a breath and savor it because it'll be a while before I'm on the road again.

All the long hours in a recording studio, all the painstaking interviews and promotion for the tour, it all comes down to this. And the payoff is so worth it.

When I strike the opening chords on my acoustic guitar to my latest single "Confusion," the crowd goes wild and Pride flags appear from all corners of the audience.

Since the track dropped as a surprise release six months ago, I've become somewhat of a queer icon. My label and public relations team have worked overtime for years trying to keep the truth of my orientation a secret, but with one song, speculation is everywhere. A simple google search will bring up countless articles and blogs questioning my sexuality.

Of course, releasing a song with the guy who broke my heart wasn't exactly subtle, but whenever I'm asked about the meaning behind the song, I point them in Radioactive's direction and to my ex, Jay, who cowrote this song. He's already an out and proud artist.

I give nonanswers, making sure I stick to ally-focused vocabulary.

It's the most freedom my label has allowed me. It's not much, but as I stare out over the crowd and see the support and love they have for this song, my heart feels full knowing I'm doing something to contribute to the community. *My community.*

People have tweeted me when they've come out to their families and thanked me for inspiring them.

Pride fills my veins knowing the song has been received so well, and as I glance offstage to where my manager and assistant are standing, my heart sinks at the reminder they're the only two people I have to share this moment with.

People I *pay* to be here.

I close my eyes and concentrate on the song when my voice cracks with an unintentional rasp.

> *You help me escape*
> *A life I can't lead*
> *A life I need to hide*

I swallow hard at the heartache attached to this song and at the empty spot next to my manager, Gideon. A spot I wish I could fill with someone who chooses to be there. Who *wants* to be there.

It's something I've craved nearly my entire career. For a while, I had it.

And then I lost it.

Because I chose this life over one filled with love.

After the song, I finish the rest of the set with the kind of energy my fans deserve from me. It involves a lot of jumping, a lot of using as much of the stage as I can so each person in the audience can get a piece of me.

"Great show," Gideon says as I finally leave the stage after my third encore.

As far as managers go, he's a good one, but he's extremely business oriented. He's your stereotypical suit. Always immaculately dressed with his phone permanently attached to his hand.

"Uh-huh."

My assistant hands me a towel to wipe the sweat from my head, and then I want to kiss her when she passes me a packet of M&M's.

We walk through the halls of the arena to my dressing room so I can shower and change before doing VIP meet and greets with fans who have paid an insane amount of money to chat with me for three minutes and get a photo.

It's hectic, but it's my life.

And I love it.

I get into fresh clothes and take the chance to grab a drink and have twenty minutes of downtime before I'm due in the VIP room. And by downtime, I mean going through all the gifts and fan mail people brought to the arena.

"How many of them are creepy this time?" I ask my assistant.

Jamie's an adorable, recent college grad with a short pixie haircut, thick-rimmed glasses, and a bubbly attitude. She hands me some handwritten letters. "Only four marriage proposals, one offer to go to Thanksgiving family dinner, and, uh, a really gross pair of underwear."

I cock my head. "Gross?"

"There was, like … stuff in them I don't even want to think about."

Gideon's towering presence looms over me. "Now that you're

home for a while, I think we need to reassess the security situation again."

Ugh. He's been on this since a fan somehow snuck past security and was in my dressing room one night during this tour.

"Why now? Because some chick sent me her used underwear? Not the first time that's happened."

"It was, uh, a guy's underwear," Jamie says.

I grin. "Did it come with a photo?"

"Harley, this is serious," Gideon says.

"No, it's not. It's fan mania. People being in my dressing room and giving me dirty underwear is nothing compared to some of the stuff we got on an Eleven tour. We once had tiny vials of blood sent on chains to wear around our necks. Now, that's fucking crazy. The current security team is fine."

If I ever need to go out, I have a driver and bodyguard on call. On tour, we have an entire team that follows me around from the venue to the hotel, and anywhere I want to go in between. It *works*.

It took my security team three seconds to get the fan out of my dressing room, so it was never a dangerous or risky situation.

I don't need someone full-time. I don't need someone living with me.

In my own home, I can be *me*. That's my safe space—*our* safe space. Mine and Evah's.

My relationship with my "fiancée" is, and always has been, a publicity stunt organized by my record label. It was a punishment of sorts for rumors spreading about me and Jay.

Apparently, letting the world know I'm gay would result in a loss of music sales so drastic that my career would be over. This is what music execs have told me for the better part of a decade. Do I believe them? Enough that I'm not going to risk everything I've sacrificed so much for.

Even when I question them by throwing artists like Sam Smith in their face, they tell me I'm no Sam Smith.

Thanks.

They remind me I'm one fifth of a complete act—a boy bander trying to make it on his own.

And I believe them. Every time.

Because I know how easy it is for careers to end.

Mason, one of the guys from Eleven, had a crappy solo album release. Music is over for him. Blake had every intention of trying to make it on his own but only got halfway through cutting his album before landing a major acting gig. He hasn't looked back since. Aside from a small group of fans, no one's asking for his next single.

It's that easy to disappear from this life, and if I throw my career away over something as trivial as who I have in my bed at night, I will lose my ever-loving shit. I don't see how it's relevant to making music.

Music is my life. Always has been.

It was there for me during my awkward preteen years when Harry Stench was being teased for being short, chubby, and, well, having the last name *Stench*. After puberty did its job, and I'd hunked out, Mom realized I had star potential. She sent in an audition video to Joystar Records, and just like that, we left Kansas and were flown out to LA. The label immediately wanted to sign me to a boy band they were putting together, and that's when they made me Harley Valentine.

I don't need anyone prying into my life and finding out that underneath it all, I'm still *Harry Stench*.

"I think you need someone full-time watching your back," Gideon says. "An NDA will mean a twenty-four-seven bodyguard wouldn't be able to talk to the press if that's what you're worrying about."

Ugh. More NDAs. Like that's what I need. I think it's at a point where if something leaked about my life, we wouldn't know who broke their contract and we couldn't sue anyway. My sexuality wasn't a well-kept secret between Eleven and the crew.

"I'll think about it," I mutter to shut Gideon up.

I love fame.

I love my life.

But sometimes it's too overwhelming. I want a break from it but then remind myself I can't stop even for a second. I have to keep pushing. Keep going.

The VIP party is like the billion others I've done. It's basically a conveyor belt of rotating fans coming up to take photos and squeal in my face. They ask about Evah and look mostly disappointed when I tell them she's visiting her parents in Kansas. Some look hopeful, like Evah being out of town means they have a chance. It's not anything I haven't heard before.

On the way out, I nod and wave to some fans lurking by the back door, and then venue security puts me into the back seat of the Escalade waiting for me.

All in all, it was a successful night, successful tour, and now I'm looking forward to doing nothing but writing songs for the new album I'm set to record in six weeks.

Twenty minutes later, my driver pulls up to my short driveway and waits in the car until I put my passcode into the gate before taking off.

The Spanish Colonial property set me back a cool ten mil, but it's big enough for Evah and me so we're not living on top of each other.

I unlock my door using an app on my phone, which still amazes me. Sure, the multimillion-dollar views of LA are breathtaking, but *I can unlock my house with an app!*

I flick on the lights and make my way to my bathroom for another shower. The guys from Eleven used to mock me for my germ phobia, but after our first ever tour, I got hit with the flu. And I don't mean the sniffly kind. I mean bedridden, fevers, vomiting, and delirium for *weeks*. I needed an IV of fluids and antibiotics for the infection I got from it. Since that happened, I shower after any meet and greet and try not to flinch if someone so much as coughs within five feet of me.

Dressed in sweats, my hair still damp, I scroll through social media on my phone while heading for the kitchen to get a snack.

I easily become lost in the world of Twitter, reading tweets about the show—egotistical maybe, but I read it for the feedback as well as the praise. If there's something I could be doing more or doing better, I want to know about it.

The fans made me who I am, and I owe everything to them.

But as my feet carry me across the cool tile, something feels off.

I get the sense I'm not alone, but Evah's not here. Unless she came home early from Kansas. I check my billions of unread messages, but none are from her.

The hairs on the back of my neck prickle.

I look up from my phone and see a guy I don't recognize sitting on a stool at my kitchen bar.

My skin breaks out in goose bumps.

I blink, thinking I'm confused or hallucinating or something. He's still there, so I blink again.

I even look around the room as if I'm the one in the wrong place. Like, it was possible for me to walk into the wrong house, shower in the wrong bathroom, and put on a stranger's sweats.

Because someone getting in, let alone looking so casual about it, doesn't make sense.

Him being here isn't even the scariest thing. It's the small smile he wears. It's … normal-looking. Cute, even. Which is why it terrifies me. He doesn't even appear to be apologetic about breaking in.

His T-shirt is old Eleven merch from a tour a few years ago, and as he stands, he slides his hand into the pocket of his ripped skinny jeans.

Seconds pass where we stare at each other.

This isn't some fan sneaking into my dressing room. This is my *home*.

Headlines from tomorrow's news flash through my head: *Harley Valentine Killed in Home Invasion.*

I'm going to die.

Breathe, Harley. Stay calm.

I glance at the counter where he was sitting, and yep, there's my knife block that usually lives about three feet to the right.

Oh shit, oh shit, oh shit.

"I thought it looked cool."

I startle at his voice, which is calm and casual, much like his demeanor. That only freaks me out more.

"Looked cool?" I manage to keep my voice flat. Somehow.

"Yeah." His smile brightens.

I don't understand because he looks so … *sane.* The kitchen lights make his pale skin glow. His dark hair is trendy. He's so average-looking that meeting him on the street wouldn't make me think twice.

But he's in my *house.* He has to be a few cards short of a full deck.

My phone is still in my hand, but I'm scared if I dial 911, he'll hear it and get to me before the cops can.

He runs a finger over my knife block which is one of those novelty things where it's in the shape of a man and the knives sit through different parts of his body. "Thought it was funny."

I swallow hard. "Ah, Evah actually bought that for me as a joke."

He frowns. "I don't know how I feel about that or how this is gonna work with her."

This keeping calm thing is hard, but I try. "How what is going to work with her?"

My hands shake. I want to put them in my pockets to cover the trembling, but I need my phone to get me out of this. I need to alert someone without actually making a phone call or being obvious that I'm texting.

My finger hovers over the home button, and that's when I remember the emergency function Gideon set up for me. If I tap the button three times fast, it'll send Gideon a recording, my location, and photos.

I don't do it yet. It only records a ten-second snippet, and I need to get this guy's name or somehow record why he's here so when Gideon gets the message, he understands I'm in danger. I don't think I'll be able to aim the camera part properly without him realizing what I'm doing, so the photo part won't help me.

I itch to press the button—to get help—but I tell myself to breathe and calm down. I need to wait for the perfect moment for it to actually help.

"Well, when you told me tonight that Evah's out of town, I thought that maybe ... you were doing it to let us all know you were available. Then on your way out when you nodded to me to follow you, I almost told myself not to do it. You're engaged, you know? It's wrong for us to hook up."

Okay, he's not only psycho but goddamn delusional.

I do it—I hit the button on my phone three times and say, "So you followed me home from the concert."

"Yeah."

"How'd you get in here?"

His eyes widen, and I watch as his hand taps along the kitchen counter closer to the knives.

"Only because I was planning to come out and get you," I say to appease him. "After my shower. Sorry I didn't make that part clear." I hope if this is still recording that Gideon can hear the edge in my voice.

Mr. Psycho lets out a loud breath. "I thought for a second I might have read this whole situation wrong."

You think?

The phone vibrates in my hand, and it's Gideon. He got the SOS message and is probably checking up on me instead of doing what I wanted him to do, which is call the LAPD.

I wonder if I can answer it without tipping this guy off. I move to put my phone in my pocket as casually as I can and hit the Answer button as I do.

"So, Evah's away, I gestured for you to follow me, and when you got here, you …"

He chuckles. "I didn't quite know what to do when you didn't leave the gate unlocked for me. I looked for a side entrance or something and then saw the gate between your yard and the neighbor's. It led me to the side of the house where the fence is lower, so I jumped it and went to your front door which was unlocked. It was easy."

Fucking app.

The fact he finds nothing wrong with what he's saying scares me most of all.

"Oh. Right."

"What's the deal with you and Evah, anyway? You're allowed to hook up when you're not together?"

I begin to think this is all a huge misunderstanding by a fan who thinks he knows me and is under the delusion we have a connection. It's definitely not the first time that's happened, though this is the first with a guy.

My heart pounds so hard my body must think I'm working out. I break into a sweat, and I worry he can see it running down my face.

I blink and try to remember what he asked. "Umm, no, Evah and I don't have a deal. I've never done this before."

The guy finally moves his hand away from the knife block. He goes to take a step closer to me, but on instinct I stumble back.

His face falls, and his jaw hardens.

"I want to get to know you," I blurt.

"What do you want to know?"

My mouth opens, but no sound comes out.

He steps closer again.

I step back. "Your name. There's a start."

It's not the thing he wanted to hear. "I told you my name when we met tonight."

I want to yell *I met a million people tonight*. How am I supposed to remember his name when I can't even remember his face or actually meeting him at all?

"Sorry." I try to laugh it off. "I'm terrible with names."

He flicks his dark hair out of his eyes. "Billy."

"Uh. Well, nice to meet you … again, Billy."

"You seem really nervous," he states.

No shit.

"L-like I said, I've n-never d-done this before." Now I'm stuttering. Brilliant.

"With any guy? I figured because of the song—"

"The song isn't about me. Common misconception." I need to shut this guy down the easiest way possible—play the straight card.

"You're seriously standing there and telling me you and Jay from Radioactive didn't have this epic romance before he went and married some other guy?"

"That's what I'm saying. We were friends, and we collaborated on a song. End of story." Not quite, but telling myself that makes it hurt less.

Oh, great, now he's singing. "*Confusing love with isolation, holding on in desperation, I thought I'd found my one, the one I'm meant to keep …* How is that not drawn from personal experience?"

"We cowrote that song. Jay did the lyrics. I wrote the melody." Now I'm flat-out lying, but hey, talking about music is better than being stabbed to death. Winning.

How the fuck am I supposed to get out of this?

"But … you invited me here."

Oh shit. Right. I already said I did that.

Keep talking. Keep him distracted.

Where the fuck is Gideon?

I want to check my phone and see if he's still on the line, but I can't draw attention to it in my pocket.

"Okay, you got me. I wanted to invite you here, but I've never been with a guy. And you're right about Evah. I don't know how she fits into all this either. And this is cheating on her, so I'm getting cold feet." Maybe I should've gone into acting instead of Blake. Although, I don't actually know how well I'm pulling this off.

The edge returns to Billy's voice. "Well, I'm here now. I went through all that effort to get in here."

A car door closes outside. It's a noise that sounds a hell of a lot like *hope.*

I hope it's Gideon or someone—*anyone*—who can help.

But most of all, I hope it's not a neighbor.

Billy tips his head toward the sound.

Keep going. Keep talking. Pretend you didn't hear anything, and don't let him think someone's here.

I step closer to him this time. "Sorry, you're right. I shouldn't have led you on."

"Then don't." His feet inch toward me.

A few more steps and he'll be on top of me.

"Wait." I hold up my hand. "Uh … wait a second. I, uh, I'm …" I'm stalling for time I don't think I have.

Disappointment fills my stomach with lead. If that was a car outside, they're not here for me or they're taking their sweet-ass time in coming to rescue me.

I swear I can hear voices too, but maybe it's the million thoughts running through my head.

I don't know what else I can do.

"You're …" He moves, and I step back.

I'm about to be backed against a wall, and then I really won't have an escape.

Pain shoots down my side as I hit a decorative table with a steel piece of art I don't remember buying but somehow have. I manage to save the art, but Billy is the closest he's been yet.

And as the gap keeps getting smaller and smaller, I close my eyes and wish for it to end quickly.

There's a beat of complete silence, and then out of nowhere, the sound of doors flying open, yelling, and stampeding feet fills my ears.

I take a peek and find a team of people in black storming into the room. With their guns pointed in our direction, one of them yells, "Get down on the ground."

The voice is so commanding, *I* almost do as it says.

Billy's quick to sink to his knees, but he stares up at me with utter disappointment, hurt, and betrayal in his green eyes.

"Hands on your head!"

He does as he's told but doesn't take his eyes off me.

I'm frozen, standing completely still as if his gaze has locked me in place.

Arms come at me from the side and drag me away. It happens so fast, I try to elbow whoever it is because my mind hasn't quite comprehended that it worked—that Gideon got people here in time.

It isn't until a woman says, "You're safe," that I relax and let her lead me wherever she's taking me.

I'm deposited on my couch, but I shake uncontrollably.

The officer's hand squeezes my shoulder. "Is there anything or anyone I can get for you?"

"Gideon," I croak. "My manager."

"The guy who called it in?"

"Yeah."

"He's outside. He got here as we were about to charge in." She talks over her radio to send him in, and I'm thankful she didn't have to leave me alone to do it.

I can't get my breathing under control.

Gideon bursts into the room and lands on his knees at my feet. "Harley?"

I sniff and wipe away tears that streak my face. I didn't realize I was crying until right now.

With a deep breath, I meet Gideon's gaze. "I'll do it. I'll hire a bodyguard."

CHAPTER 2
BRIX

GRAVEL CRUNCHES under my almost-bald tires. My shitty 1999 Honda makes a grinding noise as I park in my assigned position. I usually pull in and park my heap of junk next to Corvettes, convertible Mustangs, and Aston Martins, but today, the lot is empty.

Working for Mike Bravo Ops pays well—better than what a sergeant in the US Army earns—but medical bills cost more. There's no fighting that.

When we're all called in, and our cars are lined up, it's not hard to play a game of *one of these things is not like the other*.

I grab my bag full of stuff that'll get me through the next few weeks, take my coffee from the cupholder, and then get in the zone as I move toward HQ.

A new mission means I need my head in the game. I'm too distracted by that to notice Iris coming up the drive. I'm almost taken out by his Charger.

He's a complete show pony but decent to work with, and I'm guessing he's here for the same op.

His engine revs as he pulls his handbrake and drifts into the parking spot next to mine, kicking up gravel and dust everywhere.

Yup. Total show pony.

He's got slick brown hair, aviators, and a model face that makes all the boys and girls drool.

He's a little overstated for my tastes. Pretty guys are not my thing.

I like rugged guys. The more masculine the better. Find me a guy who has the ability to throw me around, and I'm theirs. No questions asked. No strings.

Iris catches up to me. "Any idea what the job is?"

"No idea. Boss was vague."

"You know what that means."

I nod. "Yup. It's a job we're gonna hate."

"I'm guessing recon on some bad guy where we have to stake out his place for weeks."

"Fuck. That'd be the worst."

"Aww, don't want to spend that much time with me?" Iris lifts his glasses and flutters his lashes at me.

"I love you, brother, but not that much."

He's not even offended. "That's okay. I'm better in small doses. Even my mother used to tell me that."

"That could be the saddest thing I've ever heard."

"Right? Feel sorry for me!"

I glance back at his Charger. "Yeah. So sorry for you."

"Where *does* all your money go? We're all on the same pay grade."

"Nice try."

The guys ask, but I never tell. I don't need them acting like the brothers they are. Brothers-in-arms to the core … professionally. When it comes to my personal life, it's my mess to deal with.

"You're secretly divorced, have six kids, and your ex takes all your money?"

"Nailed it, man. *Nailed it*. Their names are Brix Jr, Brix III, Brix IV, Brixley, Brixany, and … John."

He doesn't even blink. "I'm not the brains of this group for nothing."

He is far from the brains. He's the agile one we send into tight ops. The one who's so stealthy he can extract a target and take out three guys without anyone noticing until hours later.

He's the most lethal and the least sane, but I guess those things go hand in hand.

Iris claps me on the back and leads me into the house.

Travis West's mansion is our main base of operation, and in the four years I've worked for Mike Bravo Ops, I've never seen the boss anywhere but in our operation center. Supposedly, he lives at the opposite end of the house, but I've found him sleeping in our control room more times than I can count.

Today, he's in our war room.

"Take a seat." Firm and authoritative as always.

We sit opposite him, and he slides files over to us.

The company does a large range of ops, whether it be for military, government, or private clients. It ranges from extractions, intel gathering, and sometimes taking out bad men who do bad things. All *off the books* kinds of things.

Which is why the contents of my folder doesn't make much sense.

"We have to take out a pop star?" Iris asks.

Trav grumbles. "Of course you'd go there first. No. You're not taking him out. It's your job to protect him."

"From what?" I ask.

"Rabid fans," Trav says. "One broke into his house, so now he's after full security detail."

"Security …" My gaze flies to his.

"Bodyguards."

"As in glorified *babysitters*?" My voice goes high-pitched.

"Starting a new avenue for the business, boss?" Iris asks. "We're not really on the *protecting* side of things."

The opposite, actually.

"It's a favor to my cousin Gideon. He's Harley Valentine's manager."

Then something in the file catches my eye. "Live-in? We'll be living with him?"

"You will be. You're taking point. Iris will take over on Sundays, which will be your one day off."

Full-time. Live-in. With a pop star.

No, thank you.

"Am I being punished for something?" I ask.

"Punished?" Trav cocks an eyebrow. "Did you see the pay packet on this job? And you get a company car. Can't exactly protect someone in that shit box of yours."

I glance back down.

Damn, that's a lot of zeros. I'm not exactly in a position to turn it down. "Why's it so much?"

"Celebrities need to pay their employees a significant salary so they can't be tempted by a tabloid payday."

Makes sense.

"How long's the job?" I ask.

"Six months, but it could be longer. It depends on how long his next album takes to record and if they'll want you on his next tour at which time we'll reassess."

Permanent. Minimum six months.

"I can't," I blurt. That's too long. Then I look at the pay again.

I could really use this money. No, I *need* this money.

"You can't?" Iris says. "I'll do it. For that much money, I'll be his personal rent boy."

"Of course you would," I mutter.

"Iris, give us a moment."

Even though we're all no longer military, Iris follows the order as fast as if he still were. We all do it when it comes to Trav.

He's a great boss. His instincts are always on point, and we all trust him with our lives.

As soon as the door is closed behind Iris, Trav leans back in his seat.

His biceps bulge, and for a guy in his early forties, he's in better shape than I am. I may or may not have had a giant crush on the guy when I started working for him.

"You need this money," he says.

No point in arguing it. "I do. But I need it without having to be away for that long."

"How much are you in the hole?"

I try not to let my reaction show. My personal life is my own, but it's obvious to all the guys that I'm broke for a reason. I just don't know how much Trav knows.

"Over a hundred Gs." I lower my voice. "Closer to two hundred, really."

"You need this contract, and it's six months."

My knee bounces. "Six months without killing anyone. How will I survive?"

"Well, this fan is out on bail, so you might see some action."

"Here's hoping for more stalker problems, then." I realize my words after I've already said them. "I'm really doing this, aren't I?"

"You can say no."

"For that much money, I really can't." I run my hands over my buzz cut. A lot of the other guys have let their hair grow out since leaving the military, but it's order and routine for me, even now, years after being discharged. It keeps me connected to my old life that I wasn't ready to give up.

"Any questions?" Trav asks.

"Yeah. Who is Harley Valentine?"

Right after Trav gets his tears under control from laughing at my supposed ignorance, Iris comes in and I start getting it from him too.

Iris is *still* laughing.

It hasn't stopped, even on our separate drives to Valentine's place. The phone rings, and the car's Bluetooth immediately picks up.

"This line is supposed to be for emergencies," I grumble.

Take the company car, Trav said. It's better than yours, Trav said. Mine doesn't even have Bluetooth. I could escape this if I were in my own car.

"Your lack of pop culture knowledge is an emergency, bro—"

I hit End on the connection.

He calls back.

There's no escaping Iris's onslaught.

It's not my fault I live under a rock.

Iris is still shaking his head at me when we pull into the pop star's small drive and approach the secure gate.

"I think it's more disturbing that grown-ass men know boy band trivia," I point out. "I don't think you're in a position to be laughing at me."

"He's not in a boy band anymore. He's, like, a legit artist. Won two Grammys."

"You know who else has a Grammy? The guys who sang that dog song. It's not that impressive."

Iris starts singing "Who Let the Dogs Out" as he pushes the buzzer to be let into the property.

What have I done?

Now I have that stupid song in my head.

I jump Iris and get him in a headlock, covering his mouth with my hand.

He bites me.

"Fuck." I shake out the pain.

"It's okay. I don't have rabies."

It's impossible to be mad even as the bite mark darkens on my palm. Being angry at Iris would be like yelling at a puppy for peeing everywhere. He can't help it.

At least Iris is potty trained.

The gate clicks open, and I make sure it locks automatically again when we pass through it, which it does.

The brick fence is secure but easy to scale for anyone who's fit. Any of the guys in Mike Bravo could jump it without a run-up.

A man opens the door. He's shiny in the way a lot of Hollywood people are. Dark hair, tailored suit, pompous vibe.

He waves a finger between us. "Nolan Reins?"

"That'd be me." I reach out to shake his hand.

"Gideon." He moves on to Iris.

"Isaac Griffin. I'm the Sunday man."

"Come in, and I'll show you around."

"Where's the client?" I ask.

"Harley's sleeping. Finally. It's been a rough few days since the break-in. I've asked him to see someone about it, but he refuses."

We're shown around the expansive property that's terracotta tiled throughout with Spanish tile accents. There are a lot of official-looking sitting rooms and wood-paneled doors that lead to more spaces that appear untouched. A wrought-iron banister follows the stairs to a second floor, and Gideon points out Harley's bedroom as well as four other bedrooms that are empty.

The whole place is furnished to match the Spanish Colonial theme, but it looks unlived in. I was expecting maybe a party house with big sound systems and large-screen TVs everywhere.

It feels like I'm in someone's parents' house, not the house of a famous pop star.

"I'll show you to your room." Gideon leads me to modest servant's quarters while Iris checks out the security system.

I take in the double bed that takes up most of the room and the chest of drawers underneath a wide window that looks out over the backyard and pool.

Gideon watches me for a reaction. "It's not much."

"Anything is a palace after living in barracks." Hell, this is a step up even from the shitty apartment I live in now. I turn to him. "Okay, level with me. This assignment is kinda …"

"Kinda what?"

What's the right word without saying *complete bullshit*? "I guess I don't understand it. You could get any low-grade security firm to deal with this break-in, keep tabs on the guy, *and* hire three full-time body-guards for what you're paying Trav. Why hire ex-military guys who thrive on action to babysit a pop star?"

Gideon puts his hands in his pockets. "Well, one, Trav is my cousin, and he was originally going to give me some names of compa-nies who could help me, but then he said he might have a guy who's interested in the money. And two, Harley doesn't want an entire team surrounding him. He has trouble trusting people. I'm sure it's a lot more low-key than you're used to, but think of it this way, it's easy money."

"This break-in. How serious was it?"

"The guy is a delusional fan who read into a single look and a simple sentence Harley said to him. He thought he had a 'connection' with Harley, so he followed him home, jumped the fence, and … okay, the knife thing is fuzzy. Harley still doesn't know if it was an intimidation tactic, threatening, or if this guy really was genuinely admiring Harley's knives. No one was hurt, but Harley has refused full-time security up until now because he had always felt safe here. That asshole took that away from him, so it doesn't matter that he wasn't actually hurt."

"I understand."

Gideon looks doubtful, as if he doesn't believe me. "Harley's trying to appear strong, but he hasn't left the house since it happened. He hasn't slept. He's not the type of guy to accept pity, but he won't take condescension either."

"I'll keep it in mind to stay neutral and only speak of facts when it comes to the break-in."

"I would go wake him up to meet you right now, but with how little sleep he's had, I'm reluctant. He's supposed to be writing songs for his new album, but he can't think when he's had no sleep."

"It's fine. I have some stuff in my car, but I might go home and get some more clothes and belongings. I packed light. Iris … uh, Isaac can stay with Harley while I'm gone."

"Sounds good." Gideon gestures for me to go first, and we make our way back through the house.

We don't make it to the front door.

Gideon and I both freeze in our steps at the sight of what's happening in the foyer.

A guy around five nine or ten with brown hair points a gun at Iris.

Iris is calm, his hands up, and he doesn't appear to be worried, but Iris is always cool under pressure. Frighteningly so.

The guy's back is to us, and I don't think he heard us come in. His hands shake, which makes me nervous considering the safety on his gun is off, and he's clearly not in control.

Tactical instincts kick in.

My first guess is the fan who attacked Harley a few nights ago has broken his restraining order and come to finish what he started.

It all happens so fast.

I move quickly and with precision.

The loud "No" coming out of Iris's mouth barely registers as I rush the assailant and tackle him to the ground.

In the blink of an eye, I have the guy on his stomach on the tiled floor with my knee in his back and his gun in my hand.

Then laughter pierces the room. From both Iris and Gideon.

The guy beneath me groans.

"First day on the job, and you've already broken the man you were hired to protect," Iris says.

"W-wait, what?" I stare down at the guy. His head is turned to the side with his cheek pressed against the floor. I can't make out any of his features except for the ginger scruff on his face.

Gideon steps up beside me. "Nolan, I'd like you to meet Harley Valentine."

Aww, fuck.

CHAPTER 3
HARLEY

"HARLEY, this is Nolan Reins and Isaac Griffin," Gideon says. "Your new bodyguards."

The heavy weight on top of me lifts, and I let out a grunt.

"Good work, Rambo." Even I can't tell if my words are sarcastic or genuine.

On the one hand, *Hi, random stranger on top of me. How about buying me a drink first before pinning me under your hard body?* On the other, I should be thankful my new bodyguard can take down a guy with a gun. Even if that guy is me.

In my defense, I woke up disoriented from not having had much sleep the last three days, and I found another stranger in my house.

I may have overreacted. A little.

We climb to our feet, and I come face-to-face with my ... protector-slash-UFC-superstar.

And, oh hell.

Nope.

No, no, no.

This will *not* work.

I don't have a type. I haven't had the luxury of being able to figure it out being forced into a dark closet for my entire adulthood. Guys I've been attracted to in the past have come in all shapes. But whatever my type is, this guy would top them all.

Oh, fuck, do not associate the word top with ... him.

My eyes roam over his body from his black crew cut to his muscles that are as big as mountains. His tactical pants are tight, and his all-round badassness is badass.

The only reason I'm not protesting aloud to this arrangement is because this guy has to be straight.

Gay cupid could try to penetrate him with arrows, but he'd still be immune.

Damn, don't associate this guy with the word *penetrate* either.

The deep brown color of his eyes is almost black. He stares at me, cold and calculating.

While I'm looking at him in a sexual way, he's checking me out in an assessing way—probably trying to figure out what he's working with. There's not much to find behind the pop star. I'm a scared guy with a gun.

Which he now has.

"Uh, gun?" I hold out my hand.

"Yeah, no, you don't need this." In a swift move, he releases the magazine. "Someone who can't handle a gun shouldn't be holding one." He stares at it. "Even if it's unloaded."

I glance down to see the magazine is empty. I turn to Gideon. "You gave me an unloaded gun? How is that supposed to protect me?"

"I'm not an idiot. It was to make you feel safer, not to actually use."

"Hot tip," Rambo says. "Don't aim a gun at someone unless you plan to shoot them."

"I did plan to shoot him."

"With imaginary bullets?"

"He was in my house." I turn to the other muscular but prettier guy. "But I'm sorry I pointed a gun at you."

He smiles. "Not the first time I've been shot at."

"Hey, I didn't shoot." *Yet.* It was close. All that was running through my head was shoot now, think later. Not that it would've mattered anyway because it turns out the gun wasn't *loaded*.

I'm both thankful Gideon did that and a little pissed.

What if this had been a real emergency?

Bang, bang, Mr. Bad Guy. I'm shooting you with air.

The dude who broke in has really messed me up.

For the first time in all my years of fame, I truly worried for my life that night. There have been close calls before, some scary moments with intense fans, but nothing compares to being face-to-face with someone who thinks they know you and wants the fantasy.

Rambo hands my gun back to me. "Call me Brix. I'll be with you six days a week." He nods to the pretty guy. "He'll be with you on Sundays."

"Brix? As in built like a brick shithouse?" *Fitting.*

The other guy scoffs. "Nah, as in dumb as bricks."

Brix gives his partner the finger. "I go by my middle name Brixton. Even my parents never called me Nolan."

I eye him again. I can't help it. "You don't look like a Nolan."

"You can call me Iris," the other one says.

"Which stands for 'I require intensive supervision,'" Brix adds.

Iris sighs. "That is sadly true. Not that I need supervision, but that's what it stands for."

Brix leans in. "He totally needs supervision."

"Only when in the vicinity of explosives."

"Good to see you all getting along," Gideon cuts in. "I'm going to leave you to it. I have a meeting to get to."

My brow furrows. "Meeting?"

"With the label."

"What am I in trouble for now?"

"They want you to do appearances about the intruder and talk about it."

"No way."

"That's what I keep telling them. And since there's a trial coming up, you really shouldn't talk about it publicly, so I'm going to go and convince them of that for you."

I release a loud breath. Gideon really is good at his job even if he's more impersonal than Eleven's manager. Cameron Verikas was like a father figure to us, but that might've been because we were all teenagers when we started out. We needed the guidance and reassurance that he gave. Gideon lacks that, but as an almost twenty-six-year-old, I guess I'm supposed to be above all that now.

I watch as my manager leaves me alone with the two behemoths.

They're both kind of scary-looking, but apparently my dick likes that.

Who knew?

"I'm gonna take off too," Brix says. "But I'll be back soon."

"Where are you going?" I ask.

"Getting my life in order if I'm going to be away from it for months."

"Sorry for taking you away from your real life," I say. It comes out a little sarcastic, but I don't mean it to. It's annoying that I have to interrupt someone else's life so I can feel safe.

"He has no life," Iris says. "You're not taking him away from anything."

Brix doesn't even give Iris the satisfaction of reacting to his jab. He turns on his heel and says, "I'll be back in a few hours," as if Iris never said anything at all.

As soon as he's out the door, I feel Iris's gaze from across the room.

Nothing says awkward like facing the guy you were pointing a gun at not five minutes ago. Unloaded or not.

"So, how does this full-time bodyguard thing work, anyway?" I ask.

Iris shrugs. "You tell us. We're not exactly … trained in protecting."

I frown. "What are you trained in?"

"Killing."

My eyes widen, and Iris breaks into laughter.

"We're all ex-military at Mike Bravo."

"Mike Bravo," I repeat.

"The company we work for."

"The security firm?" That's what Gideon said they were.

Iris smirks. "Sure. Look, we've faced a lot scarier situations than your break-in. We'll have no problem making sure no one gets to you, but this will go a lot smoother if Gideon has instructions or protocols for us to follow."

"Umm, I don't think he left anything." I search the kitchen countertops and then the coffee table in the living room, but there's nothing.

"We could come up with our own protocol," Iris suggests.

"Shouldn't Brix be here for that?"

The look in Iris's eyes worries me. He's way too into this idea. "Oh, trust me, we'll write everything down to give to him."

"Why do I get the feeling you're doing this to fuck with Brix?"

"Me? Never. I'm totally serious and professional at all times."

I don't believe him in the slightest. "Mmhmm."

"Besides, don't you want payback for him tackling you?" He blinks at me with an innocent look on his angelic face.

"You're either really good at manipulation or terrible at it because I can see right through your act, but I still want to do it."

He winks. "Already discovered the whole extent of my charm."

I don't yet know what to make of my new bodyguards, but they're definitely not what I was expecting.

This could either be fun or a nightmare of sexual frustration.

Brix is all hard lines and strong features, and even though he tackled me, it oddly gives me faith in his ability to protect me, which kind of turns me on. Iris, on the other hand, has a slightly smaller build than Brix and is more typically attractive, but he's still a bulky meathead.

And I have to be reading into it, but Iris is a little flirty. Or it's been so long since I've had sex, I have no idea what social cues mean anymore.

That's where the problem lies. I can't find the guys who'll be watching my back for the next few months attractive. That's a distraction I don't need.

"Let's bang out some details." Iris heads in the direction of the living room. "You got a laptop?"

"Uh, no. I have my phone."

"Old-school pen and paper, it is."

"I have an endless supply of that." I write out my lyrics on paper. I've tried typing them out before, but there's something about pen and paper that connects me to the emotions in the songs better than staring at a screen or tapping away at a keyboard.

I have stationery hidden everywhere in the house like an addict hiding their stash.

Pulling open the drawer of the coffee table, I pull out blank paper and an array of pens.

Iris takes them from me. "First thing we'll need is your routine. Oh, and to organize getting a new security system. The one you have now is complete bullshit."

"No more unlocking my house with an app?"

"Aww, you want a gimmick or, you know, to not die? You pick."

"Good point."

"I propose we put code pads on all the doors with automatic locks so you don't have to remember to lock them."

"Deal."

"So, routine?"

"Right. It, uh, changes constantly. I'm usually not told until the day of because if Gideon tells me beforehand, I get confused."

"So, Gideon will have a more detailed schedule for you?"

"Yeah."

"Do you have a daily routine, like going to the gym or, I dunno, like, singing lessons or something?"

I snort. "Singing lessons? You mean vocal coaching? I'm offended you think I need it."

He winces as if he knows he's done or said something wrong. "It, I, uh, no … you don't need it … Uh, my girlfriend totally loves you."

"Oh, your *girlfriend* totally loves me." And yep, it doesn't matter if he's flirty, because as suspected, he's straight.

"Hey, at least I knew who you were."

"Brix didn't?"

Iris blinks. "I figured you guessed that when he tackled you."

"I'm so going to keep that in my back pocket for when I need it."

Iris smiles.

"By the way, I do have a vocal coach. I just wanted to see what you'd say if I put you on the spot."

Iris seems surprised. Or amused. Maybe both. "Working with you might be more fun than I expected. No, wait, correction. Watching you work with Brix will be fun."

"I get the sense he's a bit … uptight?"

"Uptight is a better word for stubborn, so sure, let's go with that."

Hmm, what happens when two stubborn men are thrust into

living together? I guess we're going to find out.

Fun times.

Before I prod Iris to elaborate, he changes the topic.

"So, you go to see your vocal coach. What other places do you frequently go to? Gym? Which grocery store do you use?"

"Umm, Angela—my vocal coach—comes to the house once a week. Twice a week when I'm cutting an album. I have a personal trainer who comes three times a week, and we work out in the gym downstairs, and my groceries are brought in by my chef who does my meal plans for the week."

"You never leave your house?"

I don't miss his condescension. "Only when I need to."

"What do you do for fun?"

My mouth opens to throw out answers, but they die on the tip of my tongue. "I work. That's my fun. Performing in front of thousands of fans is fun."

Iris writes something down I can't see from where I'm sitting.

Then I truly think about my answer. A lot would argue that being famous is fun. Glamour, glitz, and extravagance. But if I really think about the last time I went out with friends and had actual fun …

I draw a blank.

I used to go out with the guys from Eleven, but we're talking VIP sections of clubs so we wouldn't get mobbed, high security, and artificial fun environments where we were constantly paranoid about what we were doing and who was watching.

It's been a long time since I've been able to go out without that cautious voice in the back of my head warning me about impending stampedes of fans.

First-world problems, I guess.

Iris writes a few more things down on his list and then grins up at me. "How much will you care if Brix's first impression of you isn't the best?"

"You mean second impression? His first impression was me pointing a gun at you like a crazy man. How much worse can it get?"

"I'm taking that as permission to go full pop star diva on him."

I laugh. "That actually might be close to the truth."

"Definitely gonna be so much fun."

CHAPTER 4
BRIX

WHEN I RETURN to the house, laughter filters through the large empty space as soon as I open the door.

It doesn't sound like Iris, but imagining the guy from earlier today—the one on edge, the one willing to *shoot* someone—he doesn't seem like the type of person to go from erratic to laughing so easily.

Yet, when I walk through the kitchen area and into the sitting room, there's no denying the happy sound is coming from Harley Valentine's mouth.

I have to admit, it's a mesmerizing mouth. His smile lights up his whole face. Gone is the tired-looking, wrecked man I met earlier.

His stormy-blue eyes shine when he laughs, and his long, ginger-tinged lashes frame his eyes in a hypnotic way. The contrast between his brown hair and the reddish scruff on his face makes me wonder what his natural hair color is.

Either way, there's no denying he's a good-looking guy. Sharp jaw and pouty lips.

He might just be the prettiest guy I've ever seen. Even more so than Iris, which I didn't think was possible.

Though, they're sitting too close for my liking, and something wrong twinges in my gut.

Not because of the pretty thing but because Iris is known to blur lines. I don't think he'd ever cross them, but his favorite thing is blurring them.

Even if the client has a fiancée, Iris doesn't care. It's like his flirt button doesn't have an off switch.

I clear my throat, and the laughter between them dies down, but their matching mischievous smiles don't fade. "Iris, can I talk to you for a minute?"

"Sure thing, boss." He stands.

"Wait," Harley says. "Brix is your boss?"

"He's taking point on this assignment, so technically …"

Suddenly, Harley doesn't look so happy anymore. I don't know what's changed in the last ten seconds other than I've come home.

Great start, but I can't dwell on what he thinks about me right now. I know I'll need to apologize for the mix-up earlier, but that can wait.

Iris leads me into the kitchen and pulls some orange juice from the fridge. "What's up?"

I fold my arms. "Do you need me to lecture you about being professional with this guy?"

He rolls his eyes. "No, but I'm totally interested in what you have to say, so please, go ahead. Get it out of your system."

"He's our client."

"Right."

"It's our job to protect him. Not … flirt with him."

Iris puts a hand to his heart. "Oh, you poor, sex-deprived man. If you think that's flirting, I feel so, so, so, so sorry for you. Want me to give you a few pointers?"

"Fuck you."

"That's a bit direct, but I guess it could be considered flirting."

"Griffin," I snap.

He knows I'm serious when I use his last name. "I wasn't flirting. I was getting to know the guy. If I have to spend my next twenty-six Sundays with him, I figure I should get to know what type of guy he is and find out if there's a chance he'll sneak out one night and do something stupid that'll get him killed and us fired. Does he want bodyguards to begin with? Clear answer on that is no. He feels like he needs them. The poor guy never goes out and never has fun. He only has his work. So yeah, while you might be jealous of us having a laugh together—"

"I'm not jealous. I'm being *professional.*"

"Right. Like you can't say he's not the most attractive man you've ever seen."

"Not my type." *At all.*

"Uh-huh. Pretty sure anything with a pulse would be your type at this point. The last time you took someone home was …" He tries to recount the last time I hooked up with someone when the team went out. He'll be at it a while.

"What would you know? I might hook up all the time." Yeah, I don't, but fuck him for trying to turn this around on me. "All I'm saying is, you should keep your distance."

"And all I'm saying is, you shouldn't. We're not used to this kind of job, but I'm treating it like I would any other, and the only way to do a job correctly is to get as much intel on your target as possible."

"Harley Valentine isn't our target. His stalkers are."

"S-stalkers?" Harley's voice is quiet as he stands in the entryway to the kitchen.

I spin. "How long have you been standing there?"

"Long enough. What's this about stalkers? Plural?"

"Wrong choice of words. I mean your fans in general. From your file, it's not the first time one has crossed a line. That's why we're here."

Harley's chin juts out. "Well, in that case. Here are some things you're expected to do that weren't in my file."

"What is that?"

He hands me three sheets of paper with a list of ridiculous requests on it. "Think of it as a rider. Us musicians have them for everywhere we go."

I glance at Iris, who stares like it's no big deal, but he's not the one who's going to have to do these ridiculous things on a daily basis.

"Bodyguards must taste Mr. Valentine's food and any beverages before him in case of poisoning or spiking or drugging." I turn to Harley. "Have you ever been drugged before?"

"Nope, but until a few days ago, no one had ever broken into my house before either. I'm Boy Scouting it from now on. Be prepared for everything."

"Bodyguards must walk into a room and shout 'All clear' like they do in

TV and movies when it's empty. Guns don't have to be drawn but are appreciated." I shake my head. "I'm not doing that."

"It's the request of your client." Iris is trying not to laugh.

"Bodyguards are responsible for Mr. Valentine's fun-o-meter, and as such, they cannot let it fall below the level of enjoyment that a video of someone getting kicked in the nuts can bring." My gaze shoots between Harley and Iris. "Did you guys get high while I was gone?"

"Ooh, no, but we should add that to the list," Harley says. "I've never been high. We should do that. But, like, weed high. Not *high* high. And, you know, where one of you can look after me in case I think a demon is chasing me. Wait, does weed cause hallucinations?"

I blink at him. "You … You've never … You're a famous pop star. How have you never been high before?"

"Why is that so surprising? I was in a boy band for seven years where we had handlers who basically made sure we never did drugs or anything stupid that would ruin our good-boy reputations, and since we broke up, I've been working nonstop. When would I have had the opportunity to get high?"

"I could think of a million times. Backstage with friends before or after a show—"

"The only people allowed backstage with me are my manager and assistant. Next."

"At home?"

"By myself? That's sad."

No, what's sad is that a twenty-six-year-old man has never smoked a joint before.

"Might be sad, but you won't be doing it on my time either."

"Why not? You just said—"

"It's our job to protect you. Not … supply you with drugs."

"Weed is legal in California, you know."

"Still not doing it. Beg this one on my day off." I point to Iris.

"I'll gladly corrupt a sheltered pop star."

"Why am I not surprised?" I ask. "I'm gonna go get my stuff out of the car." I throw the papers on the counter. "Cut these stupid rules down to one page, and I'll consider doing them."

As I walk away, I hear Harley say, "He's kind of bossy."

"Pfft, no *kind of* about it," Iris retorts.

They really have no idea. This is just the beginning.

Harley clears his throat and stares at me across the dinner table. He arches a perfectly manicured eyebrow, and then he points to his dinner with his fork.

He's got to be fucking kidding me.

"You can't be serious."

"It's in the rules." His shiny deep blue eyes glimmer at me.

"You cooked this meal. Are you scared you're gonna poison yourself?" I ask.

This whole list thing is insane, and while he and Iris got the demands down to one page, they kept all the crazy ones.

"Actually, I only cooked the vegetables. The chicken and cream sauce were made by my chef. She freezes meals for me, and who knows, maybe she's decided to off me."

I mutter, "For fuck's sake," under my breath and reach across the table, stabbing a piece of chicken and shoving it in my mouth. "Happy?"

"Yep. Are you dying yet?"

"How long is this rider bullshit going to last?"

"I'll take that as a no." Harley shovels food into his mouth. "What?" It comes out muffled.

"Did Iris put you up to some sort of hazing or …"

He swallows. "I'm trying to make sure I get the most out of this bodyguard thing."

I don't buy it, but I also don't get a chance to question it because the front door opens. I'm out of my seat with my gun drawn in a millisecond.

"Harley?" a sweet voice calls out.

Harley appears at my back. "Calm down, Rambo. It's Evah."

The fiancée.

Miss Evah no last name. Like Cher. Or Madonna.

A glamorous woman steps into the room just as I put my gun

away.

Long blonde hair curls over her shoulders. She's in a white shirt, long beige coat, tiny denim shorts, and black stilettos.

As soon as she spots Harley, she ditches her sunglasses, showing warm brown eyes, and then the next second, she flings herself into Harley's arms.

Of course the pretty pop star has an even prettier woman by his side.

"Fucking storms. I got home as soon as I could." She sounds so relieved to be held by Harley.

"I'm thankful you got grounded in Kansas."

She shoves him. "Missed you too, asshole."

Harley kisses the top of her head. "I mean it in the best possible way. You weren't here when it all went down. I couldn't forgive myself if he hurt you because of me."

"Please, I can handle myself." Her gaze flits to mine. "Although, if that's what your new bodyguard looks like, I might regret turning down your offer to hire one for me too."

I try to hide my smile.

Harley glares at me. "This is Brix. As in dumb as bricks."

Thanks, Iris, you fucker.

I take her hand. "As in Brixton."

"It's nice to meet you." She blushes sweetly.

"Do you want something to eat?" Harley asks her.

Evah eyes the food on the table and steals a piece of Harley's broccoli. "Thanks."

"You have to eat more."

"My agent says—"

"Your agent is a dickweed, and you don't need to lose weight."

She really doesn't.

Welcome to Hollywood.

"My fragrance launch is in a week. I need to look good for the cameras. Which also means I need my beauty sleep." She kisses his cheek and turns to me. "Protect him with your life. He's important to me."

"Yes, ma'am."

Evah screws up her face. "Okay, eww, no. *Ma'am* doesn't work for me."

"Sorry. Miss … no last name."

She smiles. "Evah is fine."

"Evah," I repeat.

"Better. Goodnight."

Now she's gone again.

Harley goes back to his food, as if he doesn't care his fiancée is home after they've been apart for a week. I'd think he'd be eager to follow her to bed, but nope, he's sitting at the table, eating, while also shooting daggers my way.

"So, that's Evah," I say.

"I wanted extra protection for her too, but she's even more pigheaded than I am, and that's saying a lot."

"From what I read, she's faced death threats before."

"Oh, yeah. Big-time. All of them harmless. All women who hated that she was marrying me. Like they had a chance."

"Egotistical much?"

Harley tilts his head. "How is that egotistical?"

"Saying there's no way you'd fall for a fan. It's elitist."

"Refusing to be with people who want you because of your fame is not elitist. And sure, I suppose there are fans out there who want me for the person they think I am—the one they see in tabloids and at music awards and onstage—but all of us in Eleven worked out fast that people are far more disappointed by the reality."

"What reality is that?"

"All five of us were manufactured. Our personalities, our images, and our lives. And none of us live up to the perfection our label projects to the public. It's the price I've paid for being a teenage pop star and letting them mold me into someone else for seven years."

Well, shit. I didn't expect that deep of an answer, and I have no idea what to say to something like that.

He huffs. "And the worst part is, breaking up the boy band did nothing to change that. I'm still not who I want to be."

I twirl my fork in my hand. "Who do you want to be?"

"*Myself.*"

"And who is that?"

"Right now, I'm a scared guy with an *unloaded* gun who needs someone bigger and stronger to protect me. That's all I know for sure."

Yikes. That's a lot to unload. I stare at him blankly.

As if sensing my inability to speak, he fills the silence. "Shit, sorry. That's heavy for the first of what I assume will be many meals together."

"We don't have to eat together. That's up to you. I can be as invisible or as involved as you want."

"I don't mind," Harley says. "It's better than eating alone."

I can't help feeling sorry for the guy, though I wonder why his fiancée doesn't eat with him other than she's under the Hollywood delusion that women need to be a size zero.

Iris's words telling me we should get to know our client ring through my head, and I hate when that fucker is right.

"I do have some things to go over," I say.

"Like?"

"I'm going to need a list of everyone who has access to your house —like who's allowed to be here and when I can expect them, so, uh, we don't have a repeat of what happened today."

"So you don't tackle my vocal coach or personal trainer? Got it. I wrote a list for Iris earlier. I think it's all still in the living room."

"Okay, next thing. The gun. Have you ever used one before?"

"No." He holds up his hand. "And before you say it, I know Gideon did the right thing by not loading it."

"Did he also tell you that eighty-five percent of gunshot wounds happen because people don't know how to use a gun properly?"

"Umm ... no."

"If you really want to learn to protect yourself with a gun, I can teach you."

"Really?" His eyes light up.

There are people who have clearly worked their whole lives to get where they are, and it's obvious they've fought hard for it. Harley's not that person. Harley is the type that when he pulls a certain expression, you just know he was born to be in the spotlight because he's absolutely breathtaking.

I'm sure he has worked hard, I'm not doubting that, but with that face? He was destined for fame from the beginning.

I shake that thought off. "I figure if you ever get your hands on another gun, you should know how to use it so you don't shoot yourself … or me."

Harley laughs. "I'd like to learn. I mean, I don't see myself ever needing to use a gun again because I have you now, but I want to."

"Then we'll do it."

He finishes his meal and stands. "I'm ready for you to check my room now."

"Isn't Evah already in there?"

"We have separate rooms. She … snores."

Could be true. I doubt it because his face is doing this weird tic thing, but I'm willing to let it go for now.

Maybe they're having problems, and I'm so not here to get into that or to care.

I follow him through the house and up to the second floor. "You're still going with that ridiculous list of demands?"

"Yep. You get bonus points if you somersault into the room."

"I'm not doing that."

Then he levels me with a look. It's part pleading, part mocking, but I see a glint of fear as well. I don't think he means for me to see it, but I've seen that look before. On countless faces, in countless dangerous situations.

It's the look of trying to be strong because there's no other choice.

Breaking down isn't an option.

And now I feel even more sorry for him.

It might be mostly a joke to him, but I realize Gideon is right. The break-in has affected Harley deeper than he lets on.

"Fine," I huff, keeping up the façade.

I leave him outside his door to check his room, the connected bathroom, and his closet. I even look under his bed at his request, but when I step back out, I refuse to do what he asks.

Then he looks up at me with puppy dog eyes and a cute pout, and damn, his stormy-blue eyes are hypnotic.

I clear my throat and find myself saying, "All clear."

He breaks into the biggest smile as he heads inside his room. "Goodnight, Rambo."

"Night, Pop Star."

CHAPTER 5
HARLEY

I OVERHEARD way more than I should have earlier. Brix told Iris to keep his distance—to be professional. So, that's all I'm doing. I'm making him be the most thorough bodyguard he could possibly be.

And, okay, when he offered to train me with a gun, I was going to drop the silly demands.

But then he looked at me with something worse than disgust in his eyes. He stared at me with *sympathy* and pity on his face. My stomach did a backflip, and that's the last thing I need.

No gross mushy feelings, please.

So yeah, professional distance is good.

Making him do silly things is even better. Not only do they provide me with entertainment, but he knows they're complete bullshit.

Maybe that'll keep him from feeling sorry for me.

That aside, knowing he was in the house made me feel safe enough to fall asleep and stay asleep.

For the first time since the break-in, I've been able to catch up.

Which is probably why at midday, I'm woken up by my bodyguard asking if I'm dead. He pulls my curtains open, letting the sunlight burn my retinas as I try to wake up properly.

I roll onto my stomach and shove my head under the pillow. "You're a pretty shitty bodyguard if you have to ask if I'm still alive."

The deep, warm chuckle from the overgrown man makes my cock twitch.

Damn him.

"I brought you a breakfast burrito. A peace offering after starting on the wrong foot yesterday."

I was thinking—hoping—he was the thing that smelled like bacon. They should make bacon-scented cologne.

The promise of food is enough to get me sitting up.

I stare at the plate. "You haven't taken a bite yet."

"I'm not going to poison you. It'd be counterintuitive when I'm paid to protect you."

"Counterintuitive, maybe, but until proven otherwise, everyone in my life is now a potential psychopath."

Brix relents and takes a large bite. Melted cheese drips onto his chin, and my immediate thought is to lick it off. Luckily, I'm sitting, he's standing, and I'm nowhere near his mouth to actually do it because that would be mortifying.

"You know," he says, talking around the food, "you're gonna have to get over your trust issues sooner or later. One break-in doesn't make everyone else a potential attacker."

"Oh, you sweet summer child. You think my trust issues come from the break-in? I've had trust issues since my momager took every cent of money I earned before I was eighteen. They got worse when the person I thought was the love of my life told me I was someone to fill the loneliness while on tour. Everyone uses me for something, only now, we have the added potential for homicide. Fun times." I shovel the entire breakfast burrito into my mouth because I'm starving, while Brix watches on. "What?" A piece of egg flies from my mouth. Oops.

Brix shakes his head. "Sorry. Nothing. Not my place."

I swallow the chunk of food. "If we're going to be working closely together, and I have to spend one hundred forty-four hours with you a week, you damn well better say whatever you're thinking or we're going to be walking on eggshells around each other."

"I was just thinking for someone who seemingly has everything, your life is kinda …"

"Sad. You can say it. My life is depressing as fuck."

"Sorry."

I shrug. "Hey, I chose it. And it's not all bad. I have money, an awesome house …"

"Evah."

My gaze flies to his. "Right. I have Evah."

"How did you two meet?"

"It's an adorable story." I put on my public-ready smile because this is a bullshit story I've told the press a thousand times. "Back when I was living in Kansas and trying to make it as an artist, she'd come see my shows. Whether it was busking or school dances, she was always there. She was my first fan."

"Huh."

"Huh? That's all you have to say? Everyone loves that story."

"Everyone loves *fiction*."

I frown. "How do you know that story's not real?"

"I don't want to give away my secrets."

"Are you, like, some walking, talking lie detector?"

Brix smiles, and it softens his hard features. "No. But you have a serious tell. Your cheek kinda twitches, and a dimple appears on one side of your face." His finger almost brushes over my cheek, but he pulls his hand back. "Same thing happened last night when you said Evah snores. Which she doesn't."

"How would you know?" My voice rises.

Brix puts his hand up to get me to calm down. "Before I went to sleep, I did a perimeter check and went through the whole house. No snoring."

"The walls are thick. You probably didn't hear her."

"Mm. Maybe."

There's a reason I don't want my new bodyguards to know the truth about Evah and me. I hate stooping to cheap celebrity publicity stunts, and I hate most of all that I've had to fight this battle ever since signing with Joystar Records.

Part of me thinks I should come out and tell everyone the rumors about me are true and let the cards fall where they may.

The other part, the business-oriented, music-loving part, reminds me that without my career, I'm nothing.

I'm no one.

I may hate being *the* Harley Valentine sometimes, but it's all I have.

A few years ago, I thought I could be more. Have more.

But here I am, eighteen months after my life was supposed to start properly, and I'm still chasing something I can't reach. I don't even know what it is. All I know is, I can't fuck up now.

What's going to happen when I come out as a gay man?

There are other things at play now other than me and my consequences.

Evah is already seen by the public as some sort of fame whore. If it comes out our whole relationship has been fake, it won't only destroy me but her as well.

She was a no one when my PR team plucked her from a small town near where I grew up. Now, she's an online influencer, and one of those people who are basically famous for … well, existing.

Maybe the public has it correct and she's using me for fame, but I'm using her just as much. It's why we've gotten along so well ever since we met. We don't lie to each other because we don't have to. She's as up-front with me about what she needs as I am with her.

Our romance might not be real, but our friendship is, and I don't want to fuck that up.

She has a new perfume line coming out, she's working on one day becoming a fashion designer, and she puts up with so much crap from the public all because of me.

Our relationship made her, but it could also destroy her. Especially if it comes out she's a beard.

So, no, I'd prefer if my bodyguard didn't find out my orientation.

Though, with the sleeping arrangements, I think he already suspects.

"Okay, I'll level with you." I stand from my bed and get momentarily distracted by Brix's gaze roaming over my almost-naked form.

Is he … checking me out?

I clear my throat, and then our eyes meet.

"Level with me?" His voice is surprisingly raspy.

"My PR team set Evah and me up. But that's nowhere near as romantic as the bullshit story they spun for us."

Brix nods. His gaze travels down again, but then he quickly stops it. Up until this moment, I've been getting nothing but straight-guy vibes. Then again, I thought Iris was flirting with me yesterday, and he has a girlfriend.

This is what sex deprivation does to a guy. Next thing, I'll start thinking Evah's actually hitting on me.

Brix takes my empty plate off the bed and goes to leave my room, then he looks over his shoulder at me. "Get dressed. We're going out today."

"What? No, we're not. My vocal coach is coming at three."

"Then we have three hours to get back. Easy."

"Where are we going?"

"Grocery shopping. I need some things your kitchen doesn't have."

"Oh, give me a list. I'll send Jamie."

"Nah. It's time your sheltered ass gets a dose of normal." He turns to leave.

I don't know whether to be flattered or insulted. "Is this how it's going to be?" I call after him. "I thought I was the boss of you, not the other way around."

He spins in the doorway. "I need food. I can't leave you by yourself. Ergo, you're coming with me."

This is a bad idea.

"This isn't going to work," I say as I put on the aviators and cap Brix hands me. "Someone will recognize me."

"Not if you act like a normal person."

I eye him from his cropped hair to his muscles, tight black T-shirt, and down to his tactical pants. "You don't think you looking like … *that* will draw attention?"

"Then everyone will be looking at me, not you." Brix doesn't give me a chance to dispute that and opens his car door.

This is going to end in disaster. I can already see it.

If I wasn't Harley Valentine, all eyes would be on the gorgeousness that is my bodyguard, but I have one of the most recognizable faces on the planet. It's why I haven't gone grocery shopping in ... well, ever.

I went from my mom's house to having handlers and assistants who did all that day-to-day stuff for me. So I've never actually had to shop for food before.

I meet Brix around the front of his SUV. "Are you sure you're not doing this because you're bored already and need to see some adrenaline-inducing action? Iris implied this is not your normal type of job."

"Do you honestly think you'll be mobbed in a Safeway?"

"Ooh. This might actually be a fun lesson for you to learn."

I take off toward the entrance, sensing he's behind me every step of the way. The doors slide open, and we cross the threshold.

I pause, waiting for the inevitable.

Maybe I am out of touch with reality, because where I'm expecting to be recognized immediately, nothing happens. No one approaches.

"No mob yet," Brix mutters as he passes me.

I catch up.

"Sorry to burst your bubble and dint that ego of yours."

"Just wait. This ingenious and very original disguise of sunglasses and a cap won't shield me for long."

Brix grabs a cart and goes straight to the fridge section to pull out liquid egg whites.

"Could you be more of a stereotype?"

He huffs. "Me a stereotype? Because I have a high-protein diet? You are aware muscles don't magically appear on their own?"

"These did." I lift the hem of my shirt and show off my toned abs.

Brix scoffs. "Please." He lifts his, and holy forking fucknuggets. He has abs on top of his abs.

Super abs.

They could be their own superhero and wear their own cape.

I take the egg whites out of his hands and read the back of the carton. "How do these things work?"

Brix laughs, loud and warm, and then reaches for more.

We walk the aisles, Brix loads the cart with more healthy crap, and it's surprising how both fascinating and boring I find this experience.

"So, this is what it's like to be a normal person?"

"I guess as normal as a pop star is ever gonna get."

"I like it." I pause at the candy aisle. "But I have a question."

"Shoot … no, wait, I probably shouldn't tell you to *shoot* anything."

"Funny. So happy we're already joking about my poor choices. But no, I'm wondering when normal people go shopping, who's there to tell you to stay away from the candy?" My feet move in the direction of delicious treats.

I might have a small sugar addiction. Especially when it comes to writing an album. Back in the early Eleven days, I piled on the weight fast.

I was always a chubby kid, but then puberty hit, I grew two feet taller, and I never struggled with my weight again until being given all the food I wanted when I asked for it.

Management had to hire a personal trainer and tell everyone on staff to give me a sugar allowance. Only so many calories per day.

After a while, it became habit, but standing in front of an entire wall of candy …

I go for some Twizzlers, but Brix grabs my hand before I can reach them.

"Normal people need self-control." He tries to pull me away. "But I'm guessing in your case, it's all on me."

I slip out of his grip. "Good luck with that."

Brix tries to block me from getting to more candy, but I'm determined to win. Sugar must turn me into some sort of ninja because more candy gets thrown into the cart than Brix can put back, and I'm too busy laughing at him to notice anyone join us in the aisle.

He manages to get his arm around my waist, and he pulls me back against him.

His big body surrounds me, and I might like it a little *too* much.

That's when the piercing scream happens.

I pray for a medical emergency like someone dropping dead in the middle of the store, but no, we turn to find a girl, maybe fifteenish, her hand over her screeching mouth and a box of Milk Duds scattered all over the ground at her feet.

"Uh, it might be time to take this stuff to the cashier," I say and step away from him.

"It's one girl. Go say hi, and then she'll be on her way."

"That's not how it works."

More people converge because someone screaming is not normal.

It honestly looks like a scene from a zombie movie. Only, instead of blood falling from their mouths, it's drool, and it's contagious. My name is echoed in harsh whispers around the store. As recognition kicks in, everyone's faces drop, and the shock starts.

It's a goddamn epidemic.

"Way to go, Rambo. You're supposed to protect me, and you've walked me into a zombie horde."

"Let's get out of here." Brix ditches the cart and takes my upper arm, guiding me through the crowd of fans trying to get my attention.

I smile at all of them and shake the hands that reach for me, although with how fast Brix is dragging me, it's more like quick touches and high fives. I try not to cringe at all the germs but make sure to keep my face public ready. All these people taking photos on their cell phones will no doubt post them to social media, and God forbid I look like a psycho, tired, high, or anything but perfect. Otherwise, I'll get a phone call from Joystar's PR department.

All the while, Brix doesn't let go of my arm and guides me through the ever-growing audience of people wanting to get a glimpse of me.

It goes from a handful of people to seemingly everyone in the store. They all want to see the famous person.

Some even block the exit, knowing I have to pass them, but Brix bowls right through them.

We leave without buying anything, and once we're outside, we're quick to make a break for the car.

No one follows us, but there are a few who stand outside the store and watch us with their phones permanently attached to their hands as we drive away.

"You got hand sanitizer in here?"

"As per ridiculous rule number six hundred and eighty-five that I must be able to supply Mr. Valentine with hand sanitizer at any given moment, I put some in the glove compartment."

"I swear someone sneezed on me in there." I take out the small bottle that claims to kill ninety-nine percent of germs and wish I could bathe in the stuff.

"Question. Is your germ phobia about all germs, or do you just hate people touching you?"

"I don't hate people touching me," I argue. "It's more in situations like back there where I'm touching people's hands and I don't know if they're sick or not. I'm not germophobic, really, I'm … flu-aphobic. One bad case has scarred me for life."

"Ah. Got it. A fan could theoretically lick you so long as they didn't have flu symptoms."

"Eww, no. But *theoretically* … yes. I'm not pedantic or obsessive over it. I just feel better if I'm able to wash my hands frequently. Anyway, I want to say *I told you so* because that was far from a successful shopping trip, but seeing as you didn't get your precious protein, I think that says it clearly enough."

Brix shifts gears. He looks all badass with his lips pursed and a concentration line across his forehead. "I don't get it."

"Don't get what?"

"The mania. It's not like you're a Beatle."

"I think you're about thirty years too young to understand Beatlemania and not Eleven fandom. When Iris said you didn't know who I was, I thought he was fucking with me."

Brix side-eyes me. "I know of you … well, Eleven. I'm not dead. I just didn't know any of your names or …"

"Or any of my solo songs."

"Sorry."

As refreshing as it is to be next to someone who can't even fathom my fame, I can't help the small seed of disappointment—as if all the work I've put in these last eighteen months to broaden my horizons and gain new fans outside of twelve- to seventeen-year-old girls and their moms hasn't been enough.

Which is bullshit because Brix isn't even my target demographic. Twenty-something females? Sure. The queer community? Definitely. Hardass ex-military tough guys who look like they could break a person in half with their bare hands? Not so much.

"You shouldn't be offended," Brix says.

"I'm not." Okay, that came out defensively.

"When you first became famous, I was doing my first tour overseas. Music was the last thing on my mind. Not dying was the first."

Wow. Perspective.

"When did you get out of the military? Let me guess. You were a Marine." For some reason, he screams Marine.

"Army. Wanted to become a Ranger."

"What happened?"

"Enlisted right after high school and did six years. I was about to be promoted to staff sergeant, was almost ready mentally and physically to apply for Ranger School, and then ..." He pauses as if stuck in a memory. "Then I got offered a job at Mike Bravo, so I didn't re-up. But my point is, after six years in the army and another four working for Trav, my whole life has centered around that. My pop culture references are all from when I was a teenager."

I can't hold back the jab. "And the Beatles were from when you were a teenager?"

Brix laughs. "Fuck off."

"I don't think you're supposed to say that to your boss."

"Are you my boss, or is Gideon my boss?"

"I pay you. That means I'm your boss."

"But can you fire me without going through Gideon first?"

I hesitate because I don't know. Sure, if I was adamant and told Gideon he had to get rid of Brix, he'd do it, but I'd have to be firm and give an appropriate reason. Saying "because he told me to fuck off" would get laughed at.

"You don't know for sure, do you?" Brix taunts.

"I can't decide if I hate you more now or when you tackled me yesterday."

"I'm gonna go with yesterday. Because now you feel sorry for me. How am I supposed to get my protein intake?"

"If you don't hit your daily limit, do your biceps deflate like a balloon overnight?"

"That's exactly how it works."

I hold up my phone. "Mind if I get things done the famous-person way now?"

"By all means."

One traffic jam and an hour later, we pull into my driveway to find my assistant unloading bags of liquid egg whites from her trunk.

"I think I might like the famous way better," Brix says.

"Yeah, well, don't become accustomed to this lifestyle or you'll never want to leave."

Brix laughs. "Oh, there's no danger of that ever happening. I may have to do my own grocery shopping in my real life, but at least I get to blow shit up."

"Okay, seriously. What kind of 'security firm' does Gideon's cousin run?"

I'm met with more laughter.

CHAPTER 6
BRIX

THIS JOB IS the easiest money I've ever made. I may have underestimated the kind of fandom that follows Harley around, but with him about to cut a new album, his time has been spent at home either writing, doing vocal exercises with his coach, or working out with his personal trainer.

I've vetted each and every one of his entourage even though Gideon would have already done the same, but I know how to dig deeper than basic background checks.

Take Harley's trainer, Cooper, for instance. The biggest crime in his life is his porn subscriptions. Every time he walks into the house, I have to bite back the urge to tell him he can do better than the cheap, amateur stuff he pays for. Especially when you can find that amateur crap for free.

Words of advice: never skimp on good porn. It's what gets you through long and lonely months.

While snooping around on the internet, I might have discovered a very interesting fan theory out there about Harley.

Rumor has it, before he was engaged to Evah, he was involved with a guy named Jay from some band called Radioactive. I've never heard of them, but as we've already established, I've lived under a rock for ten years.

The song "Confusion," a song they wrote together, is totally a breakup song if I've ever heard one. I also remember Harley saying the love of his life left him while on tour, and Eleven and Radioactive did two world tours together.

I've fallen down an internet rabbit hole of Eleven fandom, and I've barely come up for air in a week.

Today's string of sites went from the Radioactive fan website where videos of the band from concerts all over the world are posted, to clicking a link a fan shared where it was a video of Harley and this Jay guy singing a duet of "Tennessee Whiskey," to finding more links to more fan blogs where there are photos of Harley and Jay eyeing each other or being in the background during interviews. Always together. Always giving each other knowing smirks.

Apparently.

I dunno. All I see is two musicians in the same space as one another. It's not really a coincidence or breaking news considering Radioactive was Eleven's opening act for two years.

People see what they want to, which is probably why I've been scouring the internet trying to figure out what's truth and what's complete bullshit.

There's only speculation in the media about Harley's sexuality, but there is an endless supply of die-hard fans who are certain Harley's gay. Or bi or pan.

With him and Evah not sharing a bed, I have to assume it's the former.

Or maybe I'm reading into it because I want to believe it.

Harley's playing with the melody of a song he's trying to write on his piano right now. I watch him as if his face holds all the answers. As if the scrunch of his brow can tell me something.

He lets out a frustrated "Gah" and bangs his head on the keys, making an awful clanging noise. "I give up."

"Maybe try a different song?"

He lifts his head and glares.

I keep my mouth shut and go back to my phone where there's a photo of Harley and Jay smiling at each other onstage.

If it is true, his ex is gorgeous. Just like him.

There's only one thing holding me back from putting it in the *truth* column, and that's why it's a secret.

It's not like there haven't been gay musicians before—there have been countless. Some of them legends. Granted, back when Freddie Mercury came out, times were not great for acceptance, but it's different now.

I don't understand why Harley wouldn't come out or confirm the rumors that he's bi.

My gaze flits between what I'm seeing on my screen and the Harley in front of me.

A balled-up piece of paper hits my head from Harley's direction. It seems he's picked up a new favorite hobby: taking out his writing frustrations on me. His aim is getting better, I'll give him that. I'll have to start swatting them away soon.

"You're staring at me again," he complains. "You know, we're inside the house. I don't think you have to be this close to me all the time. Take a break. Go make sure no one's lurking in the backyard. Or I dunno … just stop looking at me like that."

"Like what?"

"Like you want to know all my secrets."

"You have secrets?" I feign ignorance.

Harley grumbles.

"Maybe *you* should take a break," I suggest. "You haven't left the house in a week, unless Iris took you out and you guys didn't tell me about it."

"No, he basically spent his day giving me horrible suggestions for lyrics until I told him to go for a swim and leave me to … well, this." Harley points to the mess he's made on the floor. Countless discarded pieces of paper. Pens strewn everywhere.

"So take a step back."

"I can't take a break. I'm supposed to be recording in a few weeks, and I've got nothing."

"You can't force it."

"I have to. The label is under the impression I've got my shit together."

"Why would they think that?"

He grunts. "If the people who own you ask how your new songs are coming along, you tell them 'great' and hope they believe you even if you haven't started writing any."

"Why can't you tell them you need time off?"

Harley's eyes narrow. "Time … off? Do those two words even go together in the English language?"

"When was the last time you had a vacation?"

"I get to explore the cities I tour in for a day or two."

"That's not a vacation," I point out.

"The other Eleven boys and I spent a week in Barbados once."

"When was that?"

"Like …" Harley does the math. "Eight years ago." He slumps in defeat. "Okay, fine, you have a point. But more albums mean more money, and more money means the label is happy and keeps wanting to produce more of my music."

"You've been in this loop for almost a decade."

"And?"

"Why do you keep doing it and burning yourself out?"

"I'm not burned out. I need to prove myself. I need to—"

"I'm staring at two Grammys." I point to the display case along the wall of the sitting room. "There're also countless People's Choice Awards, Teen Choice Awards, MTV Video Music Awards—"

"I'm not where I want to be yet. I need …" His face scrunches, and I begin to think he has no clue what he needs. "I need more."

"Want to know what I think?"

"I don't pay you for your opinions, so no."

"Well, you don't pay me to keep my mouth shut either, so you're getting it anyway. I think you're a workaholic."

Harley starts a slow clap. "Wow. You could get a PhD in psychology with that type of power of observation."

"I've seen what burnout does to a person, and while this might be a stretch of my job title, it's my duty to protect you. Even if it's from yourself. You should go out tonight."

"I'm going out tomorrow night for Evah's thing."

"Is two nights in a row illegal?"

"No, but where would we even go? You learned last week I get recognized *everywhere*."

That's true. But I can't sit here another minute and watch him struggle to write. It's getting to me. I don't like seeing him frustrated, and that's not part of the job description.

The burnout thing is true. I witnessed it more times than I could count in the military, but while I can feign professional concern on the outside, something niggles in my subconscious, telling me it's more than that.

Intrigue maybe. To know if the rumors are true.

"You don't have Hollywood connections who can get you into a party? Maybe a club." It would be harder to protect him at a club, but I have no doubt I could handle it.

"Going out is always a logistical nightmare. Paparazzi, fans, VIP areas … it's all noise and chaos. We did that scene when we were younger, but now it makes me cringe."

"What about a friend's place?"

"The only friends I have are probably the guys, and we've lost touch since we split ways and went solo."

"So get back in touch with one of them."

Harley contemplates it and then pulls his phone out. "The only two who might be available are Denver and Blake. Ryder has his kid full-time, and Mason fell off the face of the planet about six months ago. Supposedly went back to Montana."

"Didn't I read somewhere Blake is on location shooting some action film?"

Harley's gray-blue eyes narrow at me. "You read?"

"Yes. Muscle man read good."

"No, I mean … you read tabloid and entertainment news?"

Oh, shit. "Uh, I might have this past week or so."

"How much have you read?" Hard to miss the accusation in that.

"Why? What don't you want me to find out?"

Harley stands. "You just can't believe everything you read is all. Especially online." He goes to storm out of the room, but I call after him.

"Where are you going?"

"To call Denver and get dressed. We'll go hang with him for a while."

I didn't pry much out of him, but I did get him to take a break from writing. That's more important.

Denver's Malibu home sits on a street that is filled with cars.

Harley groans. "When he said he'd invite a few people over, this is not what I was expecting."

"I guess your definition of a few differs from his?"

"Clearly. I … I don't know if I can go in there." He plays with the collar of his button down. He looks amazing in royal blue.

Not what you should be focused on, Brix.

"Why not?" I ask.

"I haven't publicly dealt with the break-in situation yet. Everyone is going to ask."

"Tell them you can't legally speak about it, which is technically true."

"I guess …"

I pull into the first available spot, about a quarter mile from Denver's house, and kill the engine. "Question. What is it about the break-in that has you uptight? Apart from the obvious that someone invaded your personal space and it was scary."

Harley seems to contemplate that. "It's admitting that I'm vulnerable and helpless, and all I did the whole time that guy was in my house was stall and wait to be rescued like some weak—"

I hold up my hand. "I'm gonna have to stop you right there. You did the right thing. If you'd tried to overpower him, you don't know what could've happened. It's not your job to stop psychos from attacking you, and in those types of situations, you need to do what you can to survive. A lot of the time, survival is doing whatever they tell you to do until you get your chance to get out."

"You sound like you speak from experience."

"There's not much I'm allowed to tell you about the kinds of jobs we've done at Mike Bravo or when I was in the army, but …" I think of something I can tell him and turn in my seat to face him. "Okay, so during one of my deployments, we were in the Middle East going from town to town and doing a sweep for possible insurgents. Someone, a child about nine years old, had tipped us off that we were about to walk into an ambush, but they couldn't tell us how many there were, where they were, or what kind of ambush. We couldn't trust that the kid was telling us the truth because over there they have been known to use children as pawns. Teenage suicide bombers. Distractions. Decoys. For all we knew, this kid was telling us to go a different direction and leading us to an actual ambush. We had the option to fight our way through or trust the child."

"What did you do?"

"We hid."

I knew that would surprise him. Harley's eyebrows shoot up.

"For three days, we squatted in the desert while drones and aerial surveillance found us a safe passage out."

"W-why are you telling me this? This makes me feel worse about my situation. You faced something monumentally huge. Like, life-threatening—"

"Harley, I told you this because you need to know it's okay to do nothing. If your attacker had gotten to you, it wouldn't have been your fault. What somebody else does is never your fault. And I bet you a hundred bucks, if you go in there and tell every single moment of your story, which, by the way, could have easily turned into a life-threatening situation, no one inside that party is gonna say, 'Oh, wow, you're a pussy for not fighting him.' You managed to keep him calm, and you talked your way to safety. That is nothing to belittle."

Harley's mouth drops open. "I …"

I'd be lying if I said leaving Harley Valentine speechless didn't warm my insides. I clap his shoulder. "You don't need to thank me for the perspective. The shocked look on your face is thanks enough."

His lips twitch. "Fine. But I'm still not comfortable talking about it."

"And you don't have to. Like I said, tell people you can't legally talk about it."

"Can we have a signal? Like, if I rub my ear, can you come shove a drink in my face and interrupt whatever conversation I'm having?"

"That isn't on the ridiculously long list of rules you have for me," I taunt. "In fact, isn't one of them, *Bodyguards should be barely seen and not heard at public events. Wear camo and be invisible.*"

Harley's lips flatten. "Which you aren't wearing, by the way, so rule already broken."

I cock a single brow at him.

He relents. "Okay, what if I scratch that one off and change it to *Bodyguards must pretend to be my friend, work as conversation buffers, and hand me a drink every time I'm uncomfortable.*"

I was gonna do it for him anyway, but I won't tell him that. "I accept those terms."

Harley goes to get out of the car. "Let's get this over with."

"Nuh-uh. Not so fast. You have to actually try to enjoy this. You need to get out of your head for a while."

"Oh, then a party is so not where you should've brought me."

"Where should I have taken you?"

"The beach."

"At night?"

"No, but for future reference, I love going to the beach … until I'm recognized."

"Noted. Let's go."

CHAPTER 7
HARLEY

THIS IS EXACTLY the type of party I hated going to when Eleven was together. The guys loved being surrounded by fans and the attention they got, but I've never liked being put under a microscope.

And in those early days, we were constantly being watched by people paid to not let us do anything stupid. We were all underage when we started out, so even drinking was frowned upon, although we tended to get away with it because at least we weren't doing blow in the bathroom.

Having that constant eye on me made me self-conscious.

Brix follows me past countless people who all follow me with their gaze but don't bother to approach. I probably know half of them to some degree, but everyone knows you don't go crazy fan on people at these parties. You're supposed to be cool and used to being around celebrities.

We make a move to greet Denver—real name Denny—who's in the middle of his living room talking to some actress I recognize from the latest teen franchise.

Age is weird in Hollywood, and these two are the reason.

Denver is taller than me and toned but not buff. He's not skinny either. But his face? He is the youngest of us Eleven guys at twenty-four now, but he still looks fifteen—how old he was when we signed to the label. He has a baby face that is both adorable and disturbingly young-looking.

The actress, Heather someone, is almost thirty, but she's playing a sixteen-year-old heroine on the big screen.

"Hey, you came." Denver clasps my hand and brings me in for a man-hug back-slap.

"You thought I wouldn't?"

"I suspected you might change your mind."

"Fair call. I probably would've bailed if not for this guy." I point next to me. "This is my friend-slash-bodyguard. Brix, this is Denver. Also part of Eleven. You may or may not have heard of him seeing as you thought I was an intruder in my own home and tackled me to the ground."

Brix scowls at me, but Denver bursts out laughing.

"Shit, did that really happen?"

Brix goes to open his mouth to verify some details—probably to tell them I was holding a gun—but I beat him to it.

"Yep. He tried to attack me, so it's something he will never live down. Ever. Even after he stops working for me, he's going to be known as the bodyguard who crash-tackled his client."

Brix turns to Denver. "I've only been working with him for a week. Is he always this dramatic?"

"Always. I don't envy you, brother, but nice to meet you."

The traitors ganging up on me shake hands.

"Ignore them. Clearly, they're both insane," I say to Heather Whatsherface. "I'm Harley."

"I know who you are. Heather Walsh."

"I know who you are." Last name not withstanding.

"Is Evah here with you?" she asks. "I love her YouTube channel and would so love to meet her."

"I'll be sure to tell her to contact your people, but she's at home tonight. Her fragrance launch is tomorrow, so she wanted to rest. Maybe I can get you a ticket."

Her eyes light up. "Really? That'd be amazing. Thank you so much. Can I get a selfie with you?"

Denver cuts in. "And I think I've lost her for the night. Thanks."

I chuckle. "Sorry, man."

"Not the first time it's happened with us. I'm going to go get a drink. Come find me later, okay?" As he backs away, he gives me a smile because he knows I'm not actually trying to steal anyone from him.

Heather looks at me with a confused scrunch in her brow. "Was that come find me later for me or you?"

I shrug. "Both?"

We take the selfie, she gushes about Evah some more, and I ask about her movie career.

Brix's big body leaves my side at one point, and his hand subtly brushes over my lower back. He tilts his head in the direction of the bar, and I give him a nod in acknowledgment.

It's hard to take my eyes off him, especially when he turns and smiles at me as if he knows I'm watching him walk away.

I force myself to break eye contact and lose myself in conversation, not noticing that he hasn't come back. It's not until we're interrupted by a guy I don't know pushing his way into our conversation that I realize Brix is nowhere to be found.

"Is it true a fan tried to kill you?" the guy asks.

Here we go.

I start scratching my ear while I talk in case Brix is in the bathroom and comes out to find me.

"Oh my God, what happened?" Heather asks.

"It was nothing like that." I pull on my ear harder.

His big looming presence appears beside me and holds out a cup, and a grin splits my face. "Drink?"

"Thank you." I go to take a sip but pause.

"I already took a sip of it for you," Brix says in my ear quietly enough no one else can hear. His warm breath on my skin has my body responding in a way it really, really shouldn't. Especially in public.

It makes me think about what it could be like to be with a man at a party like this and not care about reaching for his hand or kissing his cheek.

I know it would cause a big reaction, but in my fantasy, no one would blink an eye if I reached for Brix—wait … not Brix. It's not the first time I've dreamed about being *out,* but it is the first time the face-less stranger beside me has an identity.

I shake off that thought quickly. I have to. Brix is hot as fuck, and the last thing I need is to think about him as something more than my hot bodyguard.

Who's proving to be actually kind of nice.

No. Just hot. Hot, dumb bodyguard.

Keep telling yourself that.

When he pulls away from me, he looks smug as if he knows how much my body likes having his close.

That's something I can add. Hot, dumb, and smug. Let's not forget he's most likely straight.

Straight guys have no business being in my fantasies—for my own sanity.

"There's someone at the bar who asked to meet you," he says.

"Who?"

"I don't know? Some woman. She might be a singer."

Heather turns and scoffs. "You mean Rihanna? Yeah, she's 'just a singer.'"

I shake my head. "Don't mind this guy. He's uncultured." I lean in and kiss Heather's cheek. "I'll see you tomorrow and introduce you to Evah." I don't bother saying goodbye to the guy.

As soon as Brix and I are out of earshot, I nudge him. "You're like a ninja. Where did you go?"

"I went to the bar to get you a drink so I could pounce at the right moment. I was chilling against the wall behind you the whole time." He grins. "See, I don't even need to wear camo to be invisible."

I force myself to talk to a few more people. Brix sticks out like a sore thumb in here in his tight black T-shirt and jeans, not because of how casual he looks but because of how well he pulls it off in a room full of image snobs who are all wearing designer labels. He might not look like he fits in, but he's so confident no one would even question it. They probably assume he's doing it to be ironic.

Brix only has to save me with a drink refill two or three more times, but then I decide I'm peopled out and need to go home.

Being *on* is exhausting, and it's not like I can be myself around any of these party types.

I spot Denver in the hallway leading to his bedroom before we're about to leave.

"I'm gonna go say bye." I leave Brix near the entryway and interrupt Denver about to kiss Heather. "Sorry to cut in, guys."

Denver groans. "Oh, God, it's suddenly five years ago, and I want to kill him again."

I grip his shoulder. "You still love me. Heather, you mind if I steal him for a second?"

She smiles. "Go for it." She runs her hand down Denver's chest. "I'll be in your room."

"What's up?" Denver asks, but his eyes are glued to Heather's retreating ass.

"I just want to say I'm bailing, but thanks for, uh, inviting me and doing this." I wave my hand around.

Denver glances down at his drink. "I was surprised when you called."

"I'm the shittiest person in the world, I know. I've been busy, and—"

"Nah, I get that. I might not be as successful on my own as you are, but even my schedule is insane. And they've asked me to be a judge on some new reality talent show which will be awesome, but I don't know how I'm going to juggle it all."

"Hey, congrats. Though, how are you going to handle that? You're like a puppy and can't be mean to anyone. It's, like, physically impossible for your baby face to scowl."

To prove my point, he scowls and looks even more childlike.

"Aww, you're so cute."

Denver laughs. "Fuck you."

I lower my voice. "Thanks for the offer, but I heard you don't swing my way."

Something weird happens to Denver's face, but it's gone in a flash.

His smile falls back into place. "Well, thanks for coming. I know this isn't your scene. Never was."

"Brix thinks I need to get out of my head. I can't write, so he thought a change of scenery would help. All it's done is make me exhausted."

Denver glances toward the door where Brix waits for me. "So, full-time bodyguard … Was the stalker situation that bad?"

The urge to reach for my ear is strong, but I refrain. This is Denver. Denny. We spent seven years practically living and performing together. Out of anyone, he'd understand the most.

"It wasn't bad. Just … scary."

"Seems like a bodyguard might be good for you, though. Anyone who can get you to walk away when you're trying to write deserves a medal."

"He's ex-military. I think he has a lot of medals."

"He's also superhot."

I cock my head at him.

"Objectively speaking. Any chance of—" Denver waggles his eyebrows.

"Fuck no. As far as he's aware, I'm with Evah. And please, as if anyone who looks like him could bat for my team."

"I dunno. He's checking you out pretty hard right now."

I turn to look, but Brix is staring at us in the way a bodyguard should. "He's making sure you don't kill me for cockblocking you."

"Hmm, maybe. Speaking of which, Heather's waiting. I'm guessing you're on your way home to shower off all the cooties."

"Funny." Even if he's not far off the mark. "Though someone totally coughed earlier. Is it wrong to hope they were choking?"

Denver laughs, and we do the man-hug thing again.

"Hope you find your words," Denver says. "You always do."

Yeah, I do. Usually. Right now, I'm worried they'll never come back.

As per Brix's orders, one night out down. One more to go.

I lean against the doorjamb to Evah's room and watch as she puts on big blingy earrings. "You look amazing."

She stares at me in the mirror. "Save it for the cameras."

I approach her and put my hands on her hips. Her gold sequined gown is rough under my palms. "I'm not blowing smoke up your ass here. You really do look amazing."

She turns. "Really?"

I want to roll my eyes. "You're a beautiful girl. You know that."

"Sometimes it's nice to be reminded by someone other than myself when I do my morning affirmations in the mirror."

I think I've got it bad in Hollywood, but it's nothing on the women in this industry.

"You're going to be the most gorgeous woman there tonight."

She knows something's up. "One compliment too far, buddy. What do you want?"

"I think my bodyguard has been reading shit about me online, and now he keeps staring at me like he knows our secret. He asked about us having separate rooms."

"Tell him. It's not like he can tell anyone else. It's in his contract that he's not allowed to."

"It's not that. It's … I don't know. I don't want him to see me as weak. It's bad enough he has to babysit me, and he's already asked me why I don't tell the label I need more time to write. Imagine what he'll say when he finds out I'm not standing up to them about my sexuality."

"You think being gay is the same as being weak?"

"Don't do that. You know that's not what I mean. I feel weak about not taking control of our public narrative. Now we're in too deep, and anything we do could affect your blossoming career, and I just don't want another person knowing."

"What's one more person?"

I grunt in frustration.

Her eyes widen. "You like him."

"Please. Not possible."

"You really like him."

"That's not it. Can you please pretend you love me?"

"I do love you."

"We need to pretend like we're *in* love. Not just have platonic feelings and mutual respect for each other."

"Fine. Though I think you should tell him."

"I think you should fix your lipstick. You've got some on your teeth."

"Fuck." She turns back to the mirror and scrubs madly at the nonexistent mark with her finger.

"I'll see you in the limo." I leave her to it. She'll realize I was lying soon enough. Or she'll think she fixed it.

Gideon is standing by the car when I get outside.

"Hey, thanks for coming, but you know you didn't have to."

"I wanted to. You and Evah are kind of a package."

If we want to get technical, we are, but we're both still very much individuals, and she has her own manager-slash-agent-slash-fat-shamer.

"Business-wise, I mean." Gideon has a weird smile on his face.

"Right. Okay." I climb into the car and freeze.

Brix is already there, and now he's staring at me in the way he has been all week. Like he's trying to read the big pink neon flashing sign in my head that says "gay."

I assume that's what's in every gay man's head. That or naked men. Hmm, yeah, definitely naked men. In my head and on my Insta. If someone were to ever hack my phone, there would never be any question in the media with how many naked butts they'd find.

"You look good in a suit," Brix says.

So does he, but I'm not going to say that.

I move to sit next to him so Gideon and Evah can slide straight into the car. "I look good in everything."

Brix snorts. "Of course."

"You actually look normal. Like, a nonlethal, regular man instead of a badass."

Brix opens his jacket to show off a gun in a shoulder holster. "Still a badass."

Damn, why is that so hot?

No, not hot. Nope.

Evah can't be right. I don't like Brix. I can't have a crush on my bodyguard for a million reasons.

One, he's straight.

Two, he's straight.

Oh, and three, he's straight.

And even if he wasn't, mixing business with pleasure has blown up in my face before, and I don't want that kind of heartache again. Ever.

I can't look at Brix that way. I just can't.

Yet, when I glance at him out of the corner of my eye, he's got that smug look on his face, and his insane body in a suit and tie makes my cock thicken.

So instead of looking at him, I stare out the window.

And when Evah climbs into the car, I force myself to look at her like I want to look at Brix.

CHAPTER 8
BRIX

SOMETHING WEIRD IS HAPPENING, and I'm not sure if it cements my suspicions or squashes them.

In public, walking the red carpet and smiling, Harley and Evah make the perfect couple. They're both these stunningly attractive people, and a chemistry I haven't seen between them before sparkles in their eyes. It's as if they're putting a spell on each other and the crowd watching them.

While their interactions at home have been warm, it feels like there's only friendship between them.

The spark right now is unmistakable, but I have to wonder if it's all for show.

We enter the event room that has 4Evah in big letters everywhere.

Even though this is Evah's night, everyone swarms toward Harley.

Like at the party we went to last night, Harley is charming and smiles brightly.

He's *captivating*.

That's probably part of the Eleven charm. He was no doubt coached to be like that in public.

Harley catches my gaze, and as we lock eyes, he reaches for something. I think he's going for his ear and wants to be rescued, but no. His arm wraps around Evah, and he pulls her closer to him. I don't know why I'm disappointed he doesn't need me.

He turns his head to kiss the top of her hair, and I can practically see the women they're standing with let out a collective "Aww."

I watch them all night—for security reasons, of course—but the more I watch, the more determined Harley seems to prove something to me. Or maybe to the public.

The first thing he does when we all file back into the limo is hold out his hand for me to give him hand sanitizer.

"You know, overusing this stuff will give you cancer," I say.

"Those studies have never been proven. Everything seems to give you cancer these days. I'll take the risk."

Evah and Harley go back to their usual friendly selves on the ride home, losing that spark they fake so well.

Yet, when we get home and I check his room to give him his ridiculous "All clear," I have more solid evidence that I'm reading into things.

Instead of Evah going to her room, Harley drags her into his.

And the look he gives me as he shuts the door behind him? Yeah, there's no question about what they're doing in there.

I try not to hate that.

Which is ridiculous. She's his fiancée. They're getting married. I've known that from the beginning.

Harley's right. I shouldn't believe what I read online. I also shouldn't be disappointed their relationship is real.

My feet take me toward my room, but I pause at the door. There's no way I'm gonna be able to sleep, knowing what they're doing in there.

I tell myself it's because it's been so long since I've had sex I'm jealous I'm not getting any.

Yup, sure, let's go with that lie.

Instead of trying to go to sleep, I change out of my monkey suit and into a pair of running shorts and a tank top. I checked the newly installed security cameras in the limo on the way home, but I'll still do an in-person perimeter check. Then I'll head to the basement to hopefully sweat out the crappy emotions trying to take hold.

The side fence is lower than it should be, and anyone could easily jump it—just like the guy who broke in did.

A security alert would've been sent to my phone if the cameras picked up any movement, but sometimes technology can be a bitch. Excuse my lack of trust in it when I've seen guys get their legs blown off by IEDs while holding detection devices.

Only a few minutes have passed since I left Harley's room, got dressed, and headed outside, yet, I definitely know Evah's bedroom light was off when we arrived home.

Which makes me wonder …

I almost make a run for my room to collect my gun in case there's an intruder again, but if my suspicions are correct, no one is in there but Evah herself.

And before I can turn and make my way back to check it out, a figure appears in the window.

It's definitely Evah.

In her room.

Not in Harley's.

A wide smile spreads across my face. I'm right about them. I feel it in my gut.

I refuse to think about why that makes me so happy.

As much as I'd love to go gloat to Harley about knowing it's all fake, I have to realize there's a reason he hasn't told me. He's not letting me in yet. Not fully.

And what's a bodyguard without trust?

I'm gonna make Harley tell me himself when he thinks the time is right.

But first, I'm gonna tell Evah that it's safer if she closes her curtains at night.

I'm sipping my morning coffee when Harley makes an appearance in the kitchen.

He looks his usual self, all bright-eyed and annoyingly handsome.

"Long night?" I try not to smirk behind my coffee cup.

"Not particularly." Harley freezes. "Well, I mean, apart from, like, the usual."

"The usual," I murmur. "Must've been up most of the night. You look like you got no sleep."

He actually looks amazing in sweats and no shirt, but I'm not gonna say that.

As if sensing what I'm implying, he nods. "Oh. Right. Yeah, we didn't sleep much."

"Lucky you've got nothing to do today but write, then, I guess."

"Right." Harley pours himself a cup of coffee and takes a tub of yogurt out of the fridge.

"If I didn't say it last night, you and Evah make the perfect couple."

His eyes narrow. "Okay. Umm, thanks."

"When are you getting married?" My tone is upbeat, even by Iris's standards.

Harley scoops a giant spoon of yogurt into his mouth. "Soon." It comes out "*thoon.*"

"Oh, so there's a date set?"

"Well, uh, no. Our schedules are super busy right now, so …"

"All you're doing is writing, and now that her launch is over, she should have plenty of time. I'm surprised she isn't all bridezilla after eighteen months of being engaged."

"You've been reading shit on the internet again," Harley mumbles.

"Maybe. I'm just wondering what's keeping you lovebirds from tying the knot."

"Busy schedules. Like I said. I need to get this next album out."

"You just came off a tour. You'll produce another album and then go on tour again. Isn't that how these things work? So, wouldn't now be the perfect time for a wedding?"

"You're weird today. I'm going to get to work. I need to write at least one usable song." Harley makes his way toward the sitting room.

"Iris should be here soon, and I'll head out as soon as he gets here."

He turns back. "What are you doing on your day off?"

"The same thing I did last week."

"You didn't tell me what you did last week."

I wink. "I know."

Just like Harley is keeping something huge from me, my extracurricular activities are none of his business.

Maybe this trust thing needs to go both ways, but I haven't told anyone about my situation, and I don't plan to.

Guess I shouldn't push for him to confide in me when I have no intention of letting him in on my burden. Though I could argue as his bodyguard, I need to know things about him in order to protect him better. He doesn't need to know shit about my life.

Iris arrives as I grab my wallet, keys, and phone from my room.

"Ooh, are we writing more songs today?" Iris throws himself on the floor next to Harley.

"Have a fun day," I say on my way out.

Before I leave, I hear Iris say, "You know what rhymes with cutie? Booty. You should put some booty in there."

Harley's mumbling can be heard from the front door. "Today's going to be a long day."

Yeah, for him and me both.

The hour-and-a-half trip out to San Bernardino is far enough away to make the sickly churning feeling in my gut settle. It's enough time to put my happy face on and keep my emotions in check.

This is the one place I hate coming to but can't blow off. Especially now that my visits are down to once a week.

They've always been sporadic, but when I've been home from ops, I've been able to get out here more often.

Now, it feels like it's not enough.

He understands, though.

I park the car in the lot of the Nevaeh Care Facility, a depressing place if I ever saw one.

The outside is as gloomy as the inside, with no gardens or frills. Just a plain, dark gray building with white trim.

Inside smells like chemicals—the kind you need to disguise the scent of death—and I hate that this is the best I can afford.

Maybe one day soon when my debts are paid, I can pay to move him somewhere better. I need a year or two. Maybe less if this Harley gig becomes permanent. It's not a job I wanted to do long term initially, but it's easy, Harley's surprisingly less of a diva than I was expecting, and after another six months at it, my debts will be almost completely wiped.

My boots squeak along the long corridor.

I knock twice and let myself into room 207, and there *he* is.

The right side of his mouth quirks—it's how he smiles. It's the only movement he can manage in his face other than blinking.

I make sure not to show how much it kills me to see him like this.

He looks a hell of a lot older than he should. He's unable to speak and can barely even move.

I take my seat by his side and reach for his hand.

He squeezes it four times quickly, followed by two more.

"Hi," I reply back.

He squeezes my hand in another sequence.

M-I-S-S Y-O-U

My heart shatters.

CHAPTER 9
HARLEY

EVAH ROLLS her eyes as I drag her into my bedroom for the second night in a row and say goodnight to Brix, who just cleared my room. I think the funniest thing about that is it has become routine with him. He doesn't even question it anymore. He just does it.

It kind of takes the fun out of it, but it's still entertaining.

"This is getting ridiculous, Harley." She sits on the end of my bed while we wait a safe amount of time for Brix to go to his room. "I'm pretty sure he knows."

"Which is why we have to make it appear even more real."

"I don't think doubling down is the right way to go here."

I step up onto my bed and start jumping up and down.

"Didn't your mother ever tell you not to jump on your bed?"

"Never. Come jump with me. Ooh, and let's make sex noises while we're at it."

Evah stands. "And I'm out."

"Evah," I whine.

"You're acting insane."

I stop jumping and land on my ass. "What do you think Brix does on his day off?"

"Enjoys not having to put up with you."

I hold my heart. "You wound me, dearest fiancée."

Evah looks sheepish. "About that ..."

Damn it. I know what's coming.

Like Brix said, we've been engaged for eighteen months. The media is starting to speculate if we're ever going to get married. The original plan was for a quick wedding, but the mere engagement toned down the unwanted rumors swirling around me.

I thought the label would make us do it after my "coming out" song was released, but the backlash was a lot less than anticipated.

In fact, the suspicion surrounding my sexuality is currently working in my favor by keeping my name fresh in the media. That's another reason the label is reluctant to take it further. Right now, the mystery causes hype. Hype gets me interview requests. Interviews sell albums.

Evah and I both know this fake engagement will never make it down the aisle. My career doesn't need it. And now that 4Evah has taken off, and she's made a name and brand for herself, she doesn't need it either.

I realized that the other night when we were at her launch.

"We need to work out a way to break up without it coming back on either of us," I say.

She lets out a breath as if she was about to drop a bombshell on me that I wasn't prepared for. "We both know I'm going to take the hit on that one, but my agent says I'm in a place where it shouldn't do too much damage. Not if both our teams agree to spin it the right way."

"People will want to kill you for breaking my poor heart."

"Your poor, poor heart," she says dryly.

"Hey, maybe it'll trigger some writing inspiration. I could release hate songs like Taylor Swift."

She frowns. "You still haven't written anything?"

"Nothing I can use."

"That sucks."

"Yep." I stand and give my soon-to-be ex-fiancée a hug. "We'll work out the breaking up thing."

"Thank you. Okay, I'm going to make a break for my room."

"No, wait. You didn't answer me. Where do you think Brix goes on his day off?"

"Why do you care?"

"I want to know."

Evah puts her hands on her hips. "No."

"No?" I ask her incredulously.

"You won't even tell him that we're not actually together, so you don't get to pry into his life."

"But …" *I want to.* "Why do you have to be all *fair* and shit? You should be on my side."

"We're about to break up, remember? That means I don't have to take your side."

"No wonder we're breaking up." I hug her again. She has always given the best hugs. "It's no secret I didn't want this"—I pull back and do air quotes—"'relationship' in the beginning, but it's been kind of nice having you around."

"Nice? *Nice?* That's what you'd say about your grandmother visiting, not the awesomeness that has been my friendship."

I'll miss her making me smile. "If it weren't for you, I don't know if I would've survived the last eighteen months. You've been a true friend when I've really needed one."

"Aww. We'll still be friends."

I doubt that, but I want to believe her. Once it gets out to the public that we broke off the engagement, everyone will speculate about how bad a breakup it was. It'll be suspicious if we still see each other. It could turn into a huge *will they, won't they* thing.

It could be a publicity nightmare.

The other night at Denver's party, Heather and I talked about fan expectations, and it reminded me of that. Half of them want one thing, and the other half want the other. Some people love Evah and me together, but others hate her without even knowing her. It's inevitable we're going to piss people off no matter what.

And no amount of screaming "It's my life and my choice" will make them change their mind. Being famous means every single person in the world is allowed to have an opinion on my actions, and they're allowed to voice it publicly.

It doesn't mean we have to like it, but it's not like we can retaliate, or we look like the assholes because we're the ones in mansions and have these amazing lives that nearly everyone on the planet wants a taste of. We're not allowed to get butthurt by people telling us we suck.

Gotta say, crying into buckets of money, while good in theory, doesn't make shit better. It doesn't make it less lonely.

More first-world problems in the life of Harley Valentine.

"When do you think we should do it?" I ask her.

"I don't know. Maybe after the publicity for 4Evah dies down a little?"

I nod. "That'll give us some time to work out all the logistics."

"Goodnight." Evah kisses me on the cheek.

"Night."

As soon as she leaves my room and I'm alone again, the large, empty space of the master bedroom feels too big. Too empty.

Soon enough, Evah will find her own place and move out, and even though I should be excited at the prospect, possibly even toy with the media by being seen with men instead of her, I know not much will change.

She'll move on, but I'll still be where I have been for the past decade—working toward a goal I'm beginning to think is unachievable.

No matter how successful I get, I'll always want more.

Because hiding behind a career is easier than going for what I want.

And what I want is to be loved.

Truly loved.

Brix walks into the living room, his long, thick legs exposed in tiny shorts, his muscular arms glistening with sweat, while his black tank top shows off every impressive line and curve of his wide chest. I bet his skin tastes salty and sweet.

Dog, wrong tree.

I shake those kinds of thoughts free.

He's been downstairs in the basement gym working out, and I've been trying not to imagine what that looks like while I write … nothing.

I've still got nothing.

When I finally admitted to myself that I want to be truly loved, my dick replaced the word "loved" with "fucked" and now my little crush … no, my *lust*, for my bodyguard has tripled.

That's all it is. Lust.

After a straight guy.

That has done nothing for my inspiration even though it should be giving me angsty unrequited-love lyrics.

Fantasizing about Brix being all sweaty in the gym is even sadder than when I was pining after my ex-boyfriend while he was in love with someone else.

"How's the writing going?" Brix runs a towel over his wet head.

"Torturous." Only, I'm not talking about the writing.

"Want to take the day off? You haven't left the house since Evah's thing."

"That was, like, only a few days ago."

"Ten. It's been ten days."

I groan and lie back on the carpet. "I don't want to go out."

"Okay, diva, calm down. We don't have to go out, but you do need some vitamin D."

My gaze flies to his, and my mouth drops open. Then I realize he means actual vitamin D and not a euphemism for his dick.

"You have an amazing pool fifty feet away. We should go swimming."

Swimming.

Together.

I run my gaze over his muscles again and eye his black tank top. He wouldn't be wearing that in the pool. He'd be completely shirtless.

Bad Harley.

"I'd rather not," I croak.

"Let me rephrase. We are going swimming. If you don't get your trunks on, I'll throw you in wearing all your clothes."

"Isn't that considered assault nowadays? What if I have my phone in my pocket?"

"I'm giving you fair warning, so I'd get rid of it if I were you."

If Brix doesn't already suspect I'm gay, it'll be impossible to hide if he picks me up and throws me in the pool.

And as he steps toward me, I jump up and run toward the stairs leading to my bedroom.

"Fine. I'll go swimming."

I usually wear board shorts with nothing underneath when I swim, but that's not going to hide the inevitable hard-on I'll get watching my insanely ripped bodyguard all wet and half-naked.

I find a pair of Speedos and slip them on first and then my board-shorts over top. Yeah, this isn't going to help. I cup my package through the material.

Why does he have to be so hot?

All the way downstairs, I try to steel myself to get through this, like I'm preparing for days of mental torture. Because I am.

I can already imagine what Brix looks like with next to no clothes on. I don't need to see the real thing.

I realize that as soon as I reach outside and sink my feet into the grass in the backyard that no amount of preparing myself will be affective.

Brix is doing laps, his long arms powerful and strong. The muscles in his back contract with every stroke, and he pushes through the water as fast as a damn torpedo.

And I'm already hard.

Yep, that took zero point three seconds.

Brix hits the wall and grabs onto the side of the pool, lifting himself up to sit on the edge. His body shoots out of the water as if in slow motion. Or maybe that's my brain slowing it down so I can watch all the water rivulets drip down his skin.

Well, that filled my spank bank reserves for the next decade.

"Coming in?"

"Going to make me?" And now I'm taunting him. *Smart, Harley. Really smart.*

Brix swings his legs over the side of the pool as if to come get me, and I flinch. I do not need this man's hands on me right now.

I want them on me for sure, but nope, nope, nope.

"Okay, okay, I'm getting in." I go to the opposite side of the pool and slip into the cool water, but even the low temperature isn't enough to put out the heat in my groin. I swim around trying to get my dick to deflate.

"Enjoying your break from writing yet?"

"No," I grumble. I should've put sunblock on because the sun is high and hot today. I'm so going to burn. "I should be working."

"When was the last time you came out here and enjoyed the view?" He slips into the pool and swims to the wall that faces the wide panorama that is LA and its surroundings.

I want to fight the urge to go to him, but I know I'll lose, so I don't even pretend like I'm going to try. I swim over to him but make sure to leave a few feet between us. "I don't think I've ever used the pool before. Evah has, but …" I shrug.

"How long have you lived in this house?"

I count. "A little over a year? I bought it a few months after Eleven broke up."

"And you've never been in the pool? Doesn't that tell you you're pushing yourself too hard? Working too much?"

"I need to push that hard. I need to work that hard."

Brix's lips press together. "Why?"

That empty part of my soul screams loudly. *Because I don't have anything else.*

"I just … do."

Brix isn't satisfied with my answer, and I can't blame him. I'm not happy with it myself. But I'm not going to admit that I throw myself into music to drown out that loud noise in the back of my brain telling me that love doesn't truly exist.

I'm destined to be alone as long as my career is my first priority, so why fight it?

Brix inches closer to me, and I hold my breath. He lowers his voice. "You know what you have to do, then?"

"What?"

His lips turn upward just slightly. "Play harder."

Next thing I know I'm under the water with this big mountain of a man pushing me down.

I'm torn between enjoying the zing of pleasure from his touch and wanting to shove him and struggle against him. In the end, air wins out. Because I kind of need that.

He lets me come up, and I splutter as I hit the surface.

"I'm pretty sure drowning me is on the list of things you shouldn't do as my bodyguard."

"The question is, is it more fun than watching a video of someone getting kicked in the nuts? I'm trying to fulfill my obligations here."

Smug son of a bitch.

"It's not. I'm above this childish game, and as if I could ever win against you when you're twice my size." I blink innocently at him.

Brix looks like he might be buying my bullshit but is a bit wary. "All right," he gives in. "I won't push you under the water again." As soon as Brix's back is turned, I smile and make my move.

I attack him from behind, but immediately, I hit the water while big hands hold me down.

When I'm let up this time, Brix is grinning.

"So predictable," he taunts.

I shake out my hair, flicking water everywhere. "Really?"

"Aww, Pop Star. Do you underestimate me that much?" He steps closer to me, and my cock hardens again. I think it's confused between being turned on and genuinely worried I'm going to drown.

Because my dick thinks about these things.

I think Brix is going to grab me again, but as I look up at his face and he steps even closer, I freeze along with my breathing.

The anticipation of him touching me has neediness thrumming through my veins.

And then? The fucker splashes me and sends a wall of water my way.

I cough. "Oh, it's on."

He turns his back and tries to escape, but one thing about his size is it makes him slower than I am. I jump on his back, wrapping my legs around his waist this time.

Big mistake.

The biggest.

My cock doesn't have time to get too into it because Brix easily flips me off his back, and there I am again, under the water.

Motherfucker.

Against my better judgment, my stubborn side won't let it go. That's how my bodyguard practically waterboards me for an hour.

It's still the most fun I've had in a long time.

"Do you trust me?" Brix asks.

I look up at him from my usual spot on the floor where I'm still trying to write.

"Nope." I'm joking. It's weird how much I do trust him.

By this point, it's not a trust issue I have with telling Brix about my sexuality. It's self-preservation. I don't want him to realize I've been eye-fucking him for weeks.

His face falls, probably not realizing I was being sarcastic.

"I'm kidding. I trust you. What's up?"

"I was thinking we could hit the firing range like I promised."

"You're still trying to distract me from my work? You're a bad influence. Are we sure you're the right bodyguard for me?"

Though, I'd be lying if I said I didn't like someone fussing over me and trying to make sure I look after myself mentally. I have a chef and a personal trainer to take care of my physical needs, but I realize I've never had a handler to tame the chaos going on in my head before.

I shouldn't go with Brix, but it's clear my muse is on vacation. Or dead. "I need something to pull me out of this funk. Maybe shooting things will help."

"In my experience, shooting stuff always cheers me up, but blowing shit up is better."

My face lights up. "Do you have somewhere we can go to do that?"

"My boss has a ranch where we do training ops in the desert about three hours away. It'd be an overnight trip."

I stand. "I can write in the car."

Brix looks concerned. "Should I be worried about *how* excited you are? The other day I had to practically drag you outside to get some sun, but with the promise of explosives and gunfire, suddenly work isn't a big deal."

"I've never been high before let alone allowed to use explosives." I jump up and down, probably a little too enthusiastically. "I'll go pack!"

"I'll call the boss and check it's okay. Maybe invite some of the other guys."

"Oh, like a party?"

"Like, as witnesses. Just in case." He hits buttons on his phone and puts it on speaker.

"West," the deep voice answers.

"Hey, anyone at the ranch over the next two days?"

A heavy sigh comes through the phone. "Please tell me the diva pop star didn't piss you off and now you have to hide a body."

I snort.

"No, though it's been tempting."

I give him the finger.

"I kinda promised him I'd let him shoot things and blow shit up."

"Of course you did."

"Well, I figure it's time we all have a refresher course on explosives. Two birds ..."

"I'll call the others."

They end the call, and Brix smiles at me. "That was easy. Ready for this?"

"I'm going to be badass like you."

"Calm down, *Rambo*."

I pause. "We can't both be named Rambo. You can call me ..." I tap my chin. "Mr. Badass."

Brix laughs. "Go pack all your beauty products, Mr. Badass. We roll out in twenty."

"I'm so excited I don't even care that you're mocking me." I race to my room and pull out the small suitcase I use for short trips, but I pause outside my closet. What am I supposed to wear?

"Fuck it." I throw in a few options.

And then I grab my toiletries which, okay, do include some skin cream and hair products. It's part of my job to stay young and fresh, and—

My gaze catches my face in the mirror. With all the writing and not going out I've been doing, my facial hair is coming in thick.

The last time I shaved was for Evah's party. My ginger is showing.

I can't leave without getting rid of it.

There's a reason photos of me as a child have never surfaced on TMZ or other tabloid sites. I'm pretty sure I've burned them all. My hair was bright red growing up, and then when I hit puberty, it darkened to look more brown than red. My beard, however, gives away that I was once a bright-eyed ginger with fair skin who used to get picked on daily.

I'm midshave when Brix yells from somewhere in the house.

"Come on, Mr. Badass."

"Two minutes," I yell back.

When I make my appearance, wheeling my suitcase behind me, I'm met with Brix's damn cocky face.

"We're only going overnight."

"I didn't know what to wear. And I had to shave, and—"

"The guys are gonna eat you alive," Brix mutters.

Little does he know how appealing that sounds to me, but I'm guessing he doesn't mean it the way my dirty mind is thinking.

"What's that supposed to mean?"

"It means you're going to the middle of the desert with a bunch of ex-military dudes who will all be in cargo pants and T-shirts, not decked out in Tom Ford. They won't give a shit what you're wearing."

My mouth drops open. "I'm sorry, back it up here a sec. You didn't know my *name* but you can tell my jeans are Tom Ford?" My eyes narrow. "Who *are* you?"

"I'm the guy who's about to kick your ass out the door. Hurry up. If the others beat us there, we'll lose out on a bedroom and have to camp in the desert. I've done enough of that in my lifetime."

"Ooh, I've never been camping. Can we do that?"

Brix shudders, almost like he's cringing at the sadness that is my sheltered life. "If Iris comes, ask him."

"Hmm, he doesn't happen to come with an off switch, does he? He. Never. Stops. Talking."

Brix laughs. "We've searched for one but found nothing."

"Did you do a thorough search?"

"No one would volunteer to get *that* close to him."

I almost volunteer for the job, but I guess that whole keeping my sexuality a secret would be over then.

We get in the car, and even though I keep a paper on my lap, I don't do anything but doodle stars and shapes on it.

I'm too distracted to concentrate on words.

Ever since Evah told me we're definitely going to do the breaking up thing, my mind has been pinging back and forth on what my future looks like.

Every now and then, I feel Brix's eyes on me, but unlike Iris, who has to hate silence with how much he has the tendency to fill it, Brix only seems to talk when he needs to.

Yet, that stare. That *I know you're hiding shit from me* stare burns like a bitch.

It takes about an hour and a half of silence and his brown eyes on me before I crack.

"Evah and I are breaking up," I blurt.

Half-truth.

Brix doesn't reply right away, and when I turn to look at him, his lips press into a thin line. "Makes sense."

"That's it? That's all you have to say? Everyone loves us. We're like Hollywood's *it* couple."

"You sleep in different rooms."

"She snores."

"Oh. Right. *That.*"

I *knew* he didn't believe me.

"Either way, I'm sorry whatever arrangement you guys had isn't working out."

"Want to hear the fucked-up thing? I never wanted to marry her in the first place."

"Why not?"

"Don't get me wrong. She's a great girl, and she helped me through some heartache, but our whole relationship was a setup by the label."

"An arranged marriage?"

"Yep. It's actually more common in Hollywood than you'd think. A lot of couples are set up by their PR reps."

"Yeah, but they don't force them to get married. Why marriage?"

To keep lying or to come clean?

"It was when Eleven was breaking up. The label thought to keep me relevant and present in the public eye, the best thing to do would be to give them something to talk about."

He says, "Makes sense," again. It's his *I call bullshit* phrase without actually saying it.

I slump. "Okay, fine, that's not entirely true."

"I never said you were lying."

"You didn't have to."

Brix remains quiet, which makes me fall silent too.

It's a problem I've always had, really, admitting who I am. It goes against the image the label created for me, and I guess it's been easier to go with the narrative I was given than to lead my own.

My hand writes that down.

I read over the words over and over again, and then suddenly a song starts forming in my mind.

I may not be able to say it, but I can write it. Singing it is another question.

Lyrics pour out of me, and my usual back-and-forth of writing, then erasing, rewriting and cutting, ignites the muse inside me.

"Looks like you found your words," Brix says.

"Shh."

He laughs.

Before I know it, we're pulling up to a mansion in the middle of the desert.

Stone-wall entry, cement-rendered and modern, the house shits all over mine back in LA.

"What kind of ass-backward 'ranch' is this?" I ask.

Brix grins. "We call it the ranch because it used to be a little three-bedroom cabin on the other side of the property, but umm, let's just say Trav has been doing well these last few years."

I get out of the car and do a full circle. "I want to live here."

"I'm sure Trav could maybe keep you as a pet. Or a singing monkey. Don't know if he's a fan of boy band music, though."

"He knows who I am. That's one step up from you when we met."

"We have to talk about your standards."

I shake my head. "Nah, my standards are good. I like people who know my name more than those who don't. Pretty simple."

"Well, I know your name now."

"Just what I wanted when I put my heart and soul into my solo album. Now, if only I could hire the rest of the population who didn't buy it to be my bodyguard ..."

"Decent plan."

"Are you showing me to my room or what?" I ask.

"You mean *our* room."

"Our?" My heart beats wildly at the idea of sharing a room with Brix.

"We may be somewhere safe with a group of guys I'd trust with my life, but it's my job to be your shadow whenever you're not in your own home. Hence, one room. Unless you really do want to camp with Iris."

Camping with Iris would be the safer option. But am I going to take it?

Nope.

CHAPTER 10
BRIX

WE SETTLE into our room—one that's at the back of the house. I wanted to get to it first because it's the biggest and has a couch I can crash on while Harley takes the bed. Even if I am a good six inches taller than he is and he'd fit better on the couch. I have a feeling it wouldn't go over well if I asked for the bed.

"When do we get to blow shit up?" he asks, and I have to admit his excitement is kinda cute.

"How about we teach you how to use a gun first. The explosives can be like positive reinforcement. Do well with a gun, you get to play with C4."

"You'd make the bestest parent ever."

"At least you're willing to admit you're basically like a child."

"Where's my gun?" He's like a damn puppy.

"I'm already regretting this."

"Nah, it's going to be fun."

"Getting shot could be considered fun, I guess. Follow me."

The ranch is on acres of land in the middle of nowhere near Palm Desert with no neighbors. It means we can make as much noise as we want without alerting anyone.

Harley walks through the halls with a look of awe in his dark blue eyes. We really should call it the *mansion* instead of the ranch.

Our bed is a four-poster, and the room has a bear-skin rug. Not even joking.

Trav as a person is a basic man. Which is why when he hired a decorator and told them to "go nuts," they turned this brand-new, empty mansion with high ceilings and marble tile throughout into a pimp's heaven.

We're talking animal print everywhere, plush couches, and tacky furnishings that the designer supposedly called "retro," but it looks like there should be hookers swinging from poles and neon lights everywhere.

Trav says it's fine for what we need, but I have to secretly wonder if he *likes* how over-the-top it is.

Harley's house is decorated for beyond his years, and Trav's … well, I imagine the interior decorator he hired also works on porn sets. I could totally see porn being made here.

Maybe I'll suggest it to Trav as a backup career plan if Mike Bravo folds.

Not that it will.

Trav's too well-known and too successful in his field.

The shooting range is separate from the house and very much more in line with Trav's personality. It's barren and army green. It's within walking distance, so I take Harley through the perfectly manicured gardens.

Trav has people looking after this place, and I have to wonder how much they're paid to keep it secret.

We get to the walk-in weapons locker, and I punch in the code. I take out a Glock 26 with a red dot scope to start him on because it's small, compact, and easy to aim.

"Aww, it's a baby." Harley reaches for it.

"No touching."

He pulls his hand back fast. "Why not?"

"Lesson one. Never touch another man's gun without asking first."

"Aren't these technically your boss's guns?"

"Lesson two. Don't be a smartass to the person teaching you how to use a deadly weapon."

Harley nods. "Okay. I guess that's a fair rule."

"We'll start with this one and see how you do." I take out ammo and put it on the table, grab two sets of ear protection and glasses, and then turn toward the Kevlar. "Think I need this?"

He doesn't reply. His face says he wants to say something but is trying to hold back.

"No opinion?"

"Well, you said I'm not allowed to be a smartass, so …"

I can't help smiling. "Let's go."

There're two ranges here. One long and one short. I take Harley to set up in one of the booths on the short course.

There are metal circles that fall when hit along the back, and then other targets throughout the space.

I go through the basics, showing him the gun while it's still unloaded and pointing out everything he needs to know.

While I'm midsentence, it looks like his eyes gloss over, and I ask him to repeat what I said.

He shakes out of his stupor. "Huh?"

"That's what I thought. You do realize you're going to be shooting a gun? It's not a toy. And unlike the last one you used, this will have real bullets."

"Sorry. I know all that. I got … umm, distracted."

"The Evah thing?"

He glances away. "Sure. Uh, the Evah thing."

"Well, distraction is what we don't want when you're working with guns. Especially loaded ones."

"No shit. Sorry. I'm here. I'm focused."

Yet, I don't miss the way his gaze moves over me or the way my chest puffs out automatically.

I like him checking me out.

I like a lot of things about my client I shouldn't.

"Brix?"

It's my turn to have tuned out. I shake it off. "I was just checking you were still paying attention."

Right.

After I finish the safety briefing and show him the proper stance and how to aim the still-unloaded gun, I finally put in a ten-round magazine.

"Earplugs," I say.

When they're in place and his glasses are on, I hesitantly hand him the gun, and I'm reluctant to let it go.

Until he smiles. "I won't shoot you. I promise."

Geez, with his angelic features, he could've told me he *will* shoot me, and I'd still hand over the gun.

"Wow, it's a lot heavier." He tests it out in his hand.

"Loaded guns are like that."

Harley laughs instead of being offended.

I step away and adjust my own protective equipment.

Harley takes his position, and I see the moment he takes a deep breath and prepares himself to squeeze the trigger.

The gun goes off, Harley jolts, and his eyes widen. At least he remembers to put the gun down before turning to me.

"Whoa." His stunned expression amuses me.

"That's all you have to say?"

"It feels … weird. Powerful, but I'm not sure in a good way."

"You get used to it."

He stares out into the field. "I didn't hit anything."

No, he didn't.

"Do it again."

He picks up the gun again and takes the same stance.

"Drop your right shoulder just a bit, and make sure the dot lines up with where you want it to go."

This time the bullet hits the metal circle, but the target doesn't drop because it wasn't hit square in the middle.

"Empty the rest of the magazine," I say.

When he runs out of bullets, missing all the intended targets, he puts the gun down.

"Statistically, you should've hit something."

A middle finger is pointed in my direction. "I'm starting to think it wouldn't have mattered if the gun Gideon gave me was loaded or not. Had I shot at Iris, I would've missed."

"Probably. But if you didn't, you'd be in prison right now, so can you see why Gideon was smart to 'forget' the bullets?"

"Yeah, yeah, I get it. I'll leave being a badass up to you, Rambo."

"Here." I step up to the gun to load another magazine and hand it back to him. "We're gonna keep going until you get it."

This time when he takes his stance, I step behind him and put my hand on his shoulder and the other on his waist.

Harley's scent hits my nose—fresh with a hint of something manly. Woodsy or ... fuck, I don't know. It makes my mind fuzzy, whatever it is.

"Try again," I say.

He does, with me right behind him, and the target falls. When he turns to look at me with a smile, my breath catches.

Being this close to him—no, to *any man*—has my body responding because it's been so long, but I can't go there with Harley.

Trav would fire my ass from this job so fast he'd probably have me shipped off to some shitty surveillance gig in Baghdad as punishment before I could even blink.

And speaking of Trav.

"You're overcorrecting him now."

I flinch at the deep voice and step away from my client. "No, I'm not."

"Yeah, you are. Here." Trav approaches and pushes me out of the way. He takes my place behind Harley and does exactly the same thing I was doing to him.

"How is that any different?" I ask.

"His stance is more natural, and it doesn't look as if he's being forced into a position he's not comfortable in."

I have to wonder if he's still talking about shooting.

Harley blushes as he stares up at my boss.

Not that I can blame him. Where I'm big and solid and have been told I look like I want to kill everything, Trav is even bigger but has softer features. He's more approachable.

And that doesn't make me jealous at all. Never has.

Until possibly right now.

"Umm, hi. I'm Harley."

Trav smiles. "Trav. Brix's boss."

I want to tell him to get his charming mitts off my client.

"Try now," Trav says and steps over to where I am.

This time when Harley shoots, the target falls. And then the next one. He misses the third, but by the time the ten shots are fired, he's hit eight of ten.

Trav glows triumphantly.

"Sure, because all my coaching up until this point counts for nothing."

Trav ignores me and focuses on Harley. "Let's pack this away, and you can meet the others."

Right. The others. One of the reasons I set up this trip in the first place.

I'm starting to regret my decision. Especially when we enter the house and the rest of the team all look like they want to devour Harley. Even Angel, who I thought was more of a lesbian than Ellen DeGeneres, and Domino, who is supposedly straight.

Maybe it's the famous effect. Or maybe it's because he's Harley and he naturally draws people to him.

"Scout, Atlas, Domino, Angel, this is Harley Valentine," Trav says.

Harley waves and puts on the smile I already know is part of his public persona. There's a difference between this smile and his real one.

His real one crinkles the corners of his eyes. His public-ready face is always immaculate. Like, too perfect. It's like he says—it's manufactured.

He leans in closer to me. "Why do you all have weird names?"

I snicker. "You want their real names?"

"Is it one of those 'we'll tell you but then we'll have to kill you' things?"

"No. You already know my name is Nolan and Iris's is Isaac."

"Hmm, still better not. I'm going to struggle to remember the nicknames. But when do I get to blow shit up?"

"Priorities." I turn to Trav. "When are we heading out?"

"Where's Iris?" Trav asks.

"I'm here. I'm here." Iris's voice travels from down the hallway before he appears. There's something different about him, though. He leans against the wall, his arms crossed, and he's giving off a wicked grumpy vibe. Even when Iris is angry, I don't think I've ever seen him show it. He's the type of guy who smiles even when he shouldn't.

"What's wrong with you?" Harley asks, picking up the same thing I am.

"Nothin'. We doing this or what?"

"Let's go." Trav leads us all to his garage where two convertible off-road Jeeps await.

Harley squeezes in between Iris and me in the back of one, with Trav in the driver's seat and Angel next to him, while the others get into the second car.

The unofficial path to the site where we get to play with the big toys is bumpy to say the least. It's unpaved and rarely used, and it's mostly through desert and rough terrain.

At one particular dip, Harley grips onto my thigh before quickly taking his hand back. "Sorry. Didn't have anything to hold on to."

Iris leans in beside him. "You can hold on to me anytime you want."

And he's back. "There's the Iris we all kinda sort of love," I say.

It's a forty-minute slow drive out to the site, and every time Harley reaches for me, the urge to hold his hand is almost over-powering.

That wouldn't scream to my boss *I'm having inappropriate thoughts about my assignment.* Not at all.

With Harley's thigh brushing against mine and his hand gripping my leg, I suddenly wish I wasn't wearing long pants.

I want to know what it would feel like to have his hand on my skin—

Abort thought process. Abort!

We pull to a stop, and Harley's brow furrows. "Did we break down?"

I stand and jump out of the Jeep without opening the door. "Nope. We're here."

"But … how do you know?"

"Where we're going is about five hundred feet that way." I point.

Harley shivers as he gets out of the car. The sun is almost below the horizon now, and the switch from hot desert sun to cool desert night comes quickly.

"Did you bring a jacket?" I ask.

"I did. In my suitcase … back at the house."

Reflexively, I shrug out of mine and put it around him.

"You don't need to—"

"It's my job," I say.

"Can I point out how much of a contradiction this trip is?" Angel steps up beside us. Her long black hair sits in a braid over her shoulder, and she smiles her innocent smile which I know can turn lethal in a second. Her name ain't Angel because she's angelic. She got the nickname Angel of Death for a reason.

"Contradiction?" I ask.

"Yeah, you're supposed to protect the pop star, yet you've brought him to where he might get blown up."

I snort. "The job was too easy. Decided to up the ante so I can see some action."

"Wait, what?" Harley looks worried.

"I'm joking. You're not gonna blow up," I say.

"Hopefully," Angel adds.

Harley trains his wide eyes on me.

"She's messing with you. This is safe. Well, as safe as you can get playing with C4."

"Is C4 one of those explosives that's, like, unpredictable and can explode if you, like, drop it and stuff?"

I bark out a laugh. "No. And you watch way too many movies. Are you actually worried about being blown up? What did you think the risks would be when I brought you out here?"

"No, I get that. I guess …" He looks down at his feet. "I didn't really think about that part. I had an image in my head of pushing down this huge lever thing and something in the distance going *boom*."

Fuck, he's adorable.

Iris and I pull the chest of supplies from the back of the Jeep, and Domino and Scout do the same from theirs.

Harley sticks by my side for the walk, practically swimming in my jacket.

I try not to laugh at how many times the poor guy almost trips. "It's surprising you're not lighter on your feet."

"Ignoring you," he sings.

"Maybe bust out some of those old boy-band moves," Iris says.

"Hate you both now," Harley grumbles.

We get to the detonation site and drop our gear.

"Maybe leave the pop star here while we get it all set up?" Trav says.

I figured as much. "I'll stay with him."

Everyone else makes their way farther out to where the actual explosion will be.

I feel Harley step up next to me more than see him.

"If I haven't said it yet, thank you for bringing me out here."

"You're welcome. You needed out of that house."

Harley nods but doesn't give me the satisfaction of saying I was right. "So, what's everyone's story?"

"Their story?"

"Army, Marines, Navy …"

I smile. "Most of us were army. Scout was a Marine, and Atlas was a SEAL."

"No fucking way."

"Ugh. SEALs. They always get the gushing admirers. Rangers are just as cool as SEALs, you know. Trav was a Ranger."

"So, he's basically what you want to be when you grow up."

I huff. "Something like that." Only, I don't think I want that anymore. Becoming a Ranger was always my goal, but since joining Mike Bravo, my goals have changed. Mainly, I can't think of anything past paying off the mountain of medical bills.

Harley shivers next to me. "Are you cold? Do you want your jacket back?"

"I'm fine."

"We could share it."

"It's okay," I assure him. "I've endured more than a little cold. We don't need to … cuddle."

"Badasses don't cuddle other men?"

"I never said that." I smile at him.

He just looks confused.

I wait for him to ask, to just say the words I've been waiting for since I began working for him, but he doesn't. I've been wondering if

Gideon has said anything to Harley about Mike Bravo and what we stand for, but I've gotten the impression that Harley thinks I'm straight.

Six figures appear on the darkening horizon, making their way back to us.

"Ready to blow shit up?" I ask.

"Oh, I am so ready."

Trav approaches and makes sure we've all got our safety shit on before he hands Harley the detonator. Debris won't come this far, and the explosion is only going to make a small divot in the ground, but safety first.

"Have fun." Trav looks at Harley in that big soft way he has about him.

"Oh my God, oh my God, oh my God," Harley whispers and stares at the simple device like *it's* the explosive.

"Stage fright?" I ask.

"No. This is so cool. Do I just press this?" His thumb hovers over the red button.

I gasp and pretend to try to take it from him. "No! That's the self-destruct button."

I thought he'd know I was joking.

"The … the what?" His voice squeaks.

Clearly not.

Everyone else laughs.

"Yes, it's the red button," I say.

He glares at me. "Just so you know, I'm imagining your head as I do *this*." He hits the button.

The dry desert sand shoots up into the night sky with a cloud of smoke, sending a small wave of dust our way.

Harley's lips twist. "Is that it?"

"Disappointed?"

"I was kind of expecting a giant mushroom cloud and fire and—"

"He is the most adorablest thing ever," Angel says.

Harley, either not sensing she's being condescending or he's ignoring it, smiles at her. "Thanks. I try." He hands me the detonator. "Was still fun. Cheaper than therapy."

"More expensive, actually," Trav says. "C4 is expensive as fuck."

"Oh. Right. Well, it's cheaper for me, then."

"Worth it?" I ask.

"Worth it. Now what?"

"Now, we go again. And then again. Our objective is to get as little an explosion as we can."

Harley doesn't seem to understand. "That one was just for me?"

"Yup," Trav says. "You can thank Brix for me allowing it. Let's clean this shit up and go again."

While they go back out into the field, Harley looks at me with an expression I can't decipher.

"It's actually not too late if you wanted to head back to LA. Up to you," I say, trying to get him to stop staring at me like I did some monumental thing. All I did was ask my boss for a favor.

He shakes his head. "Let's stay. Maybe the desert will give me inspiration."

CHAPTER 11
HARLEY

INSPIRATION? This whole group could inspire me to write songs. However, those lyrics will mainly consist of waxing poetic about sculpted bodies and godlike physiques. Don't think that'll go down well with the label.

With each explosion that goes off, the more bored I get. Today has been fun, and something I'd never normally get the chance to do, which I'm grateful for, but it's all very regimented and safe, which almost takes the thrill out of it.

Of course, with high expectations comes small reward. I pictured Brix's burly teammates all dirty, and maybe shirtless, as they come running away from a bomb that's about to explode, which would all happen in slow motion through my eyes. Yeah, it doesn't happen that way.

It's much less exciting to wait for everyone to cover their faces with a bandana so we don't inhale half the desert into our lungs before they make things blow up.

They are a great group of people, though. Angel's a little feisty, but I like her. The other guys all range in attitude from Iris to Brix. Either smiley and goofy or serious and stoic.

Although, I think Brix has proved he isn't all seriousness. His small jokes, his warm smiles. I know there's someone softer on the inside.

And after we make our way back to the house for beer and poker, another side of Brix comes out I haven't really seen yet.

He's more relaxed.

He sits with his arm draped over my chair next to him while he sips from a longneck bottle.

Maybe this is what he does on his days off.

Being here, where no one knows where I am, not even Gideon because I forgot to call him—oops—Brix is practically off the clock.

It's warm here inside Trav's big boy's room. It's like a man cave but classier. It has a professional poker table, a bar in one corner, and a fireplace that's heating up the room.

Reluctantly, I slip Brix's jacket off my shoulders. I liked wearing it even if it's four sizes too big. It smells like his spicy cologne.

"Yo, Pop Star," Iris says. "You know how to play?" He shuffles a deck of cards so fast I have to wonder if he was a blackjack dealer in a past life.

"A little. I mean, not really. I guess?" I shrug. "Poor sheltered pop star again."

That is what we call bluffing.

"We'll be gentle." Iris winks.

"Beer?" One of the other guys appears beside me with a bottle.

I take it even though I don't like beer. I don't want to turn all Evah on them, but beer has so many calories and doesn't even taste that great.

When I was put on my diet back in those Eleven days, I'd always ask myself the worthiness of the calories. A piece of cake was not worth two hours on a treadmill. Caramel Frappuccino with whipped cream and extra caramel topping? Fill me up and put me on an elliptical machine. Right now.

If I can make this one drink last all night, my trainer won't kick my ass tomorrow during our session.

After I make Brix taste it first. I shove it in front of his face and stare at him expectantly.

He takes a sip, handing it straight back to me with a sarcastic smile. I didn't realize sarcasm came in a facial expression until now.

We play five-card draw, and the first few hands, I waffle and pretend I don't know what I'm doing. I mostly fold, even when I have a decent-ish hand. I'm waiting for the pot to grow nice and big before I make my move. I want to play smart.

And when the opportunity comes up, and the pot is a decent size, I try to keep my face passive.

Iris, Brix, and I are the only ones left in.

"Maybe you guys should fold and give it to me?"

Brix folds immediately. "I'm out."

Iris glances at his teammate. "Really? Giving in to him that easily? There's something about his innocent face I don't trust. He's totally bluffing."

"What's bluffing?" I ask and cock my head.

"Okay, fuck it, I'm out too." Iris throws his cards down.

"Thanks." While I start dragging my winnings toward me, I feel Brix's intense stare.

"What did you have?"

"A pair of queens. Good, no?"

Iris gapes. "A pair of … a …" He clears his throat. "Yeah … great hand."

When I do have something good, I push it hard. Bet big right off the bat.

Iris is quick to raise, probably thinking it'll be easy money. The others play too. All of them are staring at me to see what I'm going to do.

"Call."

Someone else raises, so we go around again. We lose a few, but Iris, me, and the one who's called Map … or Atlas … Globe? Whatever his name is—the one who was a SEAL—is still in.

"Two pair," Iris says. "With aces."

"Full house." The ex-SEAL puts down his cards.

"Damn. Those are both really good hands. I only have four tens." I lay my cards flat.

Brix bursts out laughing. "He's totally playing you all."

"What? Did I win?"

"You're cute as hell, but I know when you're lying, remember?" His finger trails down my cheek, and I have the sudden urge to lean into it.

Then I remember where we are.

He pulls his hand away, way too soon for my liking.

"You let everyone know my tell?" My voice is croaky, but I can blame it on being pretend angry right now.

"I'm so confused," Angel says.

"He has to have played poker before," Brix accuses.

"Fine. I have. A lot. Do you know what it's like for five guys to be on a tour bus for sometimes twelve hours at a time? It's boring."

Everyone snickers.

"Yeah, we know a little about being stuck in places for long stretches of time," Angel says.

"Oh. Duh."

One of the others, I forget his name, says, "Plus, when you're trying to avoid going out to local scenes because you know they're not your … preferred company, you hide behind game nights with 'bro-dudes.'"

"Bro-dudes," I murmur.

"Fuck buddies."

I try not to let my surprise show, but it must.

Trav leans forward. "Gideon never told you why I started this company, did he?"

"He hasn't told me much at all. I thought you were a security firm. Like a rent-a-cop place. Not … rent-a-badass."

Everyone laughs at me. I haven't decided if they think I'm funny or naïve. Probably both. Most likely the latter.

"Harley, we all identify as LGBTQ—"

Trav is cut off by another guy clearing his throat and putting his hand up.

"Okay, *most* of us do," Trav corrects. "Except Domino, but we served together, and I know for sure he doesn't give a shit who any of us fuck. Being queer in the military is still a big deal. Maybe not as much as it once was, which is great, but I got sick of the mistrust between squad members. It's why I wanted to start my own team in the private sector."

"Oh. Umm, cool." Shit, my cheek is probably twitching like crazy. "Like, I don't have a problem with … that."

It totally sounds like I do, but it's the opposite. Well, I do have one major problem.

My bodyguard? The one I've been drooling over since the minute he stepped into my house and tackled me to the ground? The guy I've been checking out and thinking he had to be straight this whole time? He's into guys. And I take it back. When I thought the universe was unfair because Brix was straight, it's even more unfair that he's into guys.

Before he was unattainable.

Now he's just … off-limits.

Fuck, my cock responds to that like it's been served a platter of ass to pick from.

Now that I know how not straight Brix is, my life just became a whole lot harder.

Literally.

I shift in my seat.

Wait.

"Iris has a girlfriend," I say stupidly.

Ryder would kick my ass for that.

Iris makes a noise like in a game show when you get the answer wrong. "Try again. I *had* a girlfriend. She broke up with me today. Thanks to this." He waves around the room. "Got sick of me always being called into work and being away." He raises his voice two octaves higher to mimic his now ex-girlfriend. *"And now you're gone Sundays too. Wah, wah, wah."*

Guess that explains his shitty attitude when he came in earlier today.

"But that's probably not what you mean when you say I have a girlfriend like I'm the worst queer guy ever for sleeping with a woman." He mockingly gasps. "They better take my card away."

"No, sorry. I realized that was a stupid thing to say the second I said it. A friend of mine always tells me there's a B in LGBTQ for a reason."

"I like them already," Iris says. "Are they fuckable?"

I laugh. "No. Not for you anyway."

When Ryder became a father, he insisted he needed to focus on Kaylee's life. As far as I'm aware, he hasn't dated anyone, of any gender, since Kaylee was born.

That's a bigger stretch than me. I haven't been with someone since

... I count back. It's been about eighteen months since Eleven broke up, and it was a few months before that when Jay and I split ... so that's ... hard. Sex math is hard. And depressing.

"The pop star is brutal," Angel says. "I like him."

Brix smirks at me. "He's a'ight."

"Just *a'ight*?" I exclaim.

There's that thing in his eyes again—that knowing suspicion I've been trying to kill by exaggerating what Evah and I have and trying to hide the truth.

I don't understand him. I don't understand the point.

Is this all to taunt me because he knows? What was the plan? Put me in a room with a bunch of hot gay guys and see if I'd crack?

We continue to play poker, but my head's no longer in it, and I end up losing all the chips I'd already won.

I force amusement at the group's shenanigans, which remind me a lot of my Eleven days. Yeah, we fought a lot, but what brothers don't? I'm sure these guys have been at each other's throats at some point too.

We all wanted out of Eleven to do our own things, but the longer we're apart, the more I realize those guys were there for me in ways others never have been. We were in the same situation together, and yeah, a lot of the time we hated it because we had no creative control, and as I explained to Brix, we were all manufactured. But we were in it *together*.

Now I feel like I'm stuck in the same loop but doing it alone.

I miss them.

Especially Ryder, who understood me on a deeper level because of our shared need to remain closeted even though we were both desperate to break free.

Brix's foot brushes against mine, and I glance at him. "You all right?"

I nod. "Tired. I might head to bed."

"Aren't all you Hollywood types known for partying?" Angel asks.

Brix scoffs. "Harley is the least Hollywood person I know."

I tap my chin. "I kind of feel like there's an insult in there somewhere."

"Not at all," Brix says. "I thought I was going to be chasing around a superstar diva all over LA, dragging him out of nightclubs, confiscating drugs, and hiding it from the media. You're slightly easier to handle than that."

"*Slightly?*"

"Well, you are making me do that ridiculous list of yours."

Iris bursts into laughter. "You're still doing that shit?" He doubles over.

"The client is insistent."

I want to smile. I really do. I like that the list of demands has become a running joke. It would be weird walking into a room without him clearing it. But that's just it. Why is he doing it when he knows it's bullshit?

Brix stands. "I'll take you to the room."

I almost say I can manage, but I've forgotten where it is.

"Night, everyone," I say on my way to follow Brix down the hallway.

We reach the room near the back of the house, but before he can enter, I pull on his forearm.

"You don't have to."

"Have to what?" He sounds genuinely concerned.

"Do this ridiculous room-checking thing. You don't have to do the list anymore."

"I don't mind. The list is ridiculous, yes, but if it makes you feel safer ..."

I pull him into the room and close the door behind us. "It's not that. I did the list because I overheard you telling Iris to be *professional*. I was being a smartass. You didn't want to be my bodyguard just as much as I didn't want to admit I needed one. And I don't understand you. Like, at all. You're this big hardass on the outside, and then you tell me things like 'Other people's actions are never your fault.' You're *nice*. And you didn't laugh when I told you that Evah and I weren't real. Or gloat. Because I know you've suspected it for a while even though I keep trying to throw you off. Then you bring me here, and introduce me to all of"—I wave my hand toward the door—"them, and I don't understand. I thought you brought me here so I could get out of my head and write, but now

… I just … I don't …" I can't breathe. "I don't get it. I don't get *you*."

"Harley …" Sympathy shines in Brix's normally dark and calculating eyes. "I brought you here so you could see that while you might not understand me, I understand you. More than you know. All of us here do."

He steps closer, and I have to fight the urge to do the same and close the gap between us. His hands find my shoulders, and I shiver. His touch sends a jolt through me.

I want more. I want to give in to that thing telling me I like being close to him.

He stares down at me with a type of expression that I'm not used to seeing directed at me. Why would Harley Valentine need sympathy? I have *everything*.

"I've been racking my brain wondering why a pop star like you would need to keep it a secret." His voice is low and gravelly, and it does things to my dick that it shouldn't.

A lot of things to do with Brix affect my cock in ways they shouldn't. The way he looks, the way he does his job … *Him*.

"My target demographic is mainly women," I choke out. "The label says—"

"I don't need to know the reason why anymore. I was missing the point. It's not *why* you're keeping it a secret but that you feel you need to at all. You're in an industry where you don't feel safe enough to be who you are without risk. Like Trav said out there, we know what that's like. Don't Ask Don't Tell may have been repealed. The military might be more accepting now, but that doesn't mean it's safe for people like us."

I groan. "There you go with the perspective thing again. All I'm risking is money. You guys actually risked your *lives*."

"And there you go again, belittling your experiences because mine are objectively worse. You have every right to feel the way you do. Trapped by your label and your career. Having to pick one or the other. Love or music. And you've been doing it for almost a decade."

He cups my face now, the weight of his big hands feeling like a blanket of protectiveness I want to wrap around me.

"You have every right to feel the way you do. And I brought you here so you could understand that you don't need to be *that* guy with me. You don't need to pretend to be in love with Evah. You don't need to put on your fake smile that makes your gorgeous face light up even though your eyes remain dead. I want you to give me your real smile. The one that makes you look older and less perfect. Less *manufactured*."

"Brix …" It comes out as a whine.

Why is he doing this? What does he *want*?

My heart squeezes.

He's saying all the words I've wanted to hear from someone nearly my entire life.

I want to believe he truly understands. He gets it. Gets *me*.

"I want you to be *the real you* around me," he whispers, his breath ghosting over my skin. "I'll still like you. Actually, I'll probably like you more. Hollywood types are not my thing."

There's a pause. A shift. For a moment, I could swear the world stops turning.

The warmth coming off him is insane.

My entire body screams to be touched, to be even closer.

We press against each other.

I risk glancing up into his eyes. They're dark and hypnotizing.

"You're valid, Harley."

Something snaps.

One minute I'm staring at him, locked in another Brix trance, and then the next, my mouth is on his.

It's not soft. It's not caring.

It's so scorching hot it's bound to leave long-lasting third-degree burns on my soul.

His kiss is as firm as the muscles under my palms as I run my hands over his chest.

His lips are as gentle as his words.

But his tongue … his tongue is as demanding as my tour rider. It's unyielding, and I melt under its demand.

I've never been kissed like this before.

Never.

The hands cupping my face move to the back of my head. One threads through my hair, and I let out a loud moan.

It's hard to breathe, but I don't want to come up for air.

I may never want to again.

CHAPTER 12
BRIX

THIS IS NOT what I brought him here for. It was not part of the plan.

Kissing him can't be part of the plan, no matter how soft his lips are.

The way he becomes pliant in my hands does things to me I've never felt before.

I thought I liked it when guys fought back, when we'd struggle for dominance until I'd give in because I love being the one who's not in control.

With Harley, the power he's giving me is intoxicating.

I never meant to kiss him, but the pain in Harley's eyes when he was rambling at me that he didn't understand—that he didn't get it—I just wanted to take it all away. His confusion, his distrust in me ... All of it.

I've never had such a primal reaction before. I have the *urge* to protect instead of the duty.

But Harley *is* my duty, and this is wrong.

"Fuck," I hiss and pull back.

And now, while he stares up at me with his stormy-blue eyes and a look of *what the fuck just happened?* I can't bring myself to step away.

I have to.

I just *can't*.

"Harley—"

"No." He pulls me in closer, our bodies molding like soft clay around one another. "Don't go and fuck this up with logic and rational thought, because after that kiss, I don't know if they even exist in this universe anymore."

That sounds about right.

I can't think at all, let alone come up with a rational thought about why we can't do this.

This time when I kiss him, I try not to get lost in him so fast. That lasts for half a second before we're back to where we were—in a frenzy of heat and need where I can't separate my actions from the debauchery in my head.

The ideas and thoughts of what I could do to Harley ping like continuous lightbulbs lighting up my brain and outshining the dark consequences of what we're getting into.

I slide my hands down his back and grip the globes of his ass over his jeans. His cock is hard against my thigh, taunting me.

When Harley moans, I break completely.

If there was any hesitance left, it's gone when Harley takes the lead and spins us to push me backward until my legs hit the edge of the bed.

Harley's surprisingly strong hands grip my hips, steadying me so I don't fall onto the mattress. His mouth breaks from mine and moves to my neck, sucking hard enough to make me go weak in the knees.

"Take off your clothes," he rumbles against my skin.

Being overpowered is something I crave. I always have. It's why I generally go for guys who are bigger than me.

I like being coaxed into submission and letting go of the control I have to maintain in my line of work.

I've always thought I needed to be forced to surrender under the touch of a stronger man's hands. Turns out it's not that at all.

Harley's stature may not scream strong or powerful, but the way he's handling me right now proves that doesn't matter. His power is in his presence, in his voice, and in his firm but not painful grip.

It has me toeing off my boots and reaching for my belt without question.

We part to take off our shirts but come back to each other without missing a beat. We're both struggling with our pants as our mouths devour. Taste. *Consume.*

I want every inch of Harley.

With a hard push, Harley has me on the mattress. I inch my way up until my head hits the pillow.

His naked body comes down on top of mine, skin on skin, and I've never been begging for it more in my life.

I fucking whimper, and I don't do that.

Harley moves on top of me, dragging his hard cock against me while he brings his mouth back to mine.

Every thrust clouds my head, taking me to that place where nothing exists but the full-body sensation of an impending orgasm.

Nothing beats the tingling in my spine, the heat in my gut, and the growing pleasure thrumming in my veins.

"I want my mouth on you," Harley breathes.

"Pretty sure you already have that." I lean up to kiss him again, but he pulls back and sits up, straddling my waist.

"I want to suck you."

The noise that leaves me is as much affirmative as it is tortured pleading.

Harley slinks down my body and lets out a breathy "Holy fuck" right at crotch level.

I want to say something cocky … probably about being so *cocky*, but I'm scared if I talk, rational thought might kick in.

Harley's breath on my skin sends a ripple through my whole body. Then his tongue moves slowly up the side of my dick, and now I'm trembling.

My hand grips his hair, and the other fists the sheet, needing to hold on to something. Anything.

The torturous lick from base to tip takes so long I'm panting by the time he reaches the head of my cock.

I need that wet heat surrounding me. I need it now.

The fucker doesn't give it to me.

Instead, he wraps his hand around my aching shaft and moves his mouth to my sac, teasing the hell out of me.

He's driving me insane.

I have an inner war going on between fighting for control and letting go. Harley takes my choice away from me.

In an instant, my hand is gone from his hair and is pinned to the bed.

Harley continues to suck my balls until I'm practically squirming.

When he finally—*finally*—gives me what I want, he's done with the teasing completely. I'm engulfed by his hot mouth as he sucks me down. I try to silence myself but can't help crying out.

The sound of wet slurps fills the room when I get my own noises under control, and that turns me on more.

I manage to lift my head and stare down at Harley focused on bobbing up and down on my cock.

It's the best thing I've seen in a long time. Maybe ever.

The sight of it alone …

Fuck.

"Harley," I warn.

He keeps going.

I tap his shoulder with my free hand. "*Harley.*"

In a second, his mouth is gone, and then he's on top of me again. His cock grinds against mine, and he closes his fist over both of us. He goes back to kissing me, hard and unforgiving. It pushes me over the edge.

Cum hits my stomach, and he swallows my moans but doesn't stop.

When he stills on top of me a few seconds later, more warmth coats my abs.

His full body weight slumps on top of me. Harley's not a small man, but compared to all the other men I've been with, he's more petite than I'm used to. No one has ever fit against me like this, and I can't say I hate it.

I might like it too much.

Because as the cum between us cools and the fog of orgasm fades, I'm filled with the icy feeling of regret.

I think we just fucked everything up.

Harley eventually rolls off me and onto his back but doesn't say anything.

We stare at the ceiling, still breathing heavy.

I don't dare move. Maybe if I lie still enough, I'll become invisible.

"Brix?" Harley's voice is soft.

"Mm?

"We should get cleaned up."

"Mm."

"You're not moving."

"Neither are you," I point out, but my eyes are still glued above me.

We fall silent again.

Neither of us move.

"You going to clear the bathroom for me?"

I feel his smile more than see it.

"If there's someone in the bathroom, they just got a good show. They probably won't attack you after that. Applaud, maybe." I hope my tone is playful. I hope to hell I'm covering that I'm freaking out, but I don't think I am.

"Okay, I'm going to go shower." As he slides out of bed, he stares over his shoulder at me. I assume in invitation.

Instead of taking him up on the offer, I nod. "You do that."

He doesn't linger. As soon as the door to the bathroom is closed behind him, I let out a loud breath and sit up.

I reach for my shirt on the ground to wipe myself off and sit back on the bed.

The shower starts in the next room, and damn it, I could really use one, but if I go in there, I know there's no way I'll be able to keep my hands to myself. Even though this whole thing was a mistake, it's one my body wants to make over and over and over again.

Fuck, what did I do?

I hang my head in my hands.

Okay, rational thought time.

Worst case is Trav takes me off this job, and it'll be a few more years to clear my debt and be able to afford a better care facility.

This was my ticket out, and I went and fucked it. *Literally.*

I fall on my back on the mattress and cover my face with my arm.

My muscles are wound tight despite the earth-shattering orgasm.

"Brix?" Harley's voice startles me, and when I look up, he's standing by my legs wearing only a towel. I didn't hear the shower shut off.

"Harley, I …" I what?

I made a mistake? *He's* a mistake? I don't want him thinking that. For someone who's loved by millions of people, Harley has shockingly low self-worth.

"I didn't mean for that to happen," I say. It's the truth. "I didn't bring you here … for that. I …"

He does the public-ready smile I hate. "I know. It's okay. We got lost in a moment. That's all."

It was more than a moment, but it would be wrong to say that out loud.

I clear my throat. "Right. A moment."

"But, uh, if we're going to forget it ever happened, I might need my bed back."

"Sorry." I pull myself up, still naked, standing in front of him now just inches away. My cock doesn't understand I'm trying to refrain and twitches, wanting more. I should really get some underwear and cover up, but I don't. "I really am sorry."

His lips form a thin line.

"I still mean every single word I said. You don't have to be someone else around me."

"Sure."

"Wait, I can't have this conversation naked." I find my boxer briefs on the floor.

"It's okay. We don't *need* the conversation."

I pull them on. "We do. If I didn't need this job, it'd be a different story. You wouldn't be able to keep me off you. But I *do* need this job."

Harley folds his arms. "Then let's talk about *that*. Why do you need it?"

I grit my teeth. "Harley—"

"No, no. You wanted the conversation, so let's have it."

"I need the money. I'm in debt. A lot of debt."

"Gambling addiction?"

I almost want to lie and say yes, but I don't. "Medical bills."

Harley schools his surprised reaction but barely. He eyes me as if trying to figure out how I'm hurt, sick, or injured. "What for?"

"I've already told you more than any of those guys know." I wave in the direction of the door.

"End of discussion, then." Harley throws himself on the bed.

I stay standing, feeling completely helpless. My head throbs, and I rub my temples.

"Goodnight, Brix."

"Goodnight." I make my way to the tiny, uncomfortable couch.

CHAPTER 13
HARLEY

"WHAT'S a word that rhymes with regret?" I ask on the way home the next day.

Brix doesn't respond.

"*Forget*. It's not exact but close enough." I scribble that down.

Brix doesn't take his eyes off the road. "I can't tell if you're being passive-aggressive or mocking."

Neither can I, if I'm being honest.

I'm not a dumbass. Hooking up with my bodyguard was stupid. Last night was a mistake, and we shouldn't have done it. I knew the minute he shut down that I had to make a clean break.

I've done the forbidden-relationship thing before. It's not as romantic as people think. Sneaking out of hotel rooms so my handlers and management team didn't find out I was fucking a member of the opening act on tour was my life for a lot longer than it should have been.

I don't want to start that again.

So, yeah, pretending it didn't happen is what's best. Even if it's not what I want.

It's better to end it now before I catch those dreaded *feelings*.

I have no desire to get my heart broken again anytime soon. The first time took long enough to get over.

Maybe I can convince my brain that last night was a wicked fantasy instead of a memory, and I can use it for when I'm alone with my hand. Because something that explosive can't be forgotten. It would be, like, blasphemous to the gods of gay sex.

"Harley?"

I turn my head toward him. "Huh?"

"Are you really okay with what happened, or do you want me to call Trav and tell him I can't work for you anymore?"

I frown. "You want to quit? Over a mishap?"

"Tackling you on my first day was a mishap. This … this was crossing basic lines that no employer and employee should ever cross."

"Didn't we already agree Gideon is your employer, not me?"

"You know what I mean."

"I do. Which is why you shouldn't quit. Like you said, you need this job. I won't mess that up for you."

"Thank you."

I pretend to write something down. "Hey, what rhymes with *fired?*"

His gaze flicks my direction, and I grin.

"At least we can joke about it already," he mumbles.

"I like joking with you. As sad as this may sound, you're not just my bodyguard. I kind of feel like … we're friends."

"Well, you did blow me. I guess that makes us friends."

"Oh, so that's what I've been doing wrong all these years. No wonder I have no friends. Blowjobs equal friendship. Got it. You should be a life coach instead of a professional badass."

Brix side-eyes me. "Why don't you have any friends? I thought you Hollywood types all had huge entourages."

"Oh, I have an entourage, but I pay them to be with me, so it feels weird to call them friends. It's not like I see them outside of them working for me."

"So why is it different with me?"

"Blowjob. Duh."

Brix laughs. "No, seriously."

I shrug. "Maybe it's because I'm with you twenty-four hours a day. The only time you get to escape is on your day off. We're friends by proximity."

"You know how to make a guy feel special."

I sigh. "I don't think I've had any real friends since I became famous."

Brix's tone changes and becomes more guarded. "What about that Jay guy?"

"Maybe he counted at first. We were friends for a while. Although, that was only because I suck at flirting with guys because I know I'm not supposed to, so it comes out all, 'Oh, hey, you like oranges? Shit, so do I!' He didn't realize I was hitting on him for about four months."

"And then you fell in love? Is he the one who left you on tour?"

I don't want to get into this with Brix, or anyone for that matter, but that doesn't stop the words from coming out. "It's kind of a messed-up story. Basically, our label didn't want us together, so we were forced to break up. I had issues letting go, and he had issues saying no to me."

"Uh-oh."

"Yep. We kept seeing each other even when we weren't supposed to, which is why my publicist came up with the whole Evah lie. That was the last straw for him. I thought we could keep doing what we'd always done, but he wasn't okay with that. Then he went and found, in his words, *true love*."

"Ouch."

"Eh. I'm not saying he didn't have a right to move on. No one likes being shoved in a closet. But I guess … I don't know. It seemed so easy and quick for him to find someone else. I have to believe our relationship wasn't as meaningful as I thought it was."

"Am I gonna have to bitch slap you upside the head for you to get it? Other people's experiences don't diminish your own. I'm gonna have that phrase cross-stitched onto a cushion for you. He may not have seen your relationship as anything more, but you did. Therefore, it matters. What you had matters."

Damn him.

I hate that he sees through that stuff. "Maybe I don't want it to matter. You don't want to waste the *love of your life* title on a guy who's now married to someone else."

Brix snorts. "What makes you think you only get one love of your life?"

"Uh, the whole construct of soul mates?"

"Pfft."

"Wow. Dignified response."

"Soul mates is a bullshit notion. There are over seven billion people on the planet, and you only get one? Only one of them is your perfect match? That's a one in seven point five billion chance of finding the *love of your life*."

"Well, when you put it like that …"

"Relationships break down. People change. Those who are truly in love can work at it for years and still end up apart. It doesn't mean they weren't in love or that they were supposed to love someone else more. It just … is what it is. Heartbreak sucks, but it's a part of life. Putting it down to destiny or fate or any other higher deity is lazy and dismissive of the effort needed to truly make a relationship work."

"That's …"

"Insightful? Philosophical?"

"*Depressing.*"

Brix bursts out laughing. "I guess it is a bit."

"I take it back. I don't think you could be a life coach."

Yet, as I put my pen to paper again, I can't help thinking about his words and what they mean.

If destiny isn't in control of our love lives, does that mean we only have ourselves to blame?

I write like a fiend for a full week. The only breaks I take are for personal training and eating. Occasionally, I sleep. Brix is in the background, slipping effortlessly into *let's pretend nothing happened* mode.

Though he's not acting differently, I swear I catch him looking at me sometimes. Or maybe that's wishful thinking. Because while I've been busy working, my words are all about him. Not directly, but he and his friends are kind of inspirational the more I think about them.

Serving in the military while hiding a secret. Protecting a country that doesn't accept them.

Though, there's also a song in there titled "Anti-Love" that basically says soul mates don't exist. That one's just for him.

I get lost in the words, in creating melodies and working with my vocal coach to make the arrangements sound the best they can.

I get so lost that when I go downstairs for my morning coffee to get started for the day, I skid to a stop when I find Gideon in my kitchen with Iris and Brix. They're all wearing suits.

My heart thuds, skips a beat, and then I'm pretty sure it keels over.

The first thought is Gideon and Iris know we fucked up and they're here to take Brix away from me, but why would they get dressed up for that? That would be a whole new level of sadism.

Their faces don't indicate I could be jumping to conclusions, though. They're all stoic and worried-looking.

"What's up?" I hate the crack in my voice.

"You forgot, didn't you?" Gideon asks.

"Forgot what?" *To keep my dick in my pants? Umm, yep.*

"Today's your intruder's court date. I messaged you about it two days ago."

"That was two days ago already?" I read it and promptly went back to writing. Not even memories of that night could bring me out of my writing frenzy.

I took that as a good sign, but Gideon's looking at me as if I've blocked it from my mind to protect me from reliving the trauma or something.

"Okay, so do I have to be there? I'm kind of on a roll, and I don't want anything to interrupt it."

"You should be there," Gideon says, "but if it's too much—"

"It's not too much. They'll probably give him a fine or probation or something stupid. I don't think I need to be there for that."

Gideon steps closer. "I think it could be good for you to see him again. A month ago, you pointed a gun at Iris because you thought he was another intruder."

"An *unloaded* gun. And he was a stranger in my house. It's not like I tried to shoot my chef thinking she was an intruder."

It's Brix's turn to try. "Iris and I will both be with you while you're there. I called him especially for this."

I throw up my hands. "Fine, I'll go. I'm not scared." *Mostly.* "I just want to write."

The front door opens, and I startle. Brix's and Gideon's concern worsens. I'm guessing I wasn't supposed to flinch at a normal, everyday sound.

Okay, so maybe I'm not exactly thrilled to go today, but I don't think not going means I'm avoiding it or some shit. It's not like I'm scared he's going to come back. Not with Brix here. I just don't want to see him or face him.

I'll go. It'll be fine. Then this whole thing will be over.

And then the interviews will start.

Ugh. I didn't think about that part. I've been happily hiding away from the world. It's rare I get to. The only time I can make excuses is when I'm writing and cutting a new album, but even then I can't disappear completely like I have since my tour ended.

I'm going to need to start appearing in public again.

Jamie enters with my dry cleaning over her shoulder. The garment bags are almost as tall as she is, and Iris, ever the gentleman, steps in to take them from her.

"Why do you all look like someone died?" she asks.

I shake off the nervous anxiety and force a smile. Then I remember Brix knows when I'm faking it, so I angle my body away from him and toward her to try to hide it. "They're worried I'm going to freak out."

"Are you going to freak out?" she asks, her voice sweet like it always is.

"Nope."

"Go you! Well, I know you have heaps of suits in your closet, but then I remembered your favorite was sent to be dry-cleaned after the tour, and I hadn't picked it up yet. I thought you might want to wear it today."

"Thank you. You're the best."

She nods. "Okay, I only have a few days left of my 'vacation,' and I left Raffy in the car, so—"

"You left your boyfriend who has the name of a dog in the car? Did you crack a window?" I joke.

"Oh, he was dying to come in, but I figured leaving him there was a better idea than him blubbering all over you like he did when he met you. He's so embarrassing. You wonder why you've only met him once."

It was hilarious. She was so excited for me to meet her new boyfriend, nonstop talking about him in that enthusiastic babble she does. But she didn't realize he was a closeted Eleven fan. He'd gushed all over me, and she was shook.

"Aww, it was cute how he told me *I* was *his* biggest fan."

She facepalms. "Embarrassing. Anyway, unless you guys need me for anything else, I better go." The pleading in her eyes makes me dismiss her immediately.

"Go for it. Thank you for going above and beyond."

Jamie works for me around the clock when I'm on tour, doing press for an album, or recording, so I try to give her as much time off as I can when I'm in my writing cave.

It's really the only vacation she gets, and even then, she's on call. Like if I need egg whites or a suit dry-cleaned. I try to make it a point not to annoy her so she can enjoy her time off, though.

Iris hands me the suit.

"When do we have to leave?" I ask.

"Go shower and get dressed. I'll make you breakfast," Brix says.

"Let me guess. Breakfast burrito. *So delicious.*"

Iris and Gideon both hide smiles as Brix simply stares at me.

"Breakfast burrito is fine," I mutter and turn on my heel.

As I leave the room, I hear Gideon ask, "Is Brix magic? Harley *never* backs down that easily."

Hmm, yeah, let's go with magic. It's not that he's so fuckable I can barely control myself around him now I've had a taste. Nope.

And I don't think about that while I'm in the shower. I don't imagine Brix's giant cock in my mouth or him coming all over my skin.

Not. At. All.

After I don't orgasm while thinking of him, I get out and change into my crisp white shirt and royal blue suit that make my dull bluish-gray eyes a little brighter.

All heads turn in my direction as I make my way back to the kitchen to find my breakfast waiting for me. With a bite taken out of it.

"Question," Gideon says. "Why did Brix cook you breakfast and then eat some of it?"

We laugh.

"I might've given Brix a list of protocols he needs to follow as a joke, and even though I've told him he can stop, he refuses to."

Gideon doesn't even question the insanity.

By the time I've eaten and we're ready to head out, I've calmed a bit, but the anxiety comes back when we all get into the car. Gideon sits up front with the driver, and I'm sandwiched between Brix and Iris much like I was in the desert.

Those first few days after the break-in, I was rattled, but since Brix has been looking after me, I haven't actually given the guy much thought.

Now, though, in my head, he's about seven feet tall and three hundred pounds of muscle. I'm sure he wasn't that big, but my mind has turned him into this Goliath of a man.

For the first time in my life, I'm thankful for LA traffic and silently hopeful we'll be too late for the hearing.

We're not that lucky.

Not only do we make it on time, we're there early enough to find the guy waiting outside the courtroom with his lawyer.

Yep, definitely not Goliath-sized. Actually, he might even be shorter than me. Not by much, but still.

My mouth dries, and my throat gets scratchy.

I falter in my steps and pause. Gideon's on one side of me, Brix on the other, and Iris is at my back. Yet I don't feel any safer.

The guy may be smaller than I remember and may look harmless, but the helplessness that had me frozen that night has me unwilling to take another step.

"You got this," Brix says.

No, I don't got this. I try to open my mouth, but it's too dry. Swallowing hurts.

"Restroom," I croak.

"This way." Brix takes my arm and gently leads me toward the bathrooms. "Wait here." He leaves me with Iris outside the men's room and reappears ten seconds later. He leans in close and smiles. "All clear."

I appreciate the running joke, but I can't bring myself to laugh at it right now.

Brix turns to Iris. "Don't let anyone in."

Iris does as he's told and blocks the door as soon as we're through it.

I pace the small area, trying to get all this excess nervous energy out.

Brix casually leans against the counter where the sinks are. "Breathe, Pop Star."

It doesn't work. I keep pacing.

"Who is he?"

My gaze snaps to his. "Who?"

"William 'Billy' Webber. Who is he?"

"He's the guy who broke in. You *know* that."

Brix shakes his head. "Nope. Well, yeah, he is, but that's not all he is. He's twenty-one. Goes to UCLA. Works part-time at Rent A Geek. His parents are divorced, he has a dog named Waffles, and he may or may not run a fan site that speculates about Harley Valentine from Eleven being gay where he notes every single instance of 'gay' behavior. He's also convinced you and Ryder were in love at one point and started the hashtag trend *Ryley4ever*."

I finally have the ability to stop my legs from pacing. "How do you know all this?"

He folds his arms, and his biceps flexing is enough of a distraction to keep me from going back to freaking out. "It's my job to protect you. You didn't think I'd research the guy who made you need protection in the first place?"

"And? What else did you find? Mental illness, he used to kill animals as a child, what?"

Brix lets out a little laugh. "No. None of that. From what I can find, he's a slightly too-obsessed fan who had his head in the clouds and got carried away on a notion that the glimmer in your eyes that you give all your fans was just for him." He lowers his voice. "I can't say I blame him."

"What?"

Brix ignores me. "Now, who are you?"

"All I am right now is confused."

"Not trying to be philosophical or deep here. Who are you to the public?"

"Harley Valentine," I say quietly.

"Harley-motherfucking-Valentine. You're a Grammy-award-winning artist with millions of fans. Your life is perfect. Blushing fiancée, millions of dollars, and you're happy, happy, happy."

"You know the fiancée thing is bullshit and about to come to an end."

He points outside. "Everyone out there doesn't. Putting your life next to Billy's, he's nothing. He has nothing. You're above it."

I finally get what he's trying to get me to see. "So I shouldn't let him have any power over me."

"Exactly. I'm going to regret the day you finally see all this shit for yourself. You won't need me anymore."

That'll never happen. Brix always manages to make me see things from another side, and I don't want to lose that. But he'll go back to his real job when I feel safe enough. I have no doubt about it.

I also don't want to think about him leaving because even though hooking up with him was a mistake, he's important to my team.

Sure. *Team.*

I tell my conscience to shut up.

"When you run out of perspective lessons, I'll still need someone to take a bite of my food for me."

Brix laughs, and I'm finally relaxed enough to laugh with him.

"Seriously, though, aren't you getting sick of babysitting me? Don't you want to go out there and blow up bad guys and collect kill numbers?"

"Kill numbers? Is that what you think we do?"

"*I don't know* what you guys do."

Brix's eyes shine with pride.

I step closer to him. "Out of curiosity, if you and Iris did have a kill list, whose would be longer?"

The sides of Brix's lips curve upward. "Whose do you think?"

"Hmm, you're more serious and you look lethal when you get all scowly, but here you are …" Another step closer. "Yet again, telling me to stop being a dramatic pop star and somehow making me get over myself."

Brix sucks in a shuddery breath as I stop in front of him, just inches away. "Don't mistake me for someone who has a heart just because I know how to do my job."

"Calming me down isn't your job, so you can't play the broody loner card," I whisper.

His dark brown eyes are trained on mine, giving away the softness inside him.

I want to kiss him. I want to kiss him hard and rough again. All it would take is pressing myself against him and claiming his lips.

Back away, Harley.

I force myself to put distance between us. "Yeah, you're not such a hardass. Iris's list is longer, for sure."

I leave the bathroom with a smile on my face.

Billy is sentenced to only one year of probation and ordered to stay away from me. While I was expecting it and it's disappointing he didn't get more, I feel safe knowing Brix has my back.

If he does ever get tired of his actionless job, I don't know what I'll do.

CHAPTER 14
BRIX

HARLEY'S SCHEDULE picks up a bit after his attacker's sentencing. A few talk shows wanted to chat about it, and Gideon said it would be good for Harley to make a few appearances in public so people don't think he's fallen off the face of the planet since his last tour ended.

Always in the spotlight. Always under a microscope.

It's no wonder he's a little neurotic.

He said something at the courthouse about me getting bored with this position, and honestly, I thought I would hate it. I took it because of the money, but I enjoy it because of Harley.

I like talking him down. I like giving him perspective.

If I were to quit Mike Bravo, Trav could replace me with another trained soldier in a flash. What I give Harley … it might not seem like much, but it makes me feel important.

Harley makes me feel important.

Everything I do for him or around him is instinctual. Instead of tactical thinking and analyzing what I should do, I just *act*.

It may not be adrenaline inducing, but it's fluid. Reflexive.

His new schedule is testing me in ways I haven't really dealt with yet.

Fans actually camp outside studios to get a glimpse of Harley. Most of them are tame and only want a selfie or an autograph, but some like to get pushy, and I have to be the bad guy and get them out of Harley's way.

I wonder if New York will be similar.

We have a few days in the Big Apple for Harley to film more late-night talk shows and make a surprise appearance at a Radioactive concert.

Harley went quiet after Gideon told him that part and hasn't really said much since.

As soon as we get on the private plane for the trip, he settles into his seat, puts his noise-canceling headphones on, a mask over his eyes, and pretends to be asleep.

I spend the five-hour flight talking to Harley's assistant, who's come on the trip with us.

It's my job to protect Harley and Jamie's job to get him anything he wants, but I'm kinda thankful for her for other reasons. Jamie being with us means it'll be easier for me to remain professional.

Because God knows how hard that's getting. Literally.

I wake up every morning aching for him.

I haven't been this horny since basic training when I'd been too scared to make a move on anyone in case they turned on me and outed me to everyone. I served post-DADT, but it's still terrifying to come out to men who are supposed to be your brothers knowing any one of them could turn their back on you in a combat situation.

Knowing Harley can't hear us because his foot taps on the floor of the plane while he listens to music, I lean across the small table between Jamie and me. "Does he always get like this before flying, or is this more about what's waiting for us on the other side of this flight?"

"What's on the other side of this flight?" She pouts innocently.

I smile. "Your coy act is good, sweetheart, but I know that Harley and Jay had a thing. And I know you know about it too."

"Oh. Well, in that case, no, this isn't a flying issue. It's definitely a Jay issue."

Not really what I wanted to hear, but it's to be expected.

"Does he still have a thing for him?"

She glances over at Harley and bites her lip. "I don't think so. He has a lot of regret when it comes to Jay. They knew they couldn't be together but kept seeing each other anyway. I know he wishes he could take that back. It dragged out the inevitable and hurt them both."

My chest twinges for him.

That's not entirely different than what happened with us. We both know we shouldn't have hooked up, but we did it anyway. If we're not careful, and I can't get my stupid attraction to him under control, it would be easy to fall into a similar pattern.

Which is why I need to stay strong. Not just for my job but for Harley.

When we arrive in New York, we go straight to the hotel where paparazzi and fans are already gathering outside. It's crazy.

We only have enough time to go up to the room and for Harley to shower and get pretty for his talk show appearance.

Like the court date, we have a chauffeured car so I can be with Harley at all times.

Outside the studio is quieter than the ones in LA, so that's something, but in the entire time I've worked for Harley, I think this is the longest he's gone without saying a full sentence to me.

When I ask him anything, he grunts one-word answers. When I pointed out how cool it is the suite has a hot tub, he gave me his publicity smile.

I want to ask if he's okay, but I think I should pull back a bit. I'm dying to help him and want him to lean on me, but maybe that's what we should be avoiding.

I'm his shadow from the moment we arrive at the studio to the second he goes onstage in front of the cameras.

Watching him answer interview questions with his Harley Valentine charm, I'm amazed how he transforms in front of an audience. From quiet and reserved to charismatic and laughing, the switch is easy for him. Years of being coached on how to speak and act have turned him into a robot.

Everyone right now would be thinking Harley has his shit together, when I know that he's faking every single second out there.

When he's asked about the stalker situation, he plays it off like it wasn't a big deal and it was a misunderstanding.

"That ended with a fan breaking into your house?"

Harley changes the subject by going to his default answer. "I'm just glad Evah wasn't there."

He's had this interview a few times now. Something I didn't know about these talk shows is they have scripts and prompts they need to follow. Harley knows what he's going to be asked, and the host knows how he's going to answer. It's up to them to make it sound natural like they're having a normal conversation.

The ever-professional and caring Harley has always turned this story on its head and made it about Evah and her brand or himself and the upcoming album he has yet to record.

"Do you have plans here in New York?" the host asks.

"Not many," Harley says breezily. "I'm in the middle of writing songs for my next album, so I'm out here looking for some inspiration."

"So you're not out here because of the rumors?"

It's brief and covered quickly, but I see it—the fear in Harley's eyes as if the show has worked out his secret and has put him on the spot right now in front of an audience, because this question doesn't follow the usual script.

"What rumors would those be?" He pulls off the coy act well.

"That there's a band who has a show at Madison Square Garden tomorrow, and that you might be in attendance."

Harley smiles. "Eh. I might be stopping by a certain concert that's happening tomorrow night."

The audience cheers.

"Singing with Radioactive?"

"Maybe." He nods. "But you know I can't tell you top secret information." He nods faster. "But let's just say, anyone who was lucky enough to score tickets to the show are in for a treat."

"And you're the treat?"

Harley laughs. "Duh. Look at me."

On anyone else? I'd say that line was cocky and … well, like Kanye. On Harley? He has this way of making it sound self-deprecating, and it's cute.

Once the interview is over and Harley leaves the stage, he lets out a loud relieved breath and falls back into moody Harley mode.

I want to reach for him. I want to massage the tension out of his shoulders. If we weren't in public and didn't have the five-foot-nothing Jamie hovering by us, I might've done it. It's probably for the best I can't.

On the way back to the hotel, I have to say something. "Do you hate New York?"

He looks at me as if I'm crazy. "What?"

"Do you hate New York? You're all grumpy."

"I'm fine."

Sounds it.

We drop Jamie off at her room and then go to ours. I clear his bedroom but then pause before letting him in.

"Are you sure you're okay?"

"Just … exhausted. The media circuit is always mentally draining. Seeing Jay is going to be shit, so I know I'm not going to get the sleep I need. My throat hurts, and I need to sing live tomorrow night, so I'm trying to rest my voice."

I wonder if there's more to it, but it's not like I can force it out of him. "Okay. I'll stop trying to get you to talk."

He slips into his room, and I go to the other bedroom in the suite.

Like him, I don't know if I'll be able to get to sleep. I imagine him in his room, tossing and turning, rumpling the sheets as he tries to get comfortable.

He'll end up on his stomach, one leg out of the sheet, his arms under his pillow, and drool on his chin.

That's how he's looked the few times I've woken him up since working for him.

Eventually, I do sleep, but I think I only get a couple of hours. I didn't close the curtains in my room, so I'm awoken as soon as the sun rises and brightens the city.

I check on Harley, and yup, he's in the exact position I thought I'd find him in. Sneaking back out of his room so I don't wake him, I take a look at what they have in the suite and find a range of teas and coffees on top of the minibar.

He said he has a sore throat, so I pick the lemon tea and make him a cup.

It tastes gross and makes me wince, but it should help.

When I take it into Harley's room, he's now awake.

"Sorry, did I wake you?" I ask.

"Nah, I was kind of in and out. I don't think I fell into a deep sleep the whole night."

"I brought you tea." I place it on his bedside table.

"You brought tea," he repeats. "For me."

"You said your throat hurts. It's lemon."

Harley sits up and reaches for the cup. He takes a sip and gags. "That's lemon? Tastes like piss."

"Do I want to know how you know what piss tastes like? I'm not really into kink shaming, but I do have my limits."

He just about chokes. "Thank you. For the piss water." He takes another sip and winces. "Okay, can I double-check you didn't piss in here?"

I laugh. "You don't trust that I already took a sip of it?"

"If you did, you never would've given it to me."

I take it from him. "I did, but if you still don't trust me." I take a gulp and swallow it down, forcing my face to remain impassive. "There. Now stop being a baby and drink your piss water."

"Just when I thought you were being nice to me."

"I'm *always* nice to you."

"Need I remind you—"

"I tackled you one time!"

"Never going to live it down," he sings.

"At least you're a bit perkier today."

"I'm a ray of pure sunshine." Harley continues to sip the gross tea, so I can only assume he wasn't exaggerating the sore throat. "I'm sorry if I've been an asshole the last twenty-four hours."

"Only the last twenty-four hours? What about all the other times?"

Harley gives me the finger.

"What time do you have to be at the arena?"

"This afternoon sometime. I'll run a soundcheck with Jay and make sure I'm where he needs me to be for the song."

"So, we have a free morning?"

"Hmm, depends."

"On?"

"If you're going to ask me to do something fun or suggest torture like … going for a run."

My face must fall or something.

"You seriously want to go for a run?" he asks.

"I figure you should try to build up some stamina to run away from your adoring fans."

Harley throws the blanket off his lap. "Fine. I'll go for a run. It's better than going to a bar this time of day."

"Is the Jay thing really that bad?"

He sighs. "No. I'm being melodramatic. No one really wants to be around their ex, do they?"

"Guess not."

Harley stands and stretches his long and lean body as he yawns. "Oh, and one more thing. If I am recognized, you're gonna have to carry me through the horde back to the hotel."

"Nah, they say the best way to train is to run like someone's chasing you. It'll be good practice for you."

"But I want to sing 'I Will Always Love You' all Whitney Houston like while you race through the streets of New York with me in your arms bridal-style. You could be my Kevin Costner and take a bullet for me."

"Your fantasies about me are fucked-up."

"Agreed." His gaze roams over my body and then back up to my face. He looks smug as he walks into his bathroom.

I'm thankful Harley's in a better mood, but this being professional thing is even harder when he's truly smiling at me.

Harley takes a deep breath and stops outside Radioactive's dressing room.

"Jamie could've told him you were here," I point out.

"I know, but when we agreed to do the collab, we promised we'd keep everything civil and wouldn't play stupid games. We're trying to be bigger people."

"Eww. I like holding grudges. Keeps you balanced."

"Holding grudges is bad for your health. Apparently. That's what I'm going with."

"When was the last time you saw him?"

He has to think about it. "Hmm, when we did promo for the single? He was on tour in Europe for a while, so that was an easy way to get out of awkward encounters."

I nod toward the door. "Need me to knock, or …"

"I've got this." Harley lowers his voice as if talking to himself. "I've *got* this." With another deep breath, he knocks.

Someone who is not the lead singer of the band I've been online stalking since reading the rumors about Harley and Jay answers the door.

This guy is older and has graying hair.

"Luce," Harley greets him.

"Harley." The guy's gaze drifts to mine and down to my backstage credentials on a lanyard around my neck but doesn't linger. "I'll let Jay know you're ready for soundcheck."

"Thanks." Harley turns on his heel and heads for the stage area.

"Who was that?"

"The Gideon of Radioactive."

"Ah."

A few minutes later, Radioactive turns up. There's three of them, but the drummer and bass player go straight onstage. Harley and Jay don't interact as they're fitted with earpieces from the stagehands.

It's kinda painful to watch. They're in the same space but both avoiding the giant elephant between them.

Jay is nothing like me physically. We both have dark hair, but that's the only thing we have in common. His hair is longer and shaggy, mine is still military short. He's the same height as Harley, I'm six three. He's thinner than Harley, and I'm, well, a tank.

It makes me wonder if Jay is Harley's actual type of guy. Artistic and broody.

I think back to our hookup and can't help wondering if the only reason it happened was because he'd found out I was gay and it was convenient.

I don't know why that thought guts me, but it does.

Even though it was a mistake, I thought it was more than *that.*

They sing their song, stopping a few times for Jay and Harley to work out where they'll be onstage at certain parts of the song.

It only takes about twenty minutes, and then we're taken to Harley's dressing room where Jamie is waiting for us.

And now Harley's back to being quiet.

He lies on the couch and throws his arm over his eyes.

I make my way over to Jamie. "Is this still because of Jay?" I whisper.

She smiles up at me. "No. This is him before any live performance. You have nothing to worry about when it comes to Jay."

"W-worry about?" I stutter because she can only mean one thing by that which means she knows we hooked up or at least that I have a thing for him. I try to play it off casually. "Should I be worried? Does Jay pose a threat toward Harley I should be aware of? Uh, profession-ally, I mean. Like a threat to his safety … just his safety."

And now I'm rambling, and, of course, she sees right through it. She doesn't call me on it, though.

"Live performances are stressful for Harley. Everyone thinks because he came from a boy band that he lip-syncs and can't actually sing. When he was with Eleven, they made sure the boys always sang live to squash any of those rumors. But the thing with that is any pitch problems, any words sung slightly off-key and the media has a field day. Harley tries to make sure every performance is perfect."

I hate he has so much pressure on him. "That's a lot to put on his own shoulders."

Harley sits up. "You know I can hear you assholes, right?"

"Well, would you have told me that's why you're acting weird?" I ask.

"No."

"Exactly. Any off behavior puts me on alert because you could become unpredictable and try to run off on me. Then you could get kidnapped by some rabid fan, dragged to their basement, and forced to sing and dance for food and water."

"That's really specific."

"It could happen."

"I'm not going to run off on you. Have I yet?"

"A fan hasn't broken into your house again yet, doesn't mean it won't happen."

"You think another one will try to get in?"

"Given the opportunity, hell yes, they would. Your fans are nuts."

Jamie clears her throat. "They prefer to be called *fanatics*."

Harley stands. "I'm fine. I just need this to go well."

"What's the worst that'll happen if you fuck up a line or two?"

"The worst? How about the media agrees with my label that Eleven never should've broken up because we're incompetent on our own?"

"That's the worst? Being told you should go back to your multi-platinum-selling band?"

"I know you're usually good with perspective, but this is one you're not going to win. Performing is different than writing. One bad performance could mean the beginning of the end of your career."

"How so?"

He holds up his fingers and counts as he goes. "Fergie singing the national anthem for the NBA. Janet Jackson at the Super Bowl."

"So maybe stay away from performing at sporting events?"

"Robin Thicke's 'Blurred Lines,' Ashlee Simpson's SNL appearance. Britney Spears's VMA performance," he continues.

I lean in toward Jamie. "By the way, what's a Fergie?"

Harley throws his hands up. "My point exactly."

Jamie giggles. "In Brix's defense, he didn't know who *you* were. He's not going to know the Black Eyed Peas."

"Ooh, they sing that 'Where Is the Love' song. I know who you're talking about now."

Harley groans. "Can I … Can I please have the room for a bit? I need to get focused and out of my head."

"Can I go watch some of the concert?" Jamie asks and bounces on her feet.

"Go for it. I don't think I need you for anything until I go onstage."

"Thanks." She bounds out of the room.

He stares at me, waiting for me to leave.

"I'll be right outside the door."

"Thank you," he murmurs.

I wait and watch as stagehands and roadies walk the corridors, all the while thinking of what Harley's doing just a few feet away from me.

The urge that always happens when he gets in his head, like when he forces himself to write and pushes until the breaking point, makes me want to go in there and distract him or do something to make him forget.

Jamie reappears sometime later, interrupting my internal battle of going inside or staying where Harley told me to.

"He'll be going on soon," Jamie says. "Is he ready?"

I knock. "Ready, Pop Star?"

The door swings open. "Ready."

He hands Jamie a bottle of water, hand sanitizer, and a mini packet of peanut M&M's.

"Performance survival kit," she says to me.

This time when Harley hits the stage, it's completely different than this afternoon during rehearsals. This afternoon was quiet and professional. No smile, just polite civility and doing as he was told.

Right now, he's in Harley Valentine mode, and he's as charismatic as he always is in front of his fans.

The crowd screams for about five minutes when he leaves us in the wings. He gives the bass player a fist bump and then throws his arm around Jay's shoulders. They stand there waiting for the audience noise to die down.

"I can't be sure," Harley says into his mic, "but I think that means they're excited I'm here."

Jay grins. "He thinks you guys are excited. He *thinks*. How about showing him how you really feel!" Jay steps away and waves his hand upward as if to say turn it up.

There's another five minutes of screaming.

"They really are nuts," I mutter.

"Harley's fans?" a voice says beside me.

"Yeah. I don't get it." I mean, I do. He's good-looking and talented and charming, but that's all superficial. It's not real. It's not the reason why *I* like him.

The guy laughs. "Funny. Neither do I." He's maybe an inch or two shorter than me, muscular, and he has brown hair and honey-colored eyes. He gives me a once-over in the same way I'm doing to him. "I heard Harley has a new shadow."

"Bodyguard. I'm Brix."

He shakes my hand. "Soren. Jay's—"

"Husband," I say. I didn't recognize him until he said his name. I've seen photos of this guy, but he looks different in person some-how. More friendly and approachable than the photos of him in hockey gear. "I know who you are."

He gives me a half-smile, understanding written all over his face. "Yeah."

Jay and Harley finish their cowritten song, and as the screams and applause go on and on, I stick my head out a tiny bit and see a sea of pride flags waving in the audience.

It makes my breath catch in my throat, and emotion clogs my chest.

"You never get used to that reaction," Soren says. "It happens every show with that song."

"It's a great song," I admit.

Harley's supposed to get off the stage now, but he doesn't. Instead he asks to borrow Jay's guitar.

"What's he doing?" I ask.

Soren sighs. "Going rogue. He has a habit of doing that."

The next thing I hear throughout the arena are the opening words to Whitney Houston's "I Will Always Love You," and I break into laughter.

Soren eyes me suspiciously. "Bodyguard, huh?"

"It's an inside joke."

"Mmhmm." He doesn't sound convinced.

I wish I could say I keep cool about it, but I don't. I can't take my eyes off Harley as he performs the shit out of the song.

Every now and then, he glances over at me waiting in the wings.

"You know, a year ago I would've assumed Harley was singing this to piss me off," Soren says. "But I don't think it's me he's staring at right now."

"Oh, it's definitely not. He's messing with me. It's his favorite pastime."

Soren leans in. "It's Harley's form of foreplay."

As a form of foreplay, it would be damn good, but Soren is wrong. Harley and I agreed we wouldn't go there again.

Still doesn't stop me from smirking as Harley finally leaves the stage. "That one was just for me?"

"As a thank-you for putting up with my shit tonight. And yesterday." He steps closer to me.

Soren coughs. "Hi, Harley."

Harley blinks and flicks his gaze toward Soren. "Oh, hey, hockey player. See you at the after-party? I need to drag my bodyguard away for a moment."

"Mmhmm, sure."

As Harley leads me away, I glance back to see Soren mouth, "Good luck."

I'm starting to think I might need it. I'll need it to stay off Harley. Because I'm sure, if he even gives the slightest sign that he's interested in a repeat, I won't be able to say no.

CHAPTER 15
HARLEY

I MIGHT ACT insane before a gig, but the high after performing makes all the neuroses worth it. It's the first time Brix has seen me like that, though. I appreciate that he cares enough to worry, but I want to show him that I'm fine. Especially now that the performance is done.

Jamie hands me my survival necessities. I drink my water, sanitize my hands, and then down my packet of M&M's, and this is all on the walk back to the dressing room.

I'd love nothing more than to leave, but part of this publicity train with the song is making it look like Jay and I are true friends, so we need to hang out a bit after the concert and be seen in public—with his husband, of course.

The song might be a queer anthem, but the label wants to make sure mainstream media paints Jay and me as some sort of bromance between gay guy and ally rather than jilted ex-lovers.

Everything in Hollywood is an illusion.

Everything.

I throw myself on the couch and take another gulp of water. The blood pumping through my veins is full of an excited energy that will take a while to come down from, but it's easy to relax into my seat and just experience it. I let the high wash over me.

Jamie hovers by the door.

"Go finish watching the rest of the concert," I say.

She lets out a little squee. "Thank you, thank you, thank you."

"Should I be offended she's a bigger fan of my ex than she is of me?" I'm joking … mostly.

Brix smiles at me. "I like this relaxed Harley better."

"If you stay on when I go on my next tour, you'll have to get used to the other Harley. He comes out before every show."

Brix sits on the armchair and rests one big foot on the coffee table. "Question."

"Yes, oh wise one? Is this going to be another lesson in perspective?"

"Nope. I just want to know when the last time you had actual fun onstage was?"

I gesture to the door. "Did you not see me out there? I was on fire. That's the reason I do this."

"That's called adrenaline. Adrenaline can easily be confused with fun. Why do you think all the guys at Mike Bravo claim to have a fun job? Because we have so much adrenaline flowing through our veins, *surviving* becomes a thrill. But that's all we're doing out there. Surviving. And when you put it that way, it's not fucking fun."

As his words register, and I truly think about it, I slump. "I hate you sometimes."

Ever since leaving Eleven, the pressure to do well has been tenfold. The more that pressure weighs down on me, the higher the payoff when I get in front of an audience, but at what cost?

The stress of it all turns me into a cold asshole.

There's no denying I've been a shithead the past two days. Having to perform with Jay added to it, but I should be able to control my crappy attitude. Especially around people like Brix and Jamie, who are on my team. They're here to help me.

Brix smiles triumphantly. "You hate me because I pointed out you're unhappy?"

"Yes! Who does that? Let me live in my oblivious depression."

Brix laughs. "Sorry, but I do have a point."

"And that is?"

"The same thing I've been trying to tell you about writing. You put way too much pressure on yourself. You need to slow down and enjoy all of this." He gestures around the room. "This is all for you.

Because you're awesome. Your songs affect lives and inspire people. Your work is loved by millions."

I wave my hand for him to keep going, but maybe he confuses it with me calling him over to me.

He stands. "You're amazing, Pop Star. You know you are." His feet stop right by mine so he's standing in front of me.

That giant cock of his, confined by his black pants, is right there. Right at eye level. I've had dreams about it. Really hot, jerk-off-inducing dreams.

He shouldn't come so close to me when I'm buzzing like this.

I want him in my mouth again. My hand. Maybe my ass, but with how big he is I'm not sure how much I'd enjoy it. I still want it.

I glance up at him. "I can remember one particularly fun time I've had recently."

"Yeah?" he asks.

"I can use my mouth for more than just singing, you know …" I hook a foot behind his leg and pull him forward.

His hands land on the couch by my head, and he hovers above me. He smells like spicy cologne and badassness. I totally know that's not technically a smell, but it describes Brix perfectly.

"I know from personal experience how talented your mouth is."

"That was *super* fun." I reach for his belt, but he stops me.

"If we do this again, there's no going back. We can't forget about logic and all that other shit this time."

"We won't."

"There's that tic again." His finger trails over the dimple in my cheek. "I'm serious, Harley. I don't want to do this back-and-forth, hot-and-cold dance. If I kiss you again, I won't be able to keep being strong."

That's a tough deal but one I'm willing to make in the heat of the moment.

I grip his shirt and pull him closer, bringing our lips mere inches apart. "Don't be strong. No regrets."

I don't exactly know what I'm agreeing to here. Just sex? Lots of sex? A casual thing with my bodyguard? I'm not sure how that will work. But right now, I'm not going to question it.

Guys should never be allowed to enter into an agreement when there's sex on the line. They'd most likely sell their souls.

Brix's lips turn up at the sides ever so slightly. "This is going to go a lot differently than last time."

"Oh?"

He brings his mouth down on mine softly, but it still hits with a strong force that knocks the wind out of me.

But before I'm ready, Brix breaks away.

It was chaste. Too quick. I assume he's doubting this.

"No, don't. No regrets. I promise."

He kisses my cheek. "Not going too far."

If I thought Brix's face while I was blowing him was unforgettable, it's nothing compared to the sight of Brix getting on his knees for me.

I shift on the couch, sinking lower and inching my ass closer to the edge.

Brix's strong hands run up my thighs, but he doesn't make a move to go any higher.

I grunt in frustration, which makes Brix smile.

"Oh, you want me to do something?"

"You know what I want," I grumble.

"I'm a military boy. I like taking direction."

"Okay. Umm …" *Great start, Harley.* "Undo my pants?"

"You sure about that?" Brix mocks. "Sounded more like a question than an order."

I clear my throat. "Undo my pants."

It must come out better because he immediately does it.

Slowly.

Really. Fucking. Slowly.

"We don't really have time to go this slow. The set only had a few songs left."

Brix looks up at me, his dark eyes shining. "I don't think I heard an order in that."

My fingers run over his short hair. "Hurry up and take my cock out."

"Mm, better."

My face heats, and I don't doubt that I'm blushing. It's not that I'm not confident in bed. I know what I like. But I've only ever been with two guys. One was an industry guy when I'd just turned eighteen and Eleven had hit it big. We both knew what it was, and there weren't feelings involved. And then there was Jay. Stolen, fleeting moments in between hiding our love.

I'm not virginal, but I don't exactly have experience in *this*—telling a partner what to do.

My cock is freed, and then Brix stares up at me expectantly. The words "Suck it" fall from my mouth, demanding and confident. I think I sound like an idiot, but Brix licks his lips and moans. I guess he really does like being bossed around.

Lowering his head, he starts soft, languidly moving over me.

I pull on what little hair he has. "Harder."

He adds a tiny bit of pressure and swirls his tongue around my hard shaft.

"Just like that."

Brix's hands are glued to my thighs, unmoving, yet they fidget as if they want to do something but aren't allowed to.

"Use your hands. Touch me."

With a shuddery breath, Brix moves one hand under my shirt and the other into my jeans to cup my balls.

I throw my head back. "More."

Brix keeps going, unchanging.

Shit. Like, do I need to be more specific? "More *everything*."

It's sensory overload as he sucks me deeper and squeezes my sac right to the border of pleasure and pain.

"Fuck, Brix."

He hums around me.

I can't take it. Heat shoots down my spine, and my mouth dries.

"I ... I ..."

His mouth drags slowly up my shaft with one hard suck until it only covers the tip of my cock. The hand on my stomach moves lower and wraps around me, giving one firm pump.

He lifts his head. "Can I swallow? Like, I'm on PrEP and have been tested recently, but you?"

"Same. Well, not the PrEP thing, because you know, if the media found out ... but I've been tested."

Brix has a disapproving line creasing his brow. I'm beginning to know it well.

Before we can get further into the super-sexy talk of STD prevention, he gives my dick another stroke, and the conversation dies. He goes back to what he was doing. It takes zero point two seconds for me to forget all about it because Brix is as good at giving head as he is at giving me perspective.

It's been so long since I've had someone's mouth on me I'm surprised I haven't already blown my load. But I'm close. So close.

My legs tremble, and I thrust up into Brix's mouth. He groans and reaches between his legs, palming his erection to try to squash it down.

The head of my dick hits the back of Brix's throat, and that's all it takes.

White heat fills my vision, making me dizzy.

"F-fuuuck." My cock pulses. Brix swallows my cum, the contracting of his throat flexing around my dick.

I gasp for breath while he licks me clean until I can't take it anymore and order him to stop. I'm overspent.

Brix stands, and I reach for him, but my arms are jelly, so I kind of lazily swipe at him instead. I should probably try to put my dick away, but ... effort.

"Lap. Sit," I pant.

The next second, he's straddling me. His big body practically squashes me, and I don't even care. His lips land on the spot right next to my mouth, catching the side of my lips. "I said I like direction, not being treated like a dog."

I ignore his weak protest. "Kiss me."

"I have cum breath."

"It's my cum, so I don't care."

"Aww, that's sweet."

"Shut up and kiss me already."

Brix laughs.

"Brix," I whine.

He kisses me hard.

He tastes like sex, and it makes me crave more. I want his cock in my mouth again. I want to taste all of him this time.

Brix cups the back of my head, and his tongue tangles with mine.

I'm about to reach for his belt when the door to the room swings open.

The voice that booms through the small space is one I know well. Intimately. I guess the concert's over. "Harley, what the fu …"

Jay, Soren, and Jamie stand there in shock.

Brix jumps off me, and that's when I realize my dick is still hanging out of my unzipped pants.

"Shit," I hiss and quickly tuck myself away.

"Ow, my eyes!" Jamie cries dramatically. "My innocent, *innocent* eyes."

"Pfft, innocent," I say.

She loses the act. "Have I mentioned lately how much I love my job? Although, if you'd waited a few seconds more, I could've snapped a pic and sold it for, like, *retirement* money."

Brix scowls, but I tug on his hand.

"She's kidding." I feel Jay's gaze on me, and I quickly drop my hand from Brix's.

I stand. "Umm …"

Jay turns to his husband beside him. "Okay, you were right. The song wasn't about me."

Soren smiles and wraps his arm around Jay. Once upon a time, my heart would've broken at the sight of that, but now I feel … nothing. I knew I was slowly getting over him, but I wasn't sure until this very second if I was there yet or not.

"I know this is hard for you to accept," Soren says to Jay. "The world not revolving around you."

Jay elbows Soren hard, but Soren laughs. "Even if that song wasn't directed at me, the label is gonna be pissed because they'll think it was. This will add fuel to the Harley and me rumors."

Damn it, he's right.

I run a hand over my hair. "Shit. I didn't think that through. It was supposed to be a joke between me and—" I gaze at Brix.

"It's not going to appear that way," Jay says.

"Yeah, I know. I'll fix it. I promise. The headlines tomorrow will not speculate anything about you and me."

"They better not. I'm finally stepping out from behind your shadow, Harley."

I can't even be pissed because he has a point. I didn't think through a lot of logistics when we were together, and I know I held him back. Instead of his band taking off on their own, I kept him as Eleven's opening act for my own selfish reasons.

It was messy.

"I really am sorry. I'll fix it right now. It's probably best we don't do that publicity op at the after-party."

"No shit," Jay scoffs and then glances at Brix. "But clearly you're already having your own after-party in here." He tries to hide his smartassness I used to love so much, but as usual, he fails.

"Jay, this is Brix. Brix, this is Jay Jackson from Radioactive. He's kind of a big deal, but you wouldn't know that." I look at Jay and am about to blurt how Brix and I met to yet another person because it is compulsory to do it to everyone he meets, but he cuts me off.

"You guys sing 'Hat Trick Heartbreak.' I love that song."

"Are you kidding me?" I screech.

Brix winks at me.

"Asshole."

Jay's gaze pings between us. "Brix? As in built like a brick shit-house? Fitting."

Of course we think the same way. Old me would've read into that, but if chasing after Jay taught me anything, it's that he and Soren are as solid as they come. They're literally *hashtag couple goals*.

And I'm … hooking up with an employee.

Fuck.

Jay smiles at me. "Despite the shitstorm it's going to bring upon us, it was a great show. Thanks for coming."

"Anytime." I give him a nod. "And I'll fix it. I promise."

On his way out, Jay gives me a thumbs-up, no doubt praising my choice of hookup. It's awkward, but hey, he's trying. And we did agree to be all supportive and civil and shit even if things aren't great between us. They probably never will be.

We hurt each other—arguably, I hurt him more—but that pain doesn't go away no matter how much you move on. I don't understand those people who try to be actual friends with an ex. Friendly, sure, but *friends*? I may be over Jay romantically, but it's still *weird*.

As soon as Jay and his husband are out the door, I drop the façade of being confident in how to fix this latest fuckup.

Brix senses my tension and approaches. "Harley—"

"I have to call Gideon." I walk to the counter where my phone is charging.

Damn, I already have six missed calls from Gideon.

He answers on the first ring when I call back. "You fucked up."

In more ways than one.

"I know. Let's do some damage control."

"Patching in the label's publicist now."

There goes the rest of my night.

"We should totally come up with something like the infamous *conscious uncoupling* wording so everyone's talking about us," Evah says. She walks across our living room and sits next to me on the couch, still in the silk nightgown she always wears to bed.

I take a deep breath. "If I haven't thanked you enough for this, I'm gonna keep saying it. Thank you."

After the concert last night where we went into *fix it* mode, my team came to the conclusion that I need to make the song about Evah —a goodbye.

We went straight to the airport and came home as soon as we were allowed to take-off. We arrived an hour ago at the crack of dawn.

"This was always the plan." Evah takes my hand. "We're just … moving it up. If we can paint it like we're both too busy right now and it's a reluctant breakup, the song makes more sense. And we could probably stay friends without too much speculation."

"I know it's not what we originally were going to do." We were supposed to plan this properly, but now we're half-assing it at the last minute to cover the fact I'm a dumbass.

"This will still work without too much backlash on either of us," Evah says.

"People are going to think you broke my heart and I'm all emo over you."

"People were always going to think that. You're the perfect guy, remember?"

Yeah. Perfect.

My gaze slowly goes to Brix, who's sitting in the armchair across the room. He's pretending not to listen, but I know he is.

Obviously, we haven't had time to digest what happened last night. Again. After we said it wasn't going to happen.

I love getting myself into messes.

We said it would be different this time. No regrets.

I'm not regretting it at all, and if it were up to me, I'd go over there right now and ask him to hold me because I know he'd make me feel better.

But I don't know if that's what he wants. Maybe what he said last night was in the heat of the moment, and today he's back to worrying about his job.

I'll have to talk to him about it, but the next few days are going to be crazy busy. Paparazzi are going to be a heavy presence on both Evah and me. And I'm due to start recording in the studio next week.

"Okay, so what can we use that's like conscious uncoupling without fully plagiarizing that?" Evah asks.

"Purposefully … breaking up." I shrug. "I don't know. Can't we just say we're both moving on and focusing on our careers right now?"

Gideon and Jamie come through the front door with takeout food for breakfast.

"How bad is it out there?" I ask.

"The street's full of paparazzi," Jamie says.

The publicist for the label put out the official statement last night that Evah and I are done. We just have to work out what to say directly to our fans.

Evah's tapping away on her phone, and I assume she's writing up a draft, but then she says, "Cognizant disentanglement."

"No," Gideon, Brix, and I say all at the same time.

"Simple language is better," Gideon says. "Besides, if you pull a Chris Martin and Gwyneth Paltrow, people will think you're trying too hard."

"But it will get attention," Evah says.

"Wait until you try to walk out of here." Gideon points outside. "You have more than enough attention from this."

We write up a brief statement that's vague but says we'll always love each other and be friends. In our case, it's true. I do love her in my own way, and we are good friends, but like all breakups in Hollywood, people will see what they want to see.

Our breakup is about to get ugly out there, and that's without us really doing anything.

The microscope on our lives just zoomed in closer.

My gaze goes to Brix's again.

I want to be the bigger person and tell him he's off the hook—that I know my lifestyle is too much—but I'm too weak. Especially when it comes to love … well, potential love. Two blowjobs don't equal love. Lust, fornication, and desire for more orgasms, sure. But not love.

Even if he is the only one who understands that the perfect guy everyone sees me as is nowhere close to the truth.

The truth is, I'm the label's puppet, and I always have been.

At this rate, I always will be because I don't know how to break free and keep everything I've worked for.

CHAPTER 16
BRIX

ALL DAY I've wanted to kiss the crap out of Harley and make him forget the shit he's enduring right now, but I haven't been able to.

He's either been with Gideon or Evah or both.

I've wanted to text him from across the room to let him know I'm here for him, but anyone could see it over his shoulder, and I've seen in the tabloids about celebrities' phones being hacked and posted all over the internet for the world to see.

Last night, after the show, being with Harley again … I don't care if it's a mistake or it puts my job in jeopardy.

His mere presence gives my life light again when it's been nothing but darkness and adrenaline for the last four years.

This was never my plan. Hell, my original plan was to go career. I was never supposed to get out of the military let alone wind up babysitting a slightly neurotic but cute as hell pop star who has me interested in his life in ways I couldn't have anticipated.

Harley needs someone in his life who's above all the Hollywood bullshit. I want to be that guy, but the longer he goes without giving me eye contact, the more I think I'm not gonna be that guy for him.

When everyone's gone for the night and I walk Harley to his room to check it like I always do, he stops me outside his door.

"You really don't have to check it for me."

"I know. I … but, uh …" *I want to.*

"I'm scared if I open this door and let you into my room, I'm not going to let you out of it."

"Like a hostage situation? I'm good at negotiating those. Just so you know." I put my arm around his back and pull him against me. "Really good."

Harley smiles. "I'm sorry the last twenty-four hours have been a mess."

"I'm sorry too," I whisper.

"You didn't do anything."

"I know, but I'm sorry you have to deal with this shit to begin with. I'm not going to rant about how the label, the public, and every single person on this planet shouldn't get a say in your life, what you do, what songs you sing, or who you sleep with, but no one cares about what they 'shouldn't' be doing. They do whatever they want anyway. I want you to know I'm here for you in spite of all that."

Harley's eyes flutter shut. "You still want to stay? With me, I mean? My life is crazy, and I'd understand if—"

I cut him off with my mouth on his, but unlike our kiss last night that was interrupted, where we were all hot and needy, this is a different type of need.

It's deeper.

It's a promise of more. Of everything I want to give him.

Chances are this thing between us isn't going to work out for a million different reasons, but that doesn't stop me from wanting it.

I want Harley Valentine. The *real* Harley Valentine.

"I want you to fuck me," I whisper against his lips.

Harley pulls back and tilts his head. "You mean … like …"

I grin. "You want specifics? I want your cock in my ass. How's that for specific?"

"You … you do that?"

"You don't? I can go either way, but I like it when a guy can overpower me and fuck me until I can't think."

"Uh, uh, umm, that's … I can do that."

"Are you sure? You don't sound too confident."

"I've, uh … I …"

"You *can't* be a virgin. I've met your ex-boyfriend. He screams sex."

"No. Not a virgin, but, like, I've only been with two guys, and in what world could I overpower you? You could snap me in half, and it's a lot of pressure, and—"

"Hey, whoa." I rub my hands up and down his arms. "We can take this slower if you want."

"No, I want to, but …"

"You had no problem taking control while you blew me." Leaning in, I run my lips along the side of his neck. "I loved the way you pinned me to the bed and took care of me."

Harley moans and throws his head back, giving me more access to his sweetly salty skin.

"Come on. I promise having sex with me isn't that intimidating." I pull him into the room and close the door behind us.

"Have you met you?"

I shuck off my shirt and undo my belt. "Not intimidating at all."

Harley swallows so hard he gulps. His gaze is on my smooth, shaved chest, and I'm almost tempted to make my pecs dance, but I want him to take what he needs from me. I want him to make the first move, to come to me, but most of all, I want him to *claim me*.

He steps forward, coming so close I'm desperate for him to reach for me and run his fingers over my bare skin.

I'm dying for it.

His long, reddish-tinged lashes blink up at me.

"Touch me," I whisper. "Do whatever you want with me."

A small smile ghosts his lips. "Whatever I want?"

"I'll let you know if you hit any limits, but I doubt you will."

Harley still looks a little unsure. He tentatively runs his hands over my chest.

"Or we don't have to take it that far," I say. "We could fool around instead. It's up to you."

"Oh, I want this. I'm just … thinking."

"That's the thing. I don't want you to think. I want you to *act*."

Harley grips the back of my neck and pulls me down so our mouths meet. I don't know where the sudden burst of confidence comes from, but I'm not complaining. At all.

His mouth is demanding and strong, and nothing—nothing—gets me going more than a struggle for power.

I push back a little with my tongue, testing to see if he'll let me, but he doesn't.

Gripping his ass, I pull him against me. Our bodies slam against one another, and I can feel how hard he is already.

Harley stumbles a little, but the next second, he turns us. In the blink of an eye, I'm on my back with the sexiest pop star on the planet on top of me.

He doesn't stop kissing me. His lower half grinds against mine, but it's not enough.

I run my hands under his shirt, dragging it up—the universal sign for *take off your fucking shirt*. But he doesn't.

He moves down my body and pulls off my pants and boxers, dumping them on the floor. His tongue traces over my inner thigh. The muscles in my legs contract and release, trembling under Harley's wandering mouth.

When he gets to the good part, so close to my cock, he detours and goes to my hip.

"No." My protest makes him laugh.

"You said I can do anything I want. I want to explore you."

"I'm more than okay with that, but could you do it a little faster?" My dick aches. I reach down to take some of that need away, but Harley swats my hand.

"Hands above your head."

"Really?" I exclaim.

He smirks up at me. Damn, he's better at this than he thought he'd be.

I do as he says, and he makes his way up my torso, his mouth leaving scorching hot kisses along my skin.

Harley sucks a nipple into his mouth, and my hips buck.

I reach for him, my hand going to the back of his head, but he grabs my forearm and pins it back above my head.

My dick leaks.

"Harley," I whine.

"Mmm?" he mocks. His eyes shine up at me.

"You need to fuck me."

"I *need* to?"

"I need you to." My voice is breathy. "And I need you to lose your clothes. And—"

Harley covers my mouth with his hand. "I need you to shut up."

He pauses for a split second, as if he's worried he crossed a line, but he's nowhere close to the fucking line.

I smile under his hand, and he relaxes on top of me.

"You can beg me all you want, but I have something else in mind. I've been thinking about your cock in my mouth ever since my first taste. Only, this time, I want all of it."

All I can do is nod because his hand is still over my mouth.

It's obvious by the way he moves to get comfortable between my legs that he has every intention of dragging this out.

The first swipe of his tongue across the pulsing head of my cock sends a shiver down my spine. The second is even more torturous. By the time he sucks me into his mouth, I'm dying.

He's in no rush, but I am. It doesn't take long for me to reach the breaking point.

I moan against his hand, and he looks up at me. Finally, he takes his hand away, only to sit up and suck a finger into his mouth.

"Legs up."

I mumble something so unintelligible even I don't know what I'm trying to say. Probably a mix of *fuck yes* and *oh my God, hurry up*.

I flatten my feet on the bed and widen my thighs. I'm practically trembling when he presses his finger against my hole. He pushes in as he lowers his head again and sucks me in as far as he can.

I want to give in to the urge to cup his head so I can fuck his face, but I don't want to test my boundaries. It's a new type of loss of control for me, and my body is loving every moment of it.

But I need release.

I don't know how long he sucks and teases me, but he seems to be an expert at getting me close only to change technique and bring me back from the edge.

"Haven't you had enough yet?" I ask.

Harley pulls off with a small laugh. "Have you?"

"I'm so far past that I'm dying."

"Dying? Really? And you think pop stars are dramatic."

I go to say something smartassy back, but before I can think of words, Harley adds a second finger and pushes against my prostate.

My body tenses, and it's all over.

Harley's mouth covers my cock just in time for the first spurts of cum to hit his tongue.

"Mmm," he hums, and I can no longer hold myself back.

I thrust up into his mouth over and over again, finally moving one of my hands from above my head to weave it into his hair.

I come down his throat, convulsing and shuddering through an intense orgasm.

I'm panting when he pulls off me, and I match his smile. His looks a lot more mischievous than the sated one I'm throwing his way.

"Roll over," he says.

"W-what?"

"*Now* I'm going to fuck you."

"Now? Not even gonna give me five minutes to recover?"

"Five minutes? Impressive refractory period."

"Oh, I'm not talking about getting it up again. I just mean to catch my fucking breath after coming so hard. I'll be lucky to get hard again at all."

Harley looks proud as he climbs off the bed. He's still completely clothed. "You have one minute for me to get undressed and grab a condom."

"No condom," I rasp. "We don't need it."

"I trust you." Harley goes to his bedside drawer to pull out lube.

I can't do anything but watch him. My muscles are broken.

"I don't see you rolling over." Harley pulls off his shirt.

"Can't," I breathe, my gaze locked on his pants as he drops them to the floor along with his underwear.

His cock springs free, long and thin, and my mouth waters. I don't know what I want more: my mouth on him again or him in my ass.

As he lubes up, it's decided. Definitely ass. Lube tastes gross.

He stands at the foot of the bed. "Minute's up."

I roll over and hold myself up on my hands and knees despite my muscles aching.

When Harley dribbles lube into my crack and preps me open enough to take him, my dick tries to get hard again but can't quite manage it. Every pass across my prostate teases and tortures me. I'm completely spent, but I want more anyway.

"Think you got another one in you?" Harley asks.

"Why don't you stop fingering me and hurry up with the fucking and find out?"

"You ready enough?"

"Enough," I choke out.

"I don't come until you do again."

"Shit, no pressure."

"Get yourself hard for me."

At his order, my hand practically flies to my cock. As I stroke myself hard and fast, Harley slams inside me.

We let out a collective moan, and my dick finally perks up a little.

"Do it again," I say.

"Sorry, what? Sounds like you just gave me an order, but that can't be right."

His words are as good as another hit against my prostate.

I'm sweaty, I'm trembling, and I'm on the brink of collapsing, but I want to do this for him. I want to come again.

I relax the arm holding me up and bury my face in a pillow, arching my ass up higher in the air.

Harley pulls out agonizingly slow and then slams back in. He repeats this over and over and coaxes me back to full hardness.

I'm still stroking, still trying to get myself off. The edge is right there, but I don't know if I can reach it.

Harley's thrusts become faster and faster until all I can hear is his hard breaths and the slapping of our bodies meeting over and over again.

I shake my head. "I don't think I can ..."

Harley's body blankets mine. He kisses my shoulder and then turns to my ear. "You can and you will, or I don't come. Do it for me because I need to let go soon."

"For you," I think aloud.

For Harley.

My pop star.

My lover.

My ... boss.

I squeeze my eyes shut. No matter how hard I try to forget that part, it keeps popping back up.

His cock is hard as steel as he slides in and out of me with ease now, picking up his pace until he's pounding into me. "The sooner you come, the sooner your ass will be full of my cum."

That's what I need to clear my mind and get there. A few more strokes of my dick, and my body shudders through another orgasm, though this one much smaller than the last.

Harley straightens back up. I chant in my head for him to come because I need to collapse. I need—

He stills inside me, and warm cum fills me up.

My body gives out and falls onto the mattress while Harley rolls onto his back beside me with the widest smile on his face.

The smile that's all *mine*.

"I want to reach out and run my finger over the adorable wrinkles your eyes get when you genuinely smile, but I can't lift my arm."

Harley laughs. "I knew you could come again."

"Are you seriously gloating right now?"

"Uh-huh. It might be the first time since we met that I was right about something."

"Hmm, true. I am usually right about *everything*."

"And so modest about it too."

"Modesty is overrated."

Harley closes his eyes. "Mmhmm."

"You tired?" I ask.

"Dead."

"Ah shit. I'm gonna lose my job if I kill you with sex."

Harley's eyes fly open. "You're not still worried about your job, are you?"

"No." Not … entirely. "Okay, yeah, but it's a risk I'm willing to take." For some reason.

The seed of guilt that was planted after last night grows. I shouldn't be willing to take the risk when I have so much on the line. Rationally, I know if this job doesn't work out, I'm only going back to how my life and bank account balance were before. It's not like I'd be losing anything.

Except … this contract is a big deal, and it's a lot of money.

But then I look at Harley's concerned gaze, and all my doubts about what we're doing go away.

"Maybe we should make some rules," Harley suggests. "Like, no matter what happens between you and me, I won't let it interfere with your job."

"Sounds like a good rule." In theory. I do wonder how that deal will go down when emotions run high.

"And keeping it between us is a given."

"Yup."

"So, also, umm, maybe you shouldn't sleep in here. In case we sleep in or whatever and Gideon comes by or something. Jamie pretty much knows after New York, but it'd be better if no one else—"

I sit up fast and then ache all over. "Right. Good point."

Harley leans up on an elbow and runs his hand down my arm. "I didn't mean you had to leave right this second."

I smile at him over my shoulder. "I'm tapping out. Two orgasms that close together can kill a guy."

"Sounds legit." He lifts his chin and pouts his lips for a kiss, and there's no way I'll deny him that.

I lean over and kiss him languidly. "Goodnight." I use my shirt to clean up but pause at throwing it in his hamper. "Guess we shouldn't get our laundry mixed up either."

"Probably not."

I throw on my pants and leave his room. I can't explain it, and I don't even know how, but this guy has given me the ability to breathe easily for the first time in four years. Which is kind of ironic considering risking it all for him should leave me stifled for air.

CHAPTER 17
HARLEY

NORMALLY, waking to someone standing over you would be creepy. It sounds creepy. But when Brix does it, it's the best wake-up call I can get. He's got a plate in his hands, and I know without looking he's made me a breakfast burrito.

I'm hungry for something else, though.

I sit up and untuck his black T-shirt from his tactical pants so I can kiss my way up his stomach.

My lips barely get to touch him before he's stepping away.

"As much as I want more, Gideon's downstairs. He's coming to the studio with us today."

I pull back. "Why is Gid— Wait, *us*? It's Sunday. Iris is coming."

"I called him and told him not to worry. I'm with you today."

This is the second Sunday he hasn't taken the day off since we started hooking up. "Don't you have stuff to do today?"

"Nothing that can't wait. Now eat your breakfast." Brix hands me the plate.

"I'm beginning to think breakfast burritos are the only thing you can cook."

"Are you complaining?"

I take a bite. "Not one fucking bit."

Brix smiles. It makes me want to kiss him.

"You can't stare at me like that. Especially in front of Gideon." I won't be able to control myself.

"I know."

I've been busy recording the album. Every day we head to the studio, and I do my thing while Brix and Jamie watch from outside the booth.

I've laid down three full tracks already, and I've put in excruciatingly long hours even though staring at Brix through the glass as I'm working is one big temptation to go home early.

"Eat up. We leave in ten," Brix says.

I watch as he walks away, taking his tight, round ass with him.

It looks good in his tactical pants. Or any pants.

No pants would be even better.

Focus, Harley.

Food, dress, leave.

I head downstairs when I'm ready to go and find the three of them waiting for me. "Why are you coming?" I ask Gideon.

"The label wants to hear what you've got so far."

"No."

"No?" Gideon asks. He seems more amused than pissed off.

"They always do this. They want to hear the songs before they're completed, and then they hate them."

"They don't hate all of them."

"Majority," I mutter. "They'll get the songs when they're done."

"This isn't negotiable, Harley."

Behind Gideon, Brix scowls. Damn, he's hot.

Nope. Focus. I need to focus because I know what the label is going to say about the songs I've already cut.

"Let me lay down something I know they'll like—a chart-topper with a dance beat. The ones I have now are ... a little off brand."

Gideon slumps. "How off brand?"

"Political, kind of a *love sucks* one, and ... uh ... sex."

Gideon rubs his chest. "You're trying to kill me, aren't you?"

"No. I'm just ... going where the inspiration is." I force myself not to glance at Brix right now.

"And where are you getting inspiration for songs about sex?"

"Maybe from my lack of getting any." Okay, yep, that was not convincing even to my own ears, but apparently, he buys it.

Gideon huffs. "Let's get to the studio, and I can see what we're working with."

This is going to be a rough day.

On our way out the door, Brix pulls me back. "They're great songs," he says low. "I can't get 'Anti-Love' out of my head."

I smile. "Well, your hatred for the concept of fate and soul mates practically wrote that song, so it's no wonder you like it."

"Problem?" Gideon calls back at us still standing in the doorway.

Brix takes the lead. "Not at all."

As a bodyguard, he's easily slipped into a protocol of his own. He's the first out of the gate, the last to get into the car, and he doesn't leave my side unless I'm in a secure part of the studio, and even then he only leaves to do a check and make sure no one's lurking outside or existing where they shouldn't be.

A poor intern on her first day got reamed for not having a pass to the studio.

Overkill, maybe, but he makes me feel safe, which I think is the point of his job more than actually protecting me.

When we arrive at the recording studio I bought a few years ago, paparazzi are there again. It's been two weeks since Evah moved out, and we've both been bombarded, but at least there are only a couple today. It's worse here than at home right now. They've pretty much given up on getting anything good other than me in a car pulling out of my driveway at home.

Brix shields me with his big body but never crosses the line into lawsuit territory. Sure, paparazzi can shove their cameras in your face, follow you, and practically stalk you, but if we touch them in any way, even their cameras, bam, assault accusations.

Brix is good at getting them to back off.

The first time he put his arm around me to shield me from them, I got worried thinking they would read into it, but it's a bodyguard loophole it seems. And it's true it is his job. If Iris had done it, I wouldn't have blinked.

We get into the studio, and I hold my breath the whole time Gideon listens to my new tracks.

His lips remain pursed through all of them, his arms folded, and he gives away nothing.

After the first listen, he asks to rehear the one I wrote about the military. It's political and will have both haters and those who defend it to the ends of the earth. The lyrics are generic enough, a basic support the troops kind of theme, but it has queer undertones like mentioning fitting in to serve and sacrificing lives for the promise of support when you're not completely accepted.

"You should sell this one," Gideon says. "It's a great song."

"I don't want to sell it."

Gideon leans against the counter. "The label will never let you put it on your next album. Not if you want the other two."

"Then I'll sell one of the other two. The sex one."

Gideon shakes his head. "That's your most marketable one so far. It could be your 'SexyBack.' That song took Justin Timberlake to the next level."

The other one is Brix's song. His destiny is bullshit theory. I want to keep that, but the message of the political song is one I want to produce and release myself.

"I want to keep all of them."

"Not going to happen," Gideon says. "Pick your battles. The other two I can convince the label. They're peppy and bouncy, and the one about fate being bullshit will be the breakup song of the year. It's not exactly on brand for you, but it's still a decent anthem for your demographic. This one about the military is *too* political. It'll alienate too many fans."

"Pitch it to them anyway."

"And if they still say no—which they will—I think you should see if Radioactive wants it. Jay's known for not giving a shit about spreading his political beliefs. He has a cause for a song like this."

I chew on my bottom lip. Not only did Jay and I write "Confusion" together, Eleven had a song he wrote, and when we were together, we'd write and help each other out all the time. If anyone else is going to sing this song and hit it out of the park, it would be him, but … I don't know.

"Isn't the point of me going solo to gain new fans and a new demographic? I can't produce the same song over and over again. The lyrics might be different, the melody slightly changed, but you know and I know, put nearly all my songs on the same backing track and you wouldn't be able to tell the difference. I want to branch out. I want to—"

"It's a risk you know the label won't go for."

I grunt in frustration.

"Leave me with it," Gideon says, "but keep Jay in mind."

I'd rather not, but I agree. "Fine. Just promise me you'll fight for it and show one hundred percent commitment to it or they'll know they can say no."

"I promise."

Gideon takes the rough tracks with him and goes to meet with the label, which means I can't concentrate during my session. I keep stumbling over my own words because I'm distracted and forcing this song out. It's the type of song the label will get excited about— something that is guaranteed to hit the charts—but my heart's not in it. It's not the type of song I want to be doing anymore.

But I understand it's a necessary evil if I want to keep selling albums.

A slight change in tone or mood can turn off even the most loyal fans.

Balance.

I need to find a balance.

I throw my head in my hands and rest my elbows on the piano in front of me.

"Want to take a break?" the producer says from the sound booth.

I lift my head to see him looking at me through the glass. I worked with Randall before when I was with Eleven, and the reason I like working with him is because he doesn't push. He never pressured us like some others did to get it done. He believes in quality over quantity and timeline.

"Yeah. Thanks."

When he leaves the sound booth, my eyes catch on Brix behind him, staring at me with that concerned scrunch in his brow again.

Jamie says something from the couch behind where he stands.

He presses the button for the intercom into the studio. "Jamie's making a coffee run. You want your usual?"

"Make it a double shot," I grumble.

When she leaves, he enters the studio and comes over to the piano.

I wish this place wasn't glass on all sides. My hands itch to reach for him and pull him against me, but it's not a question of someone possibly seeing, it's basically a definite.

"I think you should call it a day," Brix says.

"I can't. I need to get something down the label can drool over."

"No offense, but they're not going to drool over a song you're forcing. You can hear it in your voice."

"Yeah, I know. I need to get out of my head. I can get this done today."

"You could, if you push yourself, but what's the worst that could happen if you don't get it down today?"

What would be the worst? The label would be pissed. *Hello, they're going to be mad anyway.* A half-assed on brand song for them isn't going to turn it around.

"Damn it. You're right." I hate that he's always right. "You're annoying."

Brix laughs. "I know. We should go home. Just take the day to—"

"Yeah. I can write more at home." I stand.

"No, that's not what I meant. You need a *break*."

"What kind of break?"

He grins. "I know exactly where you want to go."

We drop Jamie home, thankful for the absence of any paparazzi as we arrive, and Brix runs inside to grab a bag of stuff.

When he gets back, Brix gets back in the driver's seat and heads west.

"Okay, so you aren't taking me to the ranch again," I say.

"Nope. Too far."

The closer we get to Santa Monica, the more worried I become. "We're not going somewhere super busy, are we? I'll be recognized faster than you can say, 'Oh look, I led Harley into another horde of fans.'"

Brix laughs. "Not going there." He turns south, heading away from Santa Monica.

It takes another half an hour for him to pull into a nature preserve in Rancho Palos Verdes, but the sign out front says it closes at four. It's currently five past.

"It's closed," I say.

"Not for me." We pull into the parking lot, and Brix takes a permit out of the glove compartment and puts it on the dashboard. "Trav uses this place for training, so we have special permits that allow us to use the beach when it's closed so our cars don't get towed."

I smile. "The beach. You brought me to the beach."

"You said it relaxes you."

"I thought you'd forget because it's not like I can go to the beach a lot."

"I can bring you to this one whenever you want. Even when it's open to the public, not many people come here."

We get out of the car, and Brix grabs his bag out of the back.

It's a tiny beach surrounded by high cliffs, but as we get about halfway down to the water, we realize there's no sand.

"It's high tide," Brix says, "but we can go onto those rocks over there." He points to a lower cliff that overlooks the water.

"All right, but if I break my neck, I'm pretty sure you'll be fired."

"I'm pretty sure the female population will track me down and murder me."

"Well, if you want to get technical … yeah."

We climb over some rocks and head out to the cliff, but Brix pulls up short from the edge.

"Just in case you have surprisingly horrible balance, let's sit here." He lays down towels for us from his bag. "Sorry we can't go down to the sand."

"This is perfect." I breathe in the salty air as I sit on the hard surface. "I like the water. It seems to go on forever and reminds me I'm not cooped up in a tiny studio booth. I don't like feeling … trapped."

Brix smiles. "Kinda surprising considering you never leave your house unless it's for work."

"I *can't* leave my house, and you know why. When I'm out and I'm recognized, it's not only by one person. Everyone tries to get in my face and get my attention, and then I'm more trapped than being inside."

He nods. "Yeah. I just figure there has to be a way around that."

"Like what?"

"I haven't worked it out yet. Well, I mean, there is this." He holds his arms wide.

The late-afternoon breeze is fresh, making the isolated beach seem even more deserted. We could be the only ones on the entire planet right now.

I revel in it. "This is a perfect loophole. If only we could close everywhere down when I wanted to go out."

"Maybe you could buy your own town and then pay all the people in it to pretend you're a no one."

"Brilliant idea and totally logistically sound."

"I'm here to help."

I lean back on my towel and let my skin soak up the sun. "Okay, so you know I'm all about music. I know you're all about being a badass and giving perspective to neurotic pop stars. What else is there?"

Brix mirrors my position, lying back and using his arm as a pillow. "There isn't much else. What did you want to know?"

"I take it you're still not going to tell me what you do on your usual Sundays."

"Nope."

Worth a shot. I try not to dwell on his refusal to share with me. "So that's off-limits. What about … okay, who'd you lose your virginity to?"

"Are we really doing the 'getting to know you' thing right now?"

"I can't think of anything better than being out here and wasting time with inane questions."

"You know what else is relaxing?" Brix side-eyes me. "Silence."

"No, silence is the worst. Especially when there's a constant buzz of chatter in your head."

"Maybe you should see someone about that."

"The voices? Nah, it's normal for creative types. I need to drown it out with mindless shit." I sit up to face him, but he stays lying down.

My gaze roams over his bulging muscles. Brix's shirt rises up just enough for a sliver of abs to show. My eyes travel up and meet his amused gaze.

I clear my throat. "I can go first if you want. I can't tell you his name, but I can tell you that he was a DJ for a popular radio station. I was barely eighteen. He was thirty."

"Are older guys your thing? I'm only twenty-eight. Am I too young for you?" His lips twitch.

"Jay's younger. You know that."

"I do. I guess I'm wondering what your type is."

"I don't think I have one." I stare out at the water to stop myself from saying *you. You're my type.* "Male and breathing is always sexy."

Brix laughs. "Breathing is kinda a big one for me too, but generally speaking, I like bigger guys."

"Bigger than you? You have fantasies about Sasquatch or something?" What does he see in me?

"Mm, Bigfoot. I'm getting hard just thinking about it."

I backhand his leg.

His eyes glisten with amusement. "In all honesty, until I met you, I thought I had a type. Now I'm thinking I've been going after the wrong type."

"Amen," I mumble.

"So, the radio DJ. Was it as serious as Jay?"

"God no. It was my first dirty little secret relationship that was on and off for about a year. We'd only ever be together whenever we were in his city. Like, we weren't official, obviously, and I wasn't delusional. I'd found a guy who was in the industry and would keep my secret, and he was fun to be around. I wasn't expecting a happily ever after. But it all fell to pieces when I saw him coming out of one of the other guy's hotel room during a visit. He could be with whoever he wanted when we were apart, just not one of my bandmates. That's, like, gross."

Brix's jaw ticks. "Bandmate? Are the Ryley4Ever rumors true?"

I keep my mouth shut, not confirming or denying anything.

"Did you two ever—"

"No. Hell no. I think I suggested it once when I was being emo and needed someone. Instead, he held me all night and let me cry on his shoulder." And now I'm oversharing. I clear my throat. "I mean, uh, we did masculine things like, uh—"

"Drank away your feelings with beer and went hunting."

"Yes. Let's go with that. Anyway, that night cemented our friendship and we agreed we were too much like brothers. Even the fighting. Adding sex to that … just no."

The water crashes against the cliffs, and I imagine myself floating on the waves and away from that admission.

I feel eyes on me, and I wonder what Brix sees. I wonder if he can see the loneliness I'd endured until I'd found Ryder with my pseudo-boyfriend and realized I had someone else to talk to. Someone I could confide in.

"I lost my virginity to Molly McCannon," Brix says suddenly.

My eyes widen. "Hold up. A *girl*?" I never asked him how he identifies. Not that it matters either way. I just wasn't expecting—

Brix laughs. "I was fifteen. We were both army brats and lived in military housing. It was fucking awkward, but the last puzzle piece fell into place. Her dad was transferred not long afterward, which was good, because I got out of the whole 'So, it turns out, I'm gay' conversation with her."

"Do your parents know?"

"Mom died when I was little, so I was raised by my dad, who was always the big, macho, military man. It wasn't really a secret while I was serving, so it's possible my commanding officers who knew him said something, but I'd like to think he never brought it up with me because he wasn't aware of it and not because he wanted to pretend it wasn't true."

"I understand. Not telling him, I mean. I never told my mom. And until that radio DJ, I was a bit like you. Still in denial. I'd kissed girls on tour that first year, but our handlers back then made it easy to not take it further. The other guys would have parties in their rooms with girls, and our handlers would look the other way, but I was always the good boy. I knew I was attracted to guys, but it wasn't until the DJ that I was like, 'Oh, okay, I'm *really* into dudes.'"

"And you've seriously only been with two guys?"

"Three now." I smile at him, but he doesn't return my amusement. "It was too risky to hook up."

Brix sits up so we're face to face. "Okay, I still don't get it, and I know I said I wouldn't ask why, and I guess I'm not asking you why, but asking why in general. Why can't you come out when there are other gay artists out there?"

And this just turned even heavier.

I groan. "I will never admit to saying this, so once it's out there, I'm going to deny, deny, deny. Are you ready for it? Boy bands produce crappy and shallow music. There, I said it."

Brix laughs. Hard. "You're not exactly spilling top secret intelligence there, Pop Star."

"Right, but how does it hit number one constantly? Because of the mania and the hype. They're catchy songs you get stuck in your head, and teenage girls love that. Not only did our contracts state that we couldn't come out, they also stated if we had girlfriends, we couldn't make it public knowledge. Do you know how much hate mail Evah got for being engaged to me?"

"I read that in your file."

"It's the fandom of it all. I'm trying to break away from all that, but the label has a point when they say change can't happen quickly. If the boy band image and persona they'd built for seven years changes suddenly, I could lose everything. Like Mason. His solo album tanked because he didn't re-sign with Joystar when we got out of our contracts. He went with someone who let him produce his own new sound, and it was a sound our Eleven fans didn't like. No new people were picking it up, because no matter what, we still have to fight the boy band stigma most grown-ups believe, which is that we're untalented and hiding behind an image."

"You are hiding behind an image, though."

A shiver runs through me, and it's not from the breeze coming off the water. Brix isn't saying anything I don't already know, but it leaves me cold anyway.

"We might be pigeonholed into a certain image, but we're not untalented. Those four other guys are some of the best musicians in the entire world. People can't get past the boy band thing."

Brix averts his gaze. "This might shock you, but … I'm one of those people. Or I was, until I started working for you."

"No shit," I say dryly.

"I told Iris it was sad he knew so much about you. He tried to tell me you were a legit artist, but all I could see was bad dance moves and shitty lyrics."

I should be offended, but I'm not. Because that's how it is when you're in a boy band. It's hard to break away from that mold. "Man, I'm fucking the wrong bodyguard. Iris thinks I'm a legit artist? *Iris?*"

Brix scowls. "Just so you know, if you were fucking your other bodyguard, this bodyguard would have something to say about that." He points to himself.

"Is that so?"

"Yup. And if we weren't in public right now, I'd totally kiss you and show you how much you're not fucking the wrong bodyguard."

I glance around the deserted beach. "There's no one here."

"Not worth the risk. There might not be anyone around, but that doesn't mean no one will come by. Closed beach or not."

"Mmm, give me until sunset, and then you can take me home and kiss me wherever you want."

Brix settles back on his towel, and I do the same. "You have the best ideas."

I turn my head to look at him and reach for his hand. It's a quick squeeze, something friendly, but I hope he knows how much more it is. "No, you do. Thank you for bringing me here."

"I promise to always try to bring you a dose of normal."

It's sad that's the most romantic thing anyone has ever offered me.

CHAPTER 18
BRIX

I CAN'T HELP but steal glances at Harley all the way home. A full afternoon on that cliffside has given him a relaxed vibe I've rarely seen from him.

He's wearing a permanent smile, and he's slinked back in his seat like he doesn't have a care in the world. He sings along to a song on the radio but not in the way he would if he was onstage. His voice is naturally amazing, and he always hits high notes and shows it off when he performs and in the studio, but right now he's not even trying. He's having fun with it.

I want to reach for his hand across the center console. It makes me want to pull over and do wicked things to him.

My cock is hard just thinking about doing that, and I can't wait to get back to the house so I can follow through.

I pray it's still quiet on the paparazzi front when we get home, but knowing the cameras and security system Iris set up are watching, I'll have to wait until we're inside anyway.

As we pull up to the house, I realize that's probably not an option either.

"Why's Jamie's car here?" I ask.

"I have no idea."

She usually parks on the street, but she's parked right out front. It's not a big deal, but considering she's not supposed to be here, and this is not routine, my bodyguard senses are tingling. Call it gut instinct.

I don't want to leave him out here, and I don't want to scare him, so we head inside, but I'm cautious enough to have Harley at my back.

Jamie's pacing the kitchen when we find her, and it's obvious I'm right. Something's wrong.

"What happened?" I ask.

Harley goes to step around me, but I don't let him get far. I keep him at my side.

"So, uh, my phone died, and I don't have my charger, and yours is a stupid Android—"

Harley coughs. "Awesome Android." He coughs again.

"Whatever. Anyway, I didn't know what to do, so I came here, but now I'm wondering if I should've gone to Gideon and talked to him or maybe Brix or …" She gazes at Harley sympathetically.

"What is it?" Harley asks. "You're freaking me out. Is it another stupid tabloid story?" His eyes widen. "Does someone know? Like, *know*, know."

She shakes her head. "It's not the tabloids." She has an envelope in her hands. "This came for you through the fan mail PO box."

"So I have another crazy fan. Is that all?"

If it was another harmless fan, she wouldn't be here.

"It's …" Her gaze flicks to mine. "It's from … uh, the guy. Billy Webber."

The blood drains from Harley's face.

"Fuck." I reach for the letter. "For future reference, if this shit happens, you come straight to me. I don't care if your phone is dead, your car battery died, or what the hell ever. You come to me."

"O-okay." She looks down at her feet.

That might've been harsh, but this is a security threat, no matter what the letter says. Which, as I open it and begin to read, I can't decide if this is trying to torment Harley further or reassure him somehow.

"What's it say?" Harley asks. It's obvious he's not sure if he wants to know because he makes no move to try to take it from me to read it himself.

"It's an apology. Of sorts." If victim blaming can be considered a form of an apology. "It basically says he's sorry for any stress he caused, and that it was a genuine misunderstanding. But ..."

"But?"

"But *'Your charismatic charm is hard to resist, and I had to take my chance even if it was small. You made me feel a connection that you claim wasn't there.'*"

Jamie makes a derisive noise. "If that's not a rapist's motto right there."

I glare at her. While she has a point, that doesn't help.

"I-I don't understand." Harley wraps his arms around himself. "This breaks his probation, right? He's not supposed to contact me or come near me. Can we call the cops or something?"

"Or something," I mutter.

"What?"

"This"—I hold up the letter—"violates the terms of the restraining order and his probation, so yeah, we could send him to jail if we wanted to."

"Or? It sounds like you have a better idea."

"Or we ignore it. He might be doing this to get a reaction out of you. This is a major stalker tactic here. If he wants attention and he gets it, his behavior could escalate. Or he might actually want to say he's sorry. Having him arrested for that might piss him off."

"And if we ignore him and that pisses him off?"

"Then I'll be here, and trust me, I'm begging for a reason to go after this guy. All I need is one justifiable reason."

Harley looks like he could vomit.

"Hey." I approach him and reach for his shoulders. "I'm here. I'll be here. You don't need to worry about this. That's my job."

Harley closes the small gap between us and presses himself against me.

"I'm here," I whisper into his hair. "You have nothing to worry about." I wrap my arms around him to hold him tighter.

Harley's body is tense against mine, and I want to do everything I can to reassure him that he's safe.

His lifestyle is bullshit if you ask me. Even when he gets a rare sense of normal like today at the beach, it's taken away tonight by the ugly side of fame reappearing. It's like he doesn't ever get a break from it. He has to take the great with the shit, and I dunno how he does it.

"I'm tired," he mumbles.

"Okay, let's get you to bed, and I'll order food, and—"

"No. Don't invite a stranger to the house." His gaze meets mine, and it breaks my heart. "Please."

"I can go get you guys food," Jamie says. "It's no problem."

"Thank you. Can you bring it to his room when you get back?"

"What do you feel like?" she asks.

We both say "Chinese" at the same time.

Jamie's eyes dance as her gaze flits from my face to Harley's head buried in my chest. She leaves with a smile and wave.

"Come on. I'll go check your room for you."

He doesn't let me go as we walk through the house and up the stairs to his room. It's clear, as I suspected it would be, and when I let him in, he flops down on the bed.

"I'll be back in a minute, okay?"

He sits up. "No. Can you stay? Like, stay, stay? All night? I know we haven't done that, but—"

"I'll stay." I walk over to him and cup his cheek.

The kiss I've craved giving him all day is softer and more reassuring than I'd like, but he needs that right now.

I pull back. "I just have to go get fresh clothes from my room. These smell like the beach."

He grips my shirt. "I like the way you smell."

The desperate way he clings to me lets me know I need to somehow lighten the mood. This letter could be nothing. It could be a problem too, but I don't want him to worry about it. I'll take care of it.

"I'll be two minutes tops. You can count ... wait, can you count to one hundred twenty? I assume the highest a musician can go is eight."

Finally, I get a laugh.

"Sixteen, actually. I'm giving you two minutes. If you're not back by then, I will assume you've been kidnapped."

"Please. No one can kidnap me. You've seen my guns."

"How many guns do you own?"

"Not those guns. These." I take my shirt off and flex.

Harley licks his lips. "Okay, now I don't want you to leave for an entirely different reason."

I'm glad I can cheer him up a little even if I'm barely holding it together myself. "I'll be back in two minutes."

As soon as I'm out his bedroom door, I take out my phone and hit Trav's number.

"West."

"Yeah, I'm gonna need you to tail someone."

I wake with Harley's head buried in my shoulder, my arm around him, and his leg thrown over my hip. I'm disappointed we didn't start sleeping in the same room sooner because it's an amazing way to start the day.

It's tempting to wake him up because my cock is clearly not used to having a warm body to wake up to, but Harley took forever to get to sleep last night.

He didn't want sex, but he clung to me all night like he couldn't let go. As if my presence reminded him that he's safe. I rubbed his back and held him tight until he finally drifted off. It would be mean to wake him now.

I want to do something for him though—create a distraction.

I don't want him to have to worry about the stupid letter or Billy Webber and his delusions.

Slipping out of bed carefully so I don't wake him, I slink out of his bedroom and text Jamie.

I'm gonna need you to pick something up for Harley.

What? she replies.

I send her my list, and she replies with the confused-looking emoji.

For Harley, I text.

It takes about an hour for her to get all the things I need and to come to the house, and I'm thankful Harley stays asleep the whole time.

When Jamie dumps all the stuff on the floor in the living room, she looks at me as if she's awaiting an explanation.

I take one of the Nerf guns out of the packaging and shoot a foam bullet at her. It hits her square in the chest and falls to the floor.

She looks unimpressed.

"It's fun. He needs that right now."

She cracks a smile. "I like you for him."

I shoot her again. "Thanks."

"Quit it."

"Are you gonna join us?" I pick up another gun and hold it out to her.

She doesn't hesitate. "Heck yes."

I arm myself with another gun and shove ammunition into my pockets.

"You're really sweet for doing this for him."

"Harley never gets to goof off. I figure I should give him that while I'm still working for him."

She tilts her head. "You're planning on leaving?"

She knows Harley and I are in more than a professional relationship, but we haven't really decided what we are. I don't think I have the right to get into it with his assistant when we don't know ourselves.

"My contract still has a while left. After that, it's up to Harley. Unless this Webber guy does something drastic, there isn't really a need for me."

I want to stay on longer than my initial six-month contract, but that's not up to me.

"Ready to gang up on Harley?" I ask.

"I thought you said this was supposed to be fun for him?"

"Did I say for him or fun in general? I'll be right back, and we can pick our vantage points."

I run upstairs and lay an arsenal of plastic guns for Harley to arm himself with on my side of the bed. Knowing Harley has pen and paper stashed everywhere, I find some in his bedside drawer and write:

These are the type of guns I'm comfortable with you using. Choose wisely and come find me when you wake up.

I draw a winky face at the bottom.

All my moving around the room makes him stir, so I don't think we'll be waiting long for him to come find us.

I sneak back out and am immediately hit in the shoulder with a foam bullet. But it's not from Harley.

Jamie stands at the end of the hall, and she gives me a quick salute before ducking around the corner.

Oh, so that's how it's going to be, is it?

Even though it will give both of them the advantage of shooting at me from above, I run down the stairs and hide behind one of the couches in the formal sitting room Harley never uses. There're a lot of rooms in this place that don't get used.

The creaking of Harley's door echoes off the high ceilings.

I risk a peek around the side of the couch.

Harley stands at the banister in just his boxer shorts.

I'm almost disappointed that he chose the toy crossbow. Looks cool, yeah, but he's going to be slaught—

Jamie hits him from his left but disappears before Harley can register it.

"Brix?" he asks with a confused croak in his voice.

I aim my gun for him and take my shot.

Bam, right on his nipple. Totally a happy fluke. I was aiming for his head.

"What the fuck?" Harley glances around the room, no doubt wondering where the bullets are coming from.

When he turns to go down the hall, I crawl toward the foot of the stairs.

I stand and shoot him in the back and then duck behind the wall next to the glass doors that open to the backyard.

Footsteps get louder as he comes back my way, but then I hear the click of another bullet being released followed by Harley's grunt of frustration.

"How are you doing this?" he whines. "I knew you were, like, a badass extraordinaire, but I didn't know you were a ninja."

"Just bringing you some normal, babe," I call out.

"Ah, there you are." His footsteps are faster now. Louder.

He's running down the stairs and will get to me any minute.

I quickly turn the corner and shoot, but not before Harley gets his own shot off. I dive and then scramble behind an armchair.

"Can't run, Brix." A bullet hits the cushion in front of me, and I laugh.

I think the bullet must've come from Harley until he says, "Wait … what?"

"Hi," Jamie says.

"You're on his side?" he exclaims.

"He made me do it. I swear!"

"She's lying. She jumped at the chance," I call out.

Next thing I know, we're in a three-way shoot-out, and I go down in a blaze of plastic bullets.

When Harley runs out, he tackles me and pins me to the rug.

I pretend to struggle against him, as if I couldn't easily overpower him, which makes him grin triumphantly.

"Don't get too cocky." I dig my fingers into his ribs.

"Oh shit, no." He twitches.

I roll us over so I'm on top, which turns into a wrestling match to the point we both end up with carpet burns everywhere.

It only stops when Jamie clears her throat. "Are you two done yet?"

She's now standing above us, a toy gun in each hand.

When I look around, I realize she's kicked away our weapons while we were distracted.

Harley and I throw our hands up.

"You wouldn't," Harley says.

He gets shot first.

"Hey—"

He gets shot again. Every time he tries to speak, she shoots a foam bullet at him.

Jamie laughs. "You're right, Brix. Harley needed this to forget about the stupid letter."

I make a slashing motion at my neck, but it's too late.

Harley's face falls.

Jamie realizes what she's done. "Oh, shit. Sorry."

Harley shrugs and gets to his feet. "All good. For a while there, I did forget, and it was nice."

Well, it was good while it lasted.

Harley heads toward the stairs to go back up to his room.

I stand and chase after him.

Not even caring if Jamie's still watching, I catch up to him and pull him into my arms. I lower my head and kiss him, making a silent vow to give him as much of a distraction from this bullshit as I can for as long as I can.

Any way I can.

"I know other ways to make you forget." I waggle my eyebrows.

Harley smiles. "I might need that distraction every day. All day."

"I'm prepared to make that sacrifice as long as you need me to."

"On that note," Jamie says, "I'll leave you boys to it."

Harley and I scramble to run up the stairs to his bedroom.

After a few weeks, my ass is a little tender from what I'm calling Operation Distract Harley, but that doesn't stop me from checking the time and reaching for his morning wood pressed against my side.

"You've got twenty minutes to fuck me again before Iris will be here."

I've been trying to keep Harley in his normal routines and play down his intruder-slash-now-potential-stalker situation.

It's been working and has kept his head where it should be—on anything but Billy Webber.

Trav has been following him, and while he's saying the guy isn't a threat, I want to give it a bit more time before pulling our guys off his tail.

According to Trav and the guys at Mike Bravo, Billy is a boring human being who hasn't even googled Harley in recent weeks let alone shown escalating stalker tendencies, but it eases my mind knowing we have eyes on him.

And maybe that's overkill. Maybe this is why it's a bad idea for me to be sleeping with Harley while working for him. But I've never wanted to protect anyone or anything more.

Meanwhile, I get to wake up next to Harley every morning. I get to distract him with my mouth and my body, and he has no reservations about taking the distraction.

He knows how to get me begging for him, and any hesitation about being able to overpower me went out the window the first time he fucked me.

Harley's becoming an expert at pushing my limits, and I'm loving this newfound sense of loss of control. He reaches for the lube and preps my already used hole from a few hours ago.

"You want this?" Harley says with a smirk on his lips.

He has his fingers lodged inside me while he strokes his cock which is shiny with lube.

I shake my thoughts free and concentrate on the sexy man on top of me. He deserves all my attention. "Always."

Words like that should scare me because no matter how hard I try to think of a future with Harley, reality reminds me there isn't one.

It feels like a hell of a lot more than sex, but I've never had that before, so this is all new territory.

The way Harley stares down at me as he enters me slowly. The way he leans down and kisses me softly. I know one thing for sure, *this* is completely new.

My eyes meet his.

"Thank you," he whispers. He moves in and out of me at a languid pace.

"Thank you?"

He shifts his body weight, pressing his chest against mine, and his lips land on my neck.

His hot breath on my skin sends a jolt of want down my spine. I rotate my hips beneath him, forcing him to move inside me, and he shudders.

"You've been great at distracting me." He groans and thrusts harder as if it's an involuntary movement. "And I'm thankful for it." Harley's lips meet mine.

He starts a fast pace, and every small brush against my prostate makes me harder. This is the part I get easily lost in. Where I'm needy and wanting, with Harley giving it to me as hard as he can.

Harley's hair is wet with sweat, and I run my hand through it.

"I love being inside you," he rasps against my lips.

"I love that you love being inside me."

He pulls back and reaches for my cock. "But one of these days, we're going to have to try it the other way."

It's not my first preference, but I'll do it. "I'm up for that. You think you can handle all of me?" Yeah, I'm cocky about the size of my dick. It's not really surprising.

"Probably not, but I want to try."

I pull him close and roll us over fast so I'm on top. I try to stop him from slipping out of me, but it's impossible. Sitting up, I reach back and line him up with my ass so I can sink down on him.

"I would suggest flipping right now, but Iris will be here soon, and we don't have the time I'd need to focus on you properly."

"Is that your way of telling me to hurry up and come?"

I roll my hips. "Maybe."

He sucks in a sharp breath. "Keep doing that and it won't take long at all."

I fuck myself on his dick, loving every expression Harley pulls. I can tell he's trying to hold back for me, but I don't want him to.

"Don't wait for me. Come inside me."

He grips onto my hips and thrusts upward once. Twice.

Harley falls apart beneath me while I stroke my cock until I come all over his chest.

"We really need to shower. Fast," I pant but still don't move.

Harley runs a finger over his chest and through my cum. "Yep." He laughs.

Yet, when I go to get off him, he holds me in place.

"I'm going to miss you today."

That warm, sated feeling is gone. "I'll miss you too."

"This is the first Sunday you've taken off in a month."

Five Sundays, actually. It's been five Sundays that I have been avoiding facing the man I'm responsible for, and the guilt has been eating at me. Having any sort of personal relationship with Harley means I could potentially be fucking up any chance of getting him out of that shitty care facility and into a better one.

He'll understand, though. I'll go there and tell him I've been on a mission, which isn't a lie. I've been super focused on Harley lately and making sure he feels safe while the guys investigate Webber for me, but I still feel guilty.

My commitment to Harley betrays my obligations, but I can't go back to only caring about my debts either.

Harley has a hold on me I couldn't shake even if I wanted to.

"What are you going to do?" he asks.

I shrug. "The usual."

Harley flattens his lips but lets me get up.

I kiss his forehead. "Nothing for you to worry about."

It's my responsibility. My problem. My life.

I don't know how to let people in when I've practically been on my own since my mom died.

Dad did all he could, but being in the military, he could only be there so much.

It made me the independent guy I am. I don't need anyone, only myself.

But as I look at Harley, I realize if I was going to let anyone else in, it would be him.

CHAPTER 19
HARLEY

They say it's forbidden
You're the wrong choice
But you give me a new vision
I've found a new voice.

I STARE at Brix through the glass of the recording studio as I sing the song I'm ninety percent sure will be my first actual single on the new album. It's something that's been rattling around in my brain since even before Brix and I started hooking up, but I couldn't get the right message across, and it was going down on paper all wrong.

It's a new sound but still upbeat and something my fans will like. It has meaning even if it only makes sense to me.

Brix has been so awesome to me with everything—with my tendency to overreact and be quick to freak out. He didn't even flinch at me asking him to stay with me after Billy sent me that letter.

If I was honest with him, I'd tell him I no longer need him in my bed every night. Things have calmed down, and I don't fear Billy turning up randomly anymore, but I don't want to send Brix back to his room.

Sometimes I can't tell what Brix is thinking when he watches me record, but if the heat in his eyes has anything to say, I can guess he knows this song is about him.

My big strong badass who's a soft marshmallow on the inside.

He's smarter than me and sees things in a different way.

When he speaks, my life's problems seem trivial.

I'm in awe of him.

When I sing the last note and the music fades, my eyes lock on his.

Then, out of the shadows, Gideon steps forward.

Shit. I didn't know he was here.

I can't get a read on him, but I'm guessing he's here to tell me the fate of my songs. And probably to rip this one apart.

I hang up my headphones and make my way out of the booth, all the while holding my breath.

My sound engineer claps when I enter the control room where everyone is. "That was the one, man."

My producer is surprisingly quiet.

My focus is on Gideon.

My heart's in my throat, and while I'm fairly certain I know what's coming, there's still a string of hope. A fraying string, but still.

He cracks a smile. "That's your first single."

Relief floods me. "Yes!" I jump and fist pump the air.

Everyone laughs. My producer is now smiling and clapping, and Gideon clasps my shoulder.

"It's a great song."

Jamie hugs me, and then Brix is right there. I almost forget where I am and go to step into his arms, but at least one of us has our heads screwed on. He steps back before I can get to him.

The lack of PDA has never really gotten to me before. It's always been a necessity. But right now, all I want to do is celebrate with Brix because this song was born from us.

It involves him. It *is* him.

It sucks I can't physically share it with him. My heart twinges with longing. Longing to touch him. Longing to have something real.

"I don't bring all good news, though," Gideon says, and the excitement in the room dies faster than you can say, *And the Grammy goes to …*

"The label refuses to give me the political song," I guess.

Gideon looks at his feet. "And the song about sex."

My heart sinks even more. In fact, it feels like I've been sucker punched. "You said that was my version of Timberlake's 'SexyBack.'"

"They didn't see it, but the good news is, we have artists interested in both songs."

"They're *my* songs." I don't know why I'm bothering to protest. It's a fight I won't ever win. I never have before.

"Why don't you go home and think about it. You've got two amazing songs for the album so far. Take the afternoon off."

Go home and think about it. It's another way of saying calm down and then get over it because this is happening whether you like it or not.

"I'd love to take the afternoon off, but now I have two more songs to write no thanks to you." My passive-aggressive tone might need some work because I may have overshot it.

"I fought for them," Gideon says.

"Not hard enough." I turn to the soundboard where my producer and sound engineer are. "How much material we got left to work on?"

"The instrumentals for the song you dubbed 'The piece of shit everyone will love' are done, but there're a couple of songs we're waiting for your band to finish up with."

"Fine, let's just get the fluff recorded, and then I can go home and wash all the positive happy shit off in the shower."

Brix tries to cover a laugh with a cough.

"It'll take us ten to get ready for the next track," my producer says.

"No problem. I'll go get some water." I walk out of the sound room, but Jamie is hot on my heels.

"I can get it."

I let her catch up to me. "Thanks, but I said it more as an excuse to get out of that room for a while."

She gives me her pity eyes, which I don't need. "For what it's worth, I love all the songs you've recorded so far."

"Thanks. Me too." Which is why it sucks I'm not allowed to use two of them.

I take a plastic cup and fill it from the water cooler.

"Umm ..." Jamie shifts from one foot to the other. "So, like, they're all about Brix, aren't they?"

I just about choke on my drink. Yeah, she knows—she's seen us together—but I didn't think she'd, you know, bring it up right to my face.

"Discretion, Jamie. Geez."

She looks horrified.

I touch her arm. "I'm messing with you. Sort of. And ..." My gaze goes to the closed control room door. "Yeah. They are. Although, not him entirely. The one about the troops was more about people in the military in general. Their sacrifice for God and country and all that."

"I like that he knows how to handle you."

"Thanks for calling me a diva."

"Oh, come on, you know that's not what I meant."

I nod. "I do know."

"You think he'll stay when the six months are up?"

It's not a question I haven't asked myself, but it is one I'm purposefully avoiding. "Logically, no. Unless he still needs the money. I don't know the full story, but he's in debt, and apparently this contract will get him back on his feet. He doesn't really have a reason to sign another contract to work for me after that."

"Well, there's you. He could do it for you."

Also something I've tried to tell myself, but I don't buy it. "Look at him, Jamie. He's a full-on soldier type who thrives on action. With me, he has to check my damn bedroom like I'm a five-year-old afraid of monsters under my bed."

Ugh. And this is why I've been avoiding thinking about it, because the bottom line is once his contract is over, he'll be leaving. I don't think our arrangement will change that. I can't see anyone picking me as their number one when they know I can't reciprocate. My number one has always been music.

Brix exits the control booth and makes his way over to us. He, too, has pity in his eyes. "Are you sure you want to stay and keep recording?"

No, but now I'm behind schedule. "I kind of have to if those two songs aren't going to be included on the album."

"No, you really don't. That's on the label, not on you. It's their fault if the album isn't done on time."

"I appreciate you trying on this one, I really do, but thinking like that is a good way to lose a career. If I slack off even the tiniest bit and the album is late, the only one in jeopardy of pissing people off is me. Most people can't see past the act to know who's truly behind it. I put out a half-assed project, I'm the one who gets the blame. Just like all those boy band haters who think we got a choice in what we wore or what we sang."

Brix steps forward and lowers his voice. "How much longer are you going to kill yourself for them?"

Shit, there he goes with the one question I've been asking for the last five years. The first five were good, but I was still new to the industry and had stars in my eyes while wearing rose-colored glasses.

"I don't know," I whisper.

"Fight harder for your songs, Harley. You deserve that much."

"You make it sound so easy."

"What's the worst that can happen? They threaten to drop you from the label? You walk away from a shitty situation?"

Jamie, who's been listening to all of this, butts in. "He has a point. Isn't this the last album you're contracted with them for? This could be your out to go to bigger and better labels."

"There aren't any labels bigger than Joystar."

"Okay, better labels, then," she says.

"And if I put my entire career on the line?"

"Isn't more creative freedom worth the risk?" Brix asks.

Is it?

Some fans would hate a new sound—that's a given—but it's not like I'd be completely changing my whole musical aesthetic.

Haven't I earned the right after ten years of doing what I'm told?

They say my career reset when I left the highest-grossing act of the last decade, but how long am I supposed to pay my dues?

It's time they saw my worth, and they sure as shit aren't going to see it if I don't make them.

I stand tall. "You guys are right."

And then I do either the smartest or dumbest thing I've done my entire career.

I storm into the studio control room and look my manager dead in the eyes when I say, "I'm keeping my songs."

Gideon relents. "Let me try again with the label."

"Thank you." I turn to my sound guys. "I'm not doing the shitty happy song, and I'm done for the day." On my way out, I stare at Gideon over my shoulder. "Those songs are nonnegotiable. Unless they want this to be the last Harley Valentine album on their label, they'll approve them."

Now to wait.

And maybe freak out.

Brix's heavy and familiar presence in my bed has been so easy to get used to. So easy to embrace and … miss.

My hand flies out to the cold side of my bed.

"Wha …?" Rolling over, I crack my eye open. "Brix?"

The mattress dips as my fully clothed bodyguard kneels next to me. I don't like it when he's wearing clothes.

"I kinda have to."

My eyes fly open. "Did I say the clothing thing out loud?"

Brix laughs. "Yeah. You did." He leans down and kisses my cheek. "Iris is already outside at the pool. Apparently, you're having a pool day. Doesn't that sound fun?"

I narrow my tired eyes. "You made him do that, didn't you?"

"Maybe." He leans in and captures my mouth, kissing me softly. "I'll be back as soon as I can today, okay? Try to put the label mess out of your mind."

Easier said than done because it's been days and I haven't heard anything. Good or bad. Just … nothing.

"I wish you could stay." I run my hand down his chest.

Brix smiles. "I'll only be a few hours. You can go that long without needing to worship me like I'm some sort of god."

I laugh. This is why I don't want him to go out today.

He has quickly inserted himself into an important role in my life, especially since Webber sent the letter. Everything on that front has died down since then, but Brix has been there time and time again, especially with this label bullshit and encouraging me to finally stand up for myself and what I want.

Brix and I go to bed together, wake up together, and right now as I watch him leave for his day off, I can't help but want him to come back.

I remain in bed for a while, smiling and sated, my muscles jelly, and it takes me a second to realize … this is what happy feels like.

Closing my eyes, I breathe in and take in the scents and overall feeling I rarely get to experience.

I kind of thought the smell of happiness wouldn't have so much sex in it, but apparently it does.

When I finally get up and make my way outside, the sun beats down on my skin. The clear water from my pool glistens in the light, and the view over LA is as breathtaking as it was the day Brix tried to drag me out here to enjoy it.

"You're so tense," Iris says as I stretch out on the lounger next to him. He has no problem sinking into his spot and letting his body soak up the sun. Unlike Brix, who constantly wears tactical pants and tight T-shirts, Iris is in boardshorts and no shirt.

He's a real professional kind of guy.

"This is wasting time." I could be writing. What, I don't know, but I could be doing *something*.

I need to work.

"Still haven't heard back from the label after you told them to shove your future up their ass?" Iris asks.

"What a positive way of putting it."

"Right?" Iris says, upbeat. "I think I know what your problem is."

"That I finally stood up for myself, and now I have an uncertain future, so I'm allowed to be stressed?"

"Nah, that's not it. You need a good fuck. Like, mind-blowing, phenomenal fuck."

I guarantee that is definitely *not* my problem. "I'm all good on that front. Thanks." More than good. So damn good it's the only time in the last few days when I haven't been thinking about the label heads deciding my fate.

Brix takes me away from all that. And not just with sex but by just being him.

He makes me step back and look at the broader picture. The label can take my career, but they can't take music away from me.

Music has always been my escape from reality. It's habit. It's safety.

Now I've found another type of safe in warm arms and a kind soul.

When the label does finally get back to me, no matter the outcome, the thought of having Brix there makes the stress and anxiety over their decision lessen.

I've given them empty threats before. I've refused to go onstage until I got my way and thrown diva fits. But I've never demanded something this big. I haven't had the courage.

I've always known my limits and what I can and cannot push.

Artistic control is not something many musicians get. Which is ridiculous if you think about it. The artist gets no say over their own work.

"Where are you getting phenomenal sex since your fiancée moved out?" Iris asks.

"My hand. Hey, do you know what Brix does on his days off? It's driving me nuts." Mainly because I want him home, but also, *subject change for the win!*

"I might happen to know …"

I cock an eyebrow in his direction.

He hesitates, then slumps. "Okay, no, he doesn't tell any of us anything. Getting deets on his personal life is like torturing someone who's already dead."

"Huh?"

"There's no point in trying. He won't tell you anything."

I narrow my eyes. "You say he won't tell you anything, but I kind of get the feeling you know more than you're letting on."

Iris jumps out of his seat. "Oh, I forgot. I brought you a present."

Now who's changing the subject?

"A present?" I call after his retreating ass. He keeps walking.

I check my phone while he's gone, hoping to see something from Brix, an update on when he might be home, but there's nothing.

It does freakishly start ringing in my hand, though. It's still not Brix.

I answer. "Hey, Ryder."

"Is it true you told the label to go f—fudge themselves?"

I chuckle. "Is the kid in hearing range?"

"Sure is, and she's picking up on everything Daddy says."

And this is why I don't want kids.

Ever.

"But is it true?" Ryder asks.

"Not entirely. I didn't use *those* words, but I did threaten to walk if they don't let me record the songs I want. How did you find out?"

Ryder whistles. "I never thought I'd see the day ... Harley Valentine grew some balls."

I laugh. "Fuck you. Oh, shit, am I on speaker? Hi, Kaylee, little darling."

"I'm not dumb enough to put you on speaker around my daughter."

"Smart man. But seriously, if the rumor mill is already turning—"

"I've started producing for some artists on the label."

"No shit? You're producing now? What happened to stepping away?"

He sighs through the phone. "I didn't want to step away completely. I just wanted out of the spotlight."

Even though he hasn't gone solo and hasn't done anything but be a stay-at-home dad since Eleven broke up, he's still stalked by paparazzi, almost as much as I am. He's probably the only one of us five who doesn't have to put any effort into being famous. He could come out as a bisexual unicorn and everyone would be all, "Oh, we have to buy every single he puts out!"

Or perhaps it's the mystery of why he wants to disappear into the background. It's not rocket science. He's doing it for his daughter.

"How's fading away working out for you?"

"Yeah, great. Did you see they printed Kaylee's picture in *Us Weekly*? Or was it *Who*? I don't know. Either way, it pissed me off."

Ryder is slightly overprotective of his four-year-old, but I get it. We signed up for the fame, his kid didn't. She doesn't deserve to grow up in the limelight.

Iris reappears in front of me and holds up a ... cigarette?

"Hey, Ry? I have to go. But please can you produce one of my songs?"

"Maybe I could do your whole next album after Joystar drops your ass-umptions."

"Drops my ass-umptions? Thanks so much for cheering me up over this. No, really, it's like you're hugging me through the phone."

"What are friends for?"

I laugh. "Later."

We end the call, and I glance up at Iris, who's hovering next to my chair. "Figured you could get high while you think about your future unemployment."

"Thank ... you?"

"You're welcome." He's too upbeat, either ignoring my sarcasm or missing it completely. He passes me the joint.

"And I'm supposed to smoke this? What if I have a bad reaction?"

"It's a mild strain with low THC. Your high should be tame."

"*Should* be." I stare up at him. "Is this peer pressure? Ooh, I never got to experience that as a kid. I really want to be strong so I can tell Brix I said no to drugs, but on the other hand ..." I hold it up in front of my face. "Really, how bad could it be?"

"I love the smell of corruption." Iris lights it for me, and I take a deep drag.

"Can I be considered a pothead now?" I joke. And then cough.

Iris laughs. "Total stoner. I still can't believe you've never smoked weed before. Or experienced peer pressure. Where were you at twelve?"

"I was a short, overweight redhead with pimples and the last name Stench. As you can guess, my friend circle wasn't too big. I threw everything I had into music."

Iris grabs his chest. "Wait, you mean to tell me your real name isn't Harley Valentine? My heart can't take it."

"A simple google would've told you that."

"I know. I'm messing with you. I bet it's weird when people call you Harry. When Mom calls me Isaac, I'm like, *Who? What? That's not my name.* Even when the guys call me by name, it's Griffin, my last name. Isaac feels foreign and weird and just ... no."

"How did you get the nickname Iris?" I ask and take another hit.

He waves me off. "Long and boring story from back in my basic training days. Let's just say that following orders took a while for me to get used to. A lot longer than anyone else in my squad it seemed."

"That is shocking news. You? Ignoring directions? Never would've guessed."

"Apparently, you can't charm your way through the military. I was surprised too."

"Who would've thought the military was full of rules and orders and no goofing off?"

Iris doesn't even crack a smile, as if lost in a memory. He quickly shakes it off. "How's the joint working out for you?"

"Good. I think. I don't know. I don't feel any different, but I guess I'm less … anxious? I mean, I'm still thinking about what the label will say, but I no longer care as much."

"Sounds like it's working perfectly, then."

I keep smoking it until there's nothing left, and I stub out the end.

"When is Brix coming home?" I complain.

"Mmhmm, phenomenal sex with your hand my ass," he mutters.

I don't know if I'm supposed to hear it or not. "You want me to put my hand *where*?"

Iris laughs, but it dies when an alert goes off on his phone. He looks at it and frowns. "Movement detected in the front yard."

"Like, as in Jamie's here?"

Iris bites his lip. "Not Jamie. Hang on, I'm pulling up the security cameras." He's out of his seat in an instant. "Stay here."

The backyard connects to the front through a gate. Iris opens it but pauses. He looks a little ridiculous wearing nothing but boardshorts and holding his gun. If there was someone in the front yard, I don't know how intimidated they would be.

I climb to my feet in case I have to move suddenly, but my brain goes to a million different scenarios. Like, someone's there, or another letter, or, I don't know, it could be anything.

Not knowing is the thing that's killing me. I move closer to try to see between the small gap in the fence and the house, but I can't see shit.

Then Iris comes running, looking like a crazed man and yelling at me to get down.

I don't have time to comprehend what he wants before he tackles me to the ground and covers my body with his.

"Someone threw a pipe bomb over the fence," he says, and my heart stops cold.

Where I'm expecting the blast, a bang, or anything that remotely resembles something similar to when we blew up C4 in the desert, nothing comes.

For, like, a really long time.

We lie there, Iris on top of me, with no sounds but our heavy breathing. While I'm shit scared, waiting for a detonation, I think my mind isn't truly comprehending the threat.

"Is this a bad trip from the weed? If so, I want a refund."

Iris doesn't even laugh. He's on his phone. "Trav? I need the fucking bomb squad."

That's when I understand how serious this is. No amount of weed can keep me calm after that.

A day in the life of a pop star … I guess.

I so didn't sign up for this.

CHAPTER 20
BRIX

I'M ABOUT HALFWAY home from San Bernardino when my phone rings and the car's Bluetooth picks up.

I glance at the display to find Trav's name lighting up the screen. "What's up, boss?"

"There's a ... situation."

"What kind of situation?"

"All you need to know is Harley is safe, but he's asking for you. He's, umm, a little rattled."

"What happened?" I growl.

"Just get back to his house as soon as you can. And don't crash my fucking car." He ends the call.

I hit the buttons and try to call Harley, but his phone rings out. I try Iris, but his goes right to voicemail.

Fucking fuck, fuck.

I fly down the freeway while remaining cautious enough not to hit anything. Not because of Trav's precious car but because I need to get to Harley.

The calm, rational voice in the back of my head telling me Trav said Harley's fine keeps me holding on to the tiny bit of control I have left.

I weave in and out of traffic, and not for the first time, I curse living in LA. I cut across six lanes of traffic to take the exit and get home.

Home.

Shit, that's an entirely foreign concept to me, but I feel it in my gut.

Somehow, since working for Harley, something inside me has settled. I no longer crave that adrenaline surge. No longer itch to see some action. Experiencing that in my current position means Harley's life is in danger, and that thought fills me with dread.

It's not just my duty to protect Harley, it's my instinct.

I should have been there with him. I should've …

No, he should have been with *me*.

I want him with me all the time. Even if it means showing him a part of my life I don't let anyone see.

He should know what I do with my time away from him.

Harley deserves that much.

This isn't like my other teammates where I don't tell them because I don't want them to pity me or offer to help when I'm handling it fine on my own.

It's not a burden I want to put on Harley, but the alternative is keeping it on my shoulders and carrying it alone.

I don't want to be alone anymore.

Harley gives me something I've only ever felt once before. With Harley is where I belong. I've never had that with another person before. Only the job.

Always the job.

I tease Harley about being a workaholic, but really, he and I have that in common. My life for the past ten years has been serving my country. Whether for the military or through Mike Bravo.

It might be time to focus on something for myself.

I want to give Harley and me a real chance.

Until now, I couldn't see a future with the pop star because, logically, we don't make sense.

If the public finds out about me, I'll become a target of their attention. I won't be able to protect Harley properly. If my boss or his manager finds out, I'll be fired, and Harley and Evah could be forced back together.

A future with Harley never seemed like an option to me, which means I haven't thought about it in depth.

The thing about that is, a solution was never going to land in my lap, and I'd forever think Harley and I would be a fleeting thing.

I want more for him. For us.

I've finally found someone I want to call my own, and the fact he came under threat today has me raging.

I pull onto Harley's street, and there are cop cars everywhere. And ...

Holy shit, is that the fucking bomb squad driving away?

The car hits the curb at an angle, and I block Gideon's Maserati in the driveway, but I don't care.

I'm out the door and through the courtyard gate without even turning off the engine.

Luckily, I remember to put it in park first.

Trav, Gideon, and Iris are in a huddle talking with some officers while Harley sits in his open doorway with a blanket wrapped around him.

Professional me knows I should go to Trav and Gideon first. The real me—the me that has Harley on my brain and in my heart—goes straight over to him.

I feel a million pairs of eyes on me as I cross the yard.

Harley looks up at me. "Brix?"

I pull him up and into my arms without thinking about if he's injured or not. That's when I have the sense to ease up a little. "Fuck, am I hurting you? Are you hurt?"

He shakes his head.

"Good." I go back to crushing him to me. "What happened?"

He's never held on to me so hard. "T-there was a-a b-bomb."

"A bomb?"

"H-homemade pipe bomb."

I pull back just enough to cup his face. "Where?"

Iris's voice comes from behind us. "Someone threw an inactive pipe bomb over the fence."

I force myself to pull out of Harley's arms, but he immediately trembles. Fuck that. I press against him again and hold him so he knows he's safe and that I'm here.

Only then do I turn to face three people who look more concerned about the way I'm holding on to my charge than the actual bomb threat. Behind them, the police make their way out of the gate and close it.

Being with Harley like this for them to see puts everything on the line, but Harley is hurting, and he needs me. So he can have me. All of me. Whatever he needs.

I pretend I'm not hugging him while I talk. "*Inactive* pipe bomb?"

Iris hands me his phone which plays a clip from the security camera.

On the screen, the top of a silver car is visible as it drives slowly past the house, and then something is lobbed over the fence before the car speeds off.

The angles of the cameras we have on the courtyard and the driveway don't catch what type of model the car is. Only the color.

Great, we're looking for a silver car. That narrows it down.

"It was fake," Trav says. "PVC pipes were strapped together and there was exposed wiring, but it wasn't connected to anything."

"I don't understand."

"We think it was a scare tactic," Iris says.

"Scare … who would want to scare—" The name comes to mind before I get the question out. "Billy Webber. Where is he?" The growl in my voice is feral.

"Brix, I think you and I need to speak privately," Trav says.

"Where. The. Fuck. Is. Billy?"

Trav and Iris share a glance.

"We don't know," Gideon says.

"I have Angel and Domino on it," Trav says. "You know Angel will be able to sniff him out."

That's not good enough. "I told you we pulled back surveillance too soon."

Trav has been saying for weeks that Billy is harmless. He's a creature of routine, and then suddenly a pipe bomb shows up and he's gone?

"Whoa, you were watching him?" Harley asks. "Why?"

"Ever since he sent the note. I needed to make sure he wouldn't make another move."

Harley pulls out from under my arm. "You didn't tell me."

"You didn't need to know."

He doesn't like that answer.

I turn to him and rub my hands up and down his arms. "I didn't want you to worry," I say softly.

Iris clears his throat, and when I look at him, he's staring at me as if I'm crazy.

When I glance at Trav and Gideon, I realize why. I'm showing way too much affection for someone I supposedly only work for, but I can't focus on that right now. They can yell at me and fire me after I know Harley is safe.

"I'm taking Harley to a hotel," I say.

Gideon nods. "Already booked him a room in West Hollywood near the recording studio."

"Stay here." I cup Harley's cheek with one hand. "I'll go pack for you."

Harley still looks a little pissed, but he can yell at me later too.

Everyone can yell at me after we get out of here.

I head into the house and go straight to Harley's room. I throw the suitcase he keeps in his closet for short trips onto the bed and start rummaging for clothes.

I'm not at all shocked when Trav appears in the doorway. "Not now, boss, I'm busy."

He folds his arms. "I thought you two looked a little close at the ranch."

"We are close. You can't work in this type of environment without getting close."

"That's not what I'm implying, and you know it."

I throw some socks and underwear into Harley's case and face Trav. "Am I fired?"

"I *should* kick your ass off this job if not out of Mike Bravo completely."

I balk. "Completely? We're not hurting anyone. We're not compromising the mission."

Just what I need. Not only is this stalker situation so messed up I'm barely keeping it together, but now my job—the job I need—is in jeopardy. I thought I'd be reassigned, not … not *this*.

I didn't think it was possible to be torn in two completely opposite directions before.

Protect Harley or pay off my mountain of debt. Love him or keep my career.

Wow.

Now I'm even giving myself perspective lessons.

This is exactly what made Harley and Jay break up. Harley had to choose between love and his career, and he chose wrong.

Or maybe it was right. If he'd chosen Jay, I wouldn't be here.

I wouldn't be with him.

"I can't lose my job," I say, but it's more to myself than Trav.

Maybe I need to choose my career so Harley will find the one person he's supposed to be with like his ex did.

My gut churns.

"And now I plain want to kick your ass."

I've never heard my boss so disappointed.

"How did you cross so many lines? That's not like you at all."

"Harley ... he ..."

"He what? Forced you to fuck him? Tied you down and threatened to fire you if you didn't?"

I pull back. "What? No. Nothing like that. He just ... he was just ... *him*. I can't explain it."

"It's called chemistry. That's all. I thought you, of all people, would rise above it."

"If it was basic chemistry, I would have been able to stay away. It's ... it's more than that."

But can I really call it love? I want to be with him. I don't want anything to hurt him. Is that love? I wouldn't fucking know. This is all new to me.

I've never felt this way about anyone before.

Ever.

Trav sighs. "I don't want to make this call."

"Then don't. You should have faith I can do my job."

"How can you do your job if emotion is clouding your judgment?"

"Trust me when I say I can compartmentalize."

Trav rubs his temples. "I'm leaving this up to Gideon. Harley's his client, and he has a right to know."

"Shouldn't Harley get a say in who protects him?"

"Can you stand there and honestly say your feelings for him won't get in the way of protecting him?"

"Look, I'd understand if it were teammates hooking up because out in the field it could distract from the true target, but Harley *is* my target. So how could loving him screw that up?"

Trav glances around the room. "Love. Did ... you just ... Am I in the right place? I think I'm lost. I'm looking for Nolan Brixton Reins. He's a serious workaholic with no love life and an attitude problem who's a royal pain in my ass most days."

I glare at him.

"Huh. Wow, this is weird. Of all the guys ..."

"Are you done yet?" I ask.

"Oh, no, I'm just getting started." His face lights up. "Iris is going to have a field day."

In a flash, Trav is gone, and I begin to wonder if *I'm* in the wrong room.

That can't have happened the way I think it did.

Trav is leaving it up to Gideon to decide if I'm fired or not?

I guess all I can do is hope Trav's cousin is as morbidly fascinated with my love life as my boss seems to be.

CHAPTER 21
HARLEY

AS ANGRY AS I am with Brix right now for not telling me about the surveillance on Billy Webber, when Trav comes back downstairs, I realize we have bigger problems. Like the secret *we've* been keeping from everyone.

"Hey, Gid, we need to talk," Trav says.

Oh fuck. Yep, he knows.

Gideon follows his cousin into the house while Iris stays with me.

"How are you holding up?" Iris asks, taking my attention away from where Trav and my manager have disappeared. "Want me to take you inside or somewhere you feel safe?"

I shiver, but I don't know if it's from the fake bomb or what's to come when Gideon finds out I crossed lines I shouldn't have. *Again.*

I'm really good at it.

He wasn't my manager when I started sleeping with Jay, but he knows all about it.

"I'm fine. It was a fake bomb." Am I fine, though? I think I'm still in shock. "Could Brix get taken away from me for this?"

"Taken away? He could lose his job entirely. It's obvious you guys are hooking up, and I don't understand why Brix would jeopardize his job like that. Especially when ..." His mouth slams shut.

"Especially when, what?"

"Nothing."

"You do know more than you let on about him."

Iris rolls his eyes. "Of course we all know. He thinks he's being so secretive, but he seems to forget gathering intel is what we do for a living. None of us call him on it because it's his burden to bear, and he clearly doesn't want our help. We keep asking in hopes he'll open up about it, but he doesn't. He never does."

I thought I was different, but I'm not.

Brix doesn't tell me anything either.

Maybe I've been seeing more than what's truly there between Brix and me.

He's this amazing man—the only man in my life to not make me feel like I need to be more. More for the public, more for the label, more for everyone else.

He reminds me that I'm valid. That my opinions and thoughts matter and shouldn't be censored by sales stats and fan opinion.

But what do I do for him?

I give him sex and an annoying whining pop star to deal with.

Great trade-off. It's astounding he hasn't proposed yet.

"Hey," Iris says. "Don't think that because he hasn't told you why he needs money that he doesn't have feelings for you. Brix is the type of guy to not risk his job for anything. For him to put his position at Mike Bravo on the line, you have to be something special."

That doesn't make me feel any better.

At all.

What's going to happen if he loses his job?

He'll hate me.

That thought is even more terrifying than the pipe bomb.

"Iris," Trav barks from the doorway. "We're rolling out." He turns to me. "I'll make sure my people find Billy Webber."

"Aren't the police going to arrest him? This is the second time he's broken the restraining order."

"We can't prove it was him this time," Iris says.

"He doesn't own a silver car," Trav adds. "We tailed him for weeks. He drives a crappy red Chevy."

"Like he can't borrow a car? Steal one? Do something to throw off the cops?" I say.

"We're not saying it wasn't him," Trav says. "Just that we can't prove it. The police will obviously want to talk to him, but with him disappearing ..."

"Essentially, we're helpless. Got it."

How did this become my life?

Gideon joins us. "Harley, we—"

"Need to talk. I know."

I storm into the house without even a goodbye to Iris and Trav.

"Brix is already in the living room," Gideon says.

I find him sitting on the long couch, so I go to sit next to him. I know what's coming, so there's no point in denying it.

Brix knows it too and wraps his arm around me.

"How long has this been going on?" Gideon asks.

"Long enough to know that I don't want to lose him or my job," Brix says.

I pull back. "Really? I thought ..."

I thought if it came down to it, he'd choose his career. If they gave him that option. It might be past that.

Brix doesn't just love his job, he *needs* it.

This whole time I thought my career was in trouble, that it could easily go away, but the thing is, I still have royalties coming in from the countless hits Eleven had. Not to mention my most recent album which is still selling. The future of my career might be rocky, but I'm stable right now. I have money and savings and an accountant who could keep me afloat for years even if I never released another song.

Brix, he only has this job.

"You can't fire him," I tell Gideon. "If you do, I'm going to hire him again personally instead of through Trav."

"Wouldn't that border on prostitution?"

I don't know if Gideon's being serious or not right now. He doesn't joke.

"I'd hire him as my bodyguard, dumbass."

Gideon purses his lips. "I don't like it."

"We didn't mean for it to happen," I argue. "The first time, it was—"

Brix pulls me close. "It wasn't a mistake. I know you were going to say that, and we said that's what it was, but it wasn't. It was eye-opening and amazing and ... and it made me realize there was more to you than you let anyone see. You give me so much by being next to me."

"I …" Shit, I have no idea how to respond to that. I run my hand along his thigh. "I can't let you lose your job for me."

"It's just money. I'll get more. It'll take longer to pay off my debts. The debt will always be there. You won't be if I let you go."

"Brix …" My whiny voice comes out.

Brix's shirt is soft in my hands as I grasp it in my fist. I inch closer, begging for him to kiss me, but just before our lips touch, we're interrupted.

"I'm in love with Evah," Gideon blurts.

Both Brix and I freeze and slowly turn toward my manager.

"Uh, what?" I ask.

"I know what it's like to cross lines. I know how this"—he waves a finger between us—"can happen. Emotions and real feelings make everything messy. All I need to know is if it's going to affect you guys in a professional manner."

"It hasn't yet," I say.

At the same time, Brix says, "It won't. And you know if shit goes down, Trav and Iris will have my back."

Gideon thinks about that and nods. "All right then. Are … umm … we cool?"

Is this really happening right now?

Brix gets to keep his job?

"You're in love with Evah, or you're with her?"

"Both," Gideon says.

I was not expecting that.

He's a good fifteen years older than her, but that's not really a concern in this industry.

And maybe I should care on a personal level, but Evah and I were never together. The only risk is if it got out, but clearly they know how to keep a secret, or we would've figured it out.

Hell, Brix and I should take lessons from them, but today when he came through that gate, all I wanted was to be wrapped in his arms where I knew I'd be safe.

"Uh …" Gideon runs a hand over his dark hair. "Shit, am *I* fired now?"

I laugh. "Call it even? You fuck my ex-fiancée, I fuck my body-guard, and we all pretend like it isn't weird."

"Deal. Now, let's get you two to a hotel before any other unwanted packages turn up. Or worse, paparazzi. I'm surprised TMZ hasn't caught the story yet. They're slacking."

And that's when I'm reminded of the severity of this thing, and my stomach drops.

Brix paces our basic hotel room which only serves to make me more anxious. We decided against a suite, checked in under another name, and they snuck me in so it would be harder for the tabloids to find me.

I sit on the large king bed with my back against the headboard just watching Brix do his thing.

He barks orders into the phone as if he's Trav's boss, not the other way around.

I shouldn't find that hot, but I do. All long legs and bulky arms moving back and forth in front of me. His strong, commanding voice unwavering.

If what he was talking about didn't scare me half to death, I'd be tempted to strip naked and distract him.

Unfortunately, he's talking about someone psychologically terror-izing me, so you know, my boner is a little fickle.

"Keep me updated." Brix huffs and ends the call.

He throws the phone on the bed and grunts.

"Come here." I move to my knees on the mattress and inch toward the edge of the bed.

He steps closer, making me crane my neck to look at him. "How are you doing? Are you okay?"

"I'm fine. You being your badass self makes me feel better about the whole thing."

His big, warm hands snake around my back, and he lowers his forehead to mine. "I won't let anyone hurt you."

"I trust you."

He dips his head, his lips inching closer to mine, but I hold firm.

"Even when you keep shit from me."

"I've been waiting for that." Brix pulls away from me and goes to lean against the dresser.

I sit back on the bed.

"I didn't tell you I was tailing Webber because we didn't know if there was a reason to be following him. Trav thinks I was being over-protective, but there's no such thing when it comes to you. And it seems the minute we stopped watching him, he made a move. I'm not going to apologize for not telling you because it's my job to take care of that shit for you. You're not going to get your album recorded if you're too busy worrying about your safety."

I guess he makes a point. "All right, but you've got to give me something. When it comes to work, I don't like being kept in the dark. I understand your point, so I'll let it go, but what about *you*? I know you're keeping shit from me, just like you are the rest of your team. They know your secret, by the way. They're just respectful enough not to push you."

Brix's lip twitches. "You're not going to be as respectful as them, I'm guessing."

I shake my head. "Nope. Because whatever this is between us means I should know more about your life than your work colleagues. You don't give me *anything*. All I know is your mom died and you were an army brat. You pay someone else's medical bills, unless you have some sort of illness you're hiding from me. I was thinking earlier about what you are to me, and I realized that while you're possibly the most important person in my life, I don't think you see me the same way. This life isn't so lonely and isolating when you're by my side telling me I don't need to give in to what everyone expects of me. You make me feel safe. You give me … everything. But you don't let me in."

"Harley …"

I can't look at him. "When I thought you could've been fired today, I was devastated, but I assumed if given the choice, you'd choose your job. You need the money, and I have no other reason to believe you're in this for *me*."

Brix is amazing at making me realize my worth and validity, but today I realized something else: I might not be enough for *him*.

"I need *something*, Brix."

"I'm used to being on my own." His words are mumbled and soft. "I don't know how to do"—he waves his finger between us—"this."

"I've already been in a relationship where I kept taking and taking, and I can't do it again. I can't lose another person I care about because I'm too selfish to see past what they need. But I can't give you what you need when you won't even let me know the true you. Deep scars, secrets, and all."

"I need *you*. That's what I need."

"But I—"

"Don't you get it? When you smile at me—truly smile—it's the biggest accomplishment I could ever achieve. I went into this job thinking it would be an easy six months, a big paycheck, but that it'd be boring as hell. I had no idea I'd meet someone who not only asks for my opinion but appreciates it. You give me a sense of purpose—"

"How romantic," I say dryly. "I need you to make me feel good about myself so you can feel good about yourself. That's fucked-up and codependent."

"It's not codependent. And what we have is not fucked-up. We're two guys from completely different upbringings, completely different lives, yet we see something in each other that no one else does. You think you're shallow and that there's nothing behind the pop star and the manufactured persona the label gave you, but when I look at you, I see someone who wants to be appreciated. Who wants validation and respect. I see someone who's begging to be loved."

My cheeks heat. This man, he knows how to read me so well. He can see past the PR bullshit. But he never lets me see him.

"You see that in me, but that's the thing. I let you see it. I let you in on my true self. I have no idea who you are. Not deep down."

"I'm an adrenaline junkie who's quickly realizing there's more to life than explosives and gunfire. Because of you. You've spent almost half your life being someone else, and I don't think you know who the real Harley Valentine is anymore. But I see him. I see him in the way you're still polite to your fans even when they're pushy and invasive and could potentially give you the flu. I see him in the way you want to protect Evah with all your heart even though you were never truly together. You forgave your manager, no questions asked, when he crossed a massive line. You're civil with your ex even though I can tell you were really hurt. You're the man I love to make smile. The man who gives me a sense of home. Of somewhere to belong. You dim the need for action and adrenaline that buzzes in my veins. You make me believe there's something out there for me besides working for Mike Bravo. I've never had that before."

"Why not?"

Brix thinks about that for a long time.

"Why not?" I ask again.

He folds his arms. "You know why a lot of people join the military?"

"To serve their country?"

"We sign away our *lives*. They give us what we need in exchange for willingly sacrificing ourselves in the line of duty. I'm sure there are a lot of people who do it because of their patriotic hearts, but for the majority of us, we do it because we don't have any other choice. We can't afford college. We want to get out of a no-hope town. Some of us do it because military life is all we've known growing up as army brats. I signed up for a lot of those reasons but also because I had this constant need for an adrenaline high. I never once felt a sense of purpose ... until I started working for you. This job, protecting you, it's as if I've found my true place for the first time in my life. I'm not with you for what you can give me. I'm not with you because of your music."

"Offensive." I pretend that's the reason my eyes are leaking.

Brix keeps going. "I'm not with you because you're Harley-fuck-ing-Valentine. I'm with you because I crave the real you. Your real smiles."

Damn him. He's basically saying he likes me for me, and how am I supposed to stay mad at that?

"Why'd you have to be so ..."

"So ..."

"*You.*" I can't help it, I smile.

"There it is." Brix grins triumphantly.

"Can you please come over here and kiss me after that?"

Brix reaches me in two steps. His large presence wraps warmth around me as he sinks to his knees, bringing us eye to eye where I sit on the bed. "Just so you know, the answer to that will always be yes."

I lean forward and capture his mouth with mine.

What starts out soft escalates quickly. It always does with us. Zero to sixty in the blink of an eye. Brix climbs onto the bed and pushes me back until my head hits the fluffy hotel pillow.

He blankets my body, and we move as one. We make out, groping and exploring each other. My hands trail over his muscles, the hardness that represents not only his strength but his solidness and stability.

I want to feel him everywhere. Around me. On top of me. Inside me.

I want to revel in the safety he gives me—the reassurance his commanding confidence demands.

His mouth moves to my neck and then my shoulder.

Brix makes me breathless while bringing fresh air to my stifled life.

Want and need collide in a mix of emotion I don't think I'm ready to address. But they're there anyway, growing stronger with every second he ravishes me.

He kisses his way down my chest. His teeth scrape my skin, and the sound that escapes me is guttural.

"Brix?" I breathe.

"Mmm?" His voice hums against my skin.

"I want you to fuck me."

He stops suddenly and stares up at me. "You sure?"

I nod.

"All right." Brix stands and pulls me up.

"Umm, what are we doing? Sex excursion?"

Brix smiles. "I'm gonna open you up the best way I know how."

He leads me to the bathroom and turns on the shower.

"Water is not adequate lube," I inform him. "Neither is soap."

Brix laughs. "Thanks for the sex ed class, but I know what I'm doing."

"Do you?"

"Trust me."

The weird part about that is I absolutely do. He may be keeping stuff from me, but I trust deep down that if it remotely affected me in any way, he wouldn't lie to me.

I don't know why I have blind faith in him the way I do, but if I waited for someone to give me a reason to trust them, I wouldn't trust anyone.

We strip naked and climb into the bath-shower combo. Brix pulls the shower curtain closed and then wraps me in his large arms.

I feel small against him, but I don't hate it. In a stupid way, it makes me feel treasured. Like I'm only his when he wraps his big body around me.

"You're trembling," Brix whispers.

"Anticipation."

"Not nerves?"

I shiver. "Maybe a little bit of nerves."

"I've got you." Brix turns me so my back is to his chest and my head rests on his shoulder.

This won't be just sex. Not that it ever has been between us. But there's something more going on here. Something I've been convinced is not for me or doesn't actually exist.

The illusions of Hollywood made me bitter, made me think this feeling I have—that I've only ever experienced once before—is fake just like everything else in my life.

Then Brix literally crash-tackles my life and zaps that part of me that was so near death I'm sure it had flatlined numerous times back to life.

He makes me want to believe that love conquers all.

Brix's hands wander down my sides while his lips trail over my shoulder.

My cock points straight up, begging to be touched.

"Put your hands on the wall."

I shudder but do as he says.

The water cascades down my back as I bend forward and rest my palms on the tiles.

Brix pumps shower gel into his hands and massages it over my shoulders and down my arms. My muscles contract and release as his warm fingers dig into my skin.

Then he moves to my front, slowly working his way farther down.

I let out a groan.

Brix takes his time washing all of me, covering me with the smell of flowery hotel soap. He ignores me when I snark that my cock isn't clean enough yet to try to get him to keep stroking it.

Then a foamy finger slips into my ass crack.

I tense.

Either my *that's not lube* warning is going unheard, or I really do need to trust him.

I glance over my shoulder, which only makes him smile.

"I can see we still have some minor trust issues, but I promise to rectify that."

His single finger breaches my hole, and the nerve endings that have been neglected for almost two years do a happy dance.

I bear down on his fat finger lodged inside me. He grips my hip with his free hand tight enough to bruise.

My ass clenches around his finger, and I breathe hard, trying to focus on the sensation of it slipping deeper inside me. It feels tight, but Brix takes his time, slowly moving in and out of me.

My mind gets fuzzy, and all I can feel is Brix all around me. I want him to consume all of me.

But then his warmth at my back suddenly disappears and so does his finger.

Noooo.

The water runs over me. I lean forward and lay my arm on the wall, pushing my ass out farther.

It's not a matter of wanting more. I *need* more.

I need to feel all of him.

Then Brix's big body presses against my back, and he reaches to shut the water off.

"Wait, wha—?" I go to stand upright, but Brix has me boxed in.

"Patience, Pop Star. Learn it."

"That's not going to happen anytime soon."

He grips my shoulder to hold me in place. "Stay there."

The next second, he's on his knees behind me and he spreads my ass cheeks.

If he thought I was trembling before, it's nothing compared to now. My legs threaten to give out.

I'm exposed and vulnerable, the cool air hitting my hole, but one look over my shoulder, and I know Brix is into it.

"So hot," he murmurs.

It feels like a lifetime for the first swipe of his tongue, and when it happens, I can't help squirming.

Brix chuckles, and the warm breath on my sensitive skin only intensifies the new experience. "Hold still," he complains.

"Can't help it. It feels … weird."

He looks up at me. "Have you never—"

"Nope. Ex wasn't into it. Never came up with the other guy."

Brix sighs. "So much you've missed out on."

"Are you going to give me an education on rimming?"

"Education? Nah. Religion? Hell yes."

"Confident much—"

Brix dives right in, and my body lights up like a damn Christmas tree.

"Holy fuck!"

He hums like he wants to say something but is too busy right now.

The sensation in my ass is completely overwhelming. I want to simultaneously clench and push my ass out farther.

As much as I want to keep watching Brix over my shoulder as his face is buried between my ass cheeks, I'm unsteady and can't stay twisted like this. I turn back to the wall in front of me and rest on my hands while Brix teases and probes.

I can see why this would be the best way to prep someone. Once I get used to the swirling sensation of his tongue, my ass relaxes under Brix's mouth.

He adds his fingers, and I don't think I've ever gotten to two without the help of lube before.

Heat tingles down my spine and in my gut. My cock is still standing tall, untouched and aching, but I don't want Brix to stop, and I don't want to take my hand off the wall because I don't want to smash my head against the tile.

His fingers reach my prostate, and over and over again, I'm hit with a wave of sensation I'm not used to.

My hips rock backward. "Need. More."

Instead of giving me what I want, he pulls away completely.

"No!" I breathe heavily.

My body feels wrung out already, and I haven't even come yet.

He stands and runs the tip of his hard cock along the crack of my ass. "Think you're ready for all of me?"

"Lube."

Brix laughs. "Of course." He smacks my ass. "Bed."

He helps me out of the tub, and on wobbly legs, I stumble toward the bed in the hotel suite.

I fall to my hands and knees.

"Nuh-uh. On your back."

"Oh, thank God." I flop over, narrowly missing the bottle of lube Brix throws next to me. "I don't know how long I could've held myself up for."

The mattress dips as Brix's knees hit the bed. I lift my head and watch his big body crawl toward me.

Skin on skin, he lowers himself on top of me, his hard cock lining up next to mine. His mouth leaves light kisses from my neck, down my chest, and then he latches onto a nipple.

As much as I'm loving this, he's got me all keyed up, and now he's trying to slow us down.

"Brix. I need you inside me."

Brix reaches for the lube. "Legs up."

"Yes," I hiss and grip my knees, lifting my ass off the bed.

His slippery fingers dip inside me before he adds more lube to them and pushes inside again. The thought of taking his fat cock makes me nervous, but as he stretches me and preps me, all that worry is forgotten.

That is, until I feel the head of his dick at my entrance.

Fuck, this thing is going to tear me in two.

"Nah, don't go tensing up now," Brix whispers. "You're doing so good."

I tell myself to relax.

His eyes flutter as he slowly pushes inside.

The burn rips through me, but I know it'll go away soon. I close my eyes and breathe through it.

Brix pauses. "Look at me." When I do, I melt under his deep brown gaze. "I've got you, okay?"

"Okay."

The urge to come dies down a little while he works his way in to the hilt, and when he's buried inside me, he stops.

We're connected wholly, on a completely new level, and when he moves inside me, slowly pumping in and out, I can't take my eyes off his expressive face.

Brix doesn't give away much on most days, but right now he's giving me everything.

His concern for me is etched in the set of his jaw. His affection comes through in his warm eyes. The encompassing need is in his hard breaths, as if it's taking everything in him to make sure he doesn't go too far.

"You feel amazing." The rasp in his voice makes my cock jump.

"You do too," I say softly.

I lift one of my hands and trail a finger over his hard features.

He closes his eyes as he leans into my hand.

The burn eases, and I start taking him easier now.

"As much as I want this to last forever, I don't think I'm built that way. You feel too good. This is …" He shudders.

I lower my legs and wrap them under his ass, pushing him deeper.

"Oh, fuck." The soft, affectionate look in his eyes turns dark and heavy.

Brix's thrusts increase, and he appears on the brink of losing it.

That's a bigger turn-on than anything he's done to me. And that's including the eye-opening rimming.

"I like doing this to you," I say.

"I …" He doesn't finish his sentence.

I can tell he's close. I wrap my hand around my dick and pump hard and fast.

Brix mimics my action with an added roll of his hips.

I shoot toward the edge just waiting for the crash. His hard cock moves in and out and seems to get harder and harder inside me.

He's losing himself and his rhythmic tempo, starting to fuck me in earnest.

My head's swimming, losing more and more brain cells with every hit against my prostate.

He's sweating all over me, and I lean up to lick his salty-sweet neck.

"Brix," I whisper against his skin. Or perhaps I mumble, "Blergph." I don't know anymore.

And when he stills and comes inside me, I fall apart with him.

We lock eyes, and I have the most intense orgasm of my life, but it has nothing to do with the sex.

It's all Brix.

CHAPTER 22
BRIX

WHETHER IT'S BEING LOCKED AWAY for days in one hotel room, the promise of giving each other more pieces of ourselves, or the new way we've been making love and exploring each other's bodies, all I know is I feel undeniably closer to Harley since we checked in.

The only person we've seen in days is Jamie when she came by to drop off Harley's phone charger I may or may not have forgotten to put in his bag.

It's given us the opportunity to connect in a way I don't fully understand, but I do know I want more of it.

I kiss my way along Harley's naked shoulder. We're lying on our sides, me spooning him, and my hand skims his stomach, brushing over the head of his cock.

He moans but doesn't open his eyes. "How long will we be holed up in this hotel room?"

"Until they find Webber."

"That could be weeks." Harley doesn't sound too upset about that.

I kiss the back of his head. "Could be."

"What an absolute shame." He reaches behind him, gripping the back of my head and pulling me closer.

Our morning breaths mingle, but I don't give a shit. I kiss him hard. Our tongues tangle, and Harley rolls over to face me.

"Is this your plan? Distract me for weeks with your mouth and your dick?"

"Has it been working?"

"It has. To a degree."

I climb on top of him. "I'm gonna have to up my game, then. You want my ass again?"

"You're such a cock slut." He squeezes my ass cheek.

"Mmm, maybe you should call me that while you're balls-deep inside me." I reach for the lube, but when I come back to Harley, he's staring up at me with a serious expression.

"Do you … like, prefer that? Bottoming, I mean. Not being called a slut."

"I like both those things."

"If you don't want to top—"

"Topping isn't my first choice, never has been, but I get in the mood every now and then. Like when I want to show a certain someone what he means to me." I lean in and kiss his cheek.

There goes another one of Harley's imperfect smiles. "You showed me real good."

"You recover from that okay?" I smirk.

"I'm just going to say it. It's a good thing you like bottoming because I think I can only handle your weapon of ass destruction every once in a while."

I lose myself laughing. "Weapon of …" I laugh more.

"It's not a total exaggeration."

"You're adorable."

We go back to kissing, and Harley's hard cock beneath me is more than an invitation. I want to blow him and get him so achingly needy for my ass, he'll be begging for it.

I make my way down his body, teasing him, going as slow as I can. We have all the time in the world to—

There's a knock at the door. "Room service."

I look up at Harley. "Did you order room service in your sleep?"

"If you'd asked me that nine years ago, the answer could have been yes, but not this time. Maybe Gideon did for us?"

"Wait here."

It's amazing how fast an erection can die. I grab a robe and throw it over my naked body.

My Glock sits on the dresser, so I take that with me too.

Through the peephole in the door, I only see a cart of food. Either no one's there or they're purposefully staying out of sight.

I open it a crack, keeping my gun ready, but there's no one there. At all. I move the cart out of the way and step into the corridor.

No one.

There's a card next to the food that says *From Joystar Records.*

I put the safety on my gun and check under the cart and around it for anything suspicious, but when I find nothing, I pull the cart into the room, more confused than ever.

Under the cloches is an array of foods. Bacon, sausage, eggs, and hash browns under one, a stack of pancakes under another, and a small fruit plate.

Harley appears from the bedroom, unfortunately dressed, but that's probably for the best.

Something doesn't sit right. It's a gut feeling—the same gut feeling I had when Webber sent the letter.

Harley reaches for a piece of cantaloupe, but I stop his hand from going anywhere near his mouth.

"Did Gideon tell the label we were here?" I ask.

He drops the fruit. "Not that I know of. They're still being dicks about the album. But ... I mean, he could have?"

"Don't eat anything," I order and rush into the bedroom to find my phone.

Gideon picks up on the third ring. "Brix? Is everything okay?"

"Did you tell the label what hotel we're at?"

"No, but I was about to call you guys. It was leaked in a tabloid. Someone saw Harley walking through the lobby."

"Shit," I hiss, then remember something. "Wait, Harley hasn't been to the lobby. We came straight up from the basement and haven't left the room."

We were careful not to let anyone see him arriving and have made sure he hasn't answered the door when we've ordered takeout or room service. Yet, somehow, he was still recognized somewhere.

"Did anyone see you?" Gideon asks.

"One guy in the elevator, but he gave no indication he recognized Harley. And that was days ago."

"Harley has one of the most recognizable faces on the planet," he reminds me. "It could've been a staff member or anyone."

"We have to move him somewhere else," I say. "Somewhere safe."

"Do you know where you could go?"

Hotels aren't safe. Public places aren't safe. "I'll call Trav."

"Keep me updated."

We end the call, but instead of calling right away, I start packing. I can call Trav from the road.

"How did your belongings get spread from one end of the room to the other already?" I call out to Harley.

"Umm, Brix?" My man's voice is trembling and scared, and I tell myself to try to stay composed.

When I look up, he's holding the card that was on the cart. "What is it?"

He holds it out to me.

On the inside, in the same script, is written: *You can't run.*

My heart stops dead, but I can't let Harley know how much I'm panicking. I need to be bodyguard Brix right now, not boyfriend Brix.

"We need to leave whatever we haven't packed yet and go." I quickly zip up his suitcase even though there's still clothes scattered around the place.

I throw on my pants and shirt from yesterday as fast as humanly possible. My duffle bag sits by the door, still practically untouched from when we arrived. It's been a clothing-optional few days.

"It's him, isn't it?" Harley croaks.

"We don't know that for sure." Oh yeah, we know it for sure. I just don't want to freak Harley out more than I have to.

"I thought it was weird that it said it was from the label. It doesn't sound like something the label would do. Especially because we're in the middle of disputing the next album."

"Maybe it's a peace offering from them, but we need to be extra cautious."

"A peace offering that says I can't run? Please tell me what you think is going on."

I sigh. "We need to leave, and we need to leave right now. That's what's going on."

"Where are we going? Back to the house?"

"No. I'll call Trav, and we'll go to one of the Mike Bravo safe houses."

"What about the album?" He's *still* thinking about work? I shouldn't be surprised. Harley is his job.

"On hold."

Harley screws up his face.

"For now," I clarify. "You can't do anything until you hear back from the label anyway."

Harley wrings his hands and chokes out an "Okay."

I approach him. "Remember what I promised you? I won't let anyone hurt you. Ever. Everything will be okay. I promise." After a quick kiss to the top of his head, I clear the room in record time.

Getting to the car is an entirely different story.

On our way to the elevators, a trio of twenty-something women come from the opposite direction. It'll take less than a second for them to recognize Harley, so I grab his arm and turn him toward the stairs.

"We're on the twenty-second floor," he complains.

"Look on the bright side. You'll get your cardio in for the day."

I put my Glock in the waistband of my pants and take Harley's suitcase from him.

At about the fifteenth floor, the loud bang of a door closing filters up the stairwell, making us pause.

"What do we do?" Harley whispers.

I peek over the railing as two kids' laughs echo around us. Then another door opens and closes.

"Keep going."

My heart pounds, and as much as I'd like to blame exertion from running down the stairs holding my duffle bag and Harley's luggage, I know it's because I'm worried for Harley.

Someone wants to hurt him which makes me ragey. I want to be out there looking for this guy, but I also don't want to leave Harley's side.

Harley's sweating by the time we get to the fifth floor and glaring at me like he does his personal trainer.

"At least it's down and not up."

"Shut up," he mumbles.

It's hilarious, but I don't dare laugh.

We finally make it to the car in the underground parking garage, but I tell Harley to stay back as I check it out.

I check under the hood, under the body, and then the driver's side for any loose wiring or signs the car's been tampered with.

There's no such thing as being too careful when it comes to Harley's life.

"Are car bombs really a thing?" Harley asks. He sounds more doubtful than scared, so that's a bonus.

"In my line of work? Yeah. But right now, I'm just being cautious. No one should know this car, but no one should've known we were at this hotel either."

We leave the hotel and get on the road with no real direction of where we're going.

"Do you want breakfast? We can get something on the way."

He shakes his head.

"I've gotta call Trav. Do you want me to pull over so you don't have to listen?"

"No. I need to. I want to know what you find out."

"Good or bad?"

He chews his bottom lip. "Good or bad."

"Just know, no matter what, I've got it, okay? I can handle anything this guy throws our way."

Harley gives a small nod.

I hit Trav's number on my phone, and it connects to the Bluetooth.

"His bank transactions show he's still in the LA area, but we still haven't found him," he answers.

Harley's eyes widen. Fucking great. Yeah, maybe this is a reason I shouldn't have let him listen.

"Harley's here with me," I say.

Harley glares at me in warning.

"What?" I play innocent. "It's rude to have people on speaker without letting them know who's in the room."

"Uh … Right," Trav says cautiously. "Was that all?"

"No." I update him on the hotel situation and about being overly cautious.

"Go to the ranch. It's far, but no one can follow you out there. Unless you've got a tail. Do you have a tail?"

"Not that I can tell, but I'll keep an eye out."

"We'll keep looking for Webber. Did you check out at the hotel?"

"Not yet. I was going to call Gideon to handle it."

"I'll go. I want to look at their security footage and see who delivered the food."

Harley looks sick again, his skin paling.

"Thanks," I mutter.

"Hang in there, Harley." Trav ends the call.

I shift lanes and head for the desert.

Harley looks out the window and remains quiet for a long time. Soft music plays on the radio, but it's not until one of Harley's songs comes on that he speaks.

"How did this become my life? Here I am, *on the radio*, singing this misguided song about happiness when in reality, I'm running and hiding from a potential crazy person who wants to hurt me because … why? Because I embarrassed him? Rejected him? Because he was convicted? What does Billy Webber want from me?"

I wish I had a better answer for him. "There are a lot of psychos out there. It's surprising this is the first time something like this has happened considering *how* famous you are."

"I'm beginning to wonder if it's worth it."

"Fame?"

"I love performing, and I love music, but all this"—he waves his hand around—"destroys the love I once had for the job. When I'm not fighting with the label, I'm hiding from fans. I can't remember the last time it *fulfilled* me. Probably back in the early Eleven days before fame got to our heads."

"Maybe when all this dies down, you should call the guys and get together."

Harley huffs. "Yeah, like that's ever going to happen. I've barely heard from them since we split. Especially Blake and Mason."

"Maybe *you* should make the effort. You're arguably the most successful."

"Except, is that true? I have the Grammys they don't, I have the successful album, but what do I have to show for it? I'm fighting with the label, my next album might not even happen with how long they're taking to make a decision after my ultimatum, and I'm ..." He looks over at me. "I'll be alone. Eventually."

"Is that what you really think? Even after the last few days?"

Harley turns and stares out the window. "I don't know what to think anymore. I don't expect you to lay your whole life out for me right away, but ..."

As if being given a sign by a deity I've never believed in, the literal sign for the San Bernardino exit appears, and my fingers itch to take it.

I promised Harley I'd give him more of me. Yet, here he is still doubting my commitment to him.

This might not be the most ideal time to do it, but I also can't think of a better way to show Harley how serious I am and to distract him from this mess for a while.

"Detour."

When I pull off the freeway, Harley turns around in his seat to stare out the rear window. "Are we being followed?"

"No."

"Then where are we going?"

I glance at him out of the corner of my eye. "Somewhere I should've told you about a long time ago."

I just wish I could've given warning.

The care facility isn't far from the exit, and it only takes those few minutes for panic to set in.

I don't know how *he'll* react when I introduce him to Harley. I don't know if he'll immediately know how head over heels I am for my pop star boyfriend.

I don't know if this will be the final nail in his coffin.

The last time I tried to come out to him, *this* happened.

"Nevaeh Care Facility," Harley says. "Wait, is this ..." His gaze flies to mine.

I turn into a parking space and grip the steering wheel hard. "Harley, I want you to meet my dad."

I hold my breath.

"D-dad?" Harley asks.

I can tell he's confused. It's habit to talk about my dad in the past tense, as if he's dead instead of the truth which is he's trapped inside a body that doesn't work.

I clear my throat. "Four and a half years ago, Dad had a major stroke. I was deployed at the time, and he was recently retired and had moved off base and set up in a little house outside of Barstow. His neighbors were the ones who found him unconscious in the front yard, but they didn't know to send him to a VA hospital. The ambulance took him to the closest one which happened to be some big private hospital that costs about a thousand dollars a minute. The VA didn't cover it. And because I was overseas, it was months before I could move him."

"Your medical bills," Harley says.

"Yup."

"He's the reason you took the job with Trav."

"Trav pays more money than the military, and I figured, timing-wise, I had to take it. If I re-upped, I wouldn't be able to be close to Dad or pay for his care. There was a huge waiting list to get him into a VA care facility and a whole lot of red tape. None of them were close to me, which is how he ended up here. It's all I can afford so close to LA."

Harley squeezes my arm. "I'm so sorry."

I turn to Harley, and my vision blurs. Tears of guilt threaten to spill over. "The reason I don't tell anyone is because it's always been just me and Dad, you know? When Mom died, he did the best he could. He transferred to a training position, and he did everything he could to be close to me. Now it's my job to do the same for him. This is where I come on my Sundays off."

Harley leans across the seats to hug me or kiss me, I don't know.

I stop him before he can reach me. "I'm not out to him."

"That's okay. I'm not out to the world. Call it even?"

I manage a small laugh. "I wanted to tell him. I Skyped with him the night before the stroke. I'd had a near miss—a guy in my squad stepped on an IED and lost his legs. I was about twenty feet from the explosion. I was right behind that guy, and I'd never felt so close to dying before. It … it scared me enough to want to die with no secrets hanging over my head. I wasn't officially out in the army, but I had hooked up with guys on base before. I don't think it was a huge secret, and for all I knew, one of my superiors had already told Dad. But I'd decided he deserved to hear it from me. Especially if I was going to come home in a coffin."

Harley lets me talk, staring at me with sympathy but not pity. "What happened when you tried to tell him?"

"I stuttered like a moron and told him I had something big I'd been sitting on for a while. Something weird happened with his eyes —like he was having trouble concentrating. He said he had a headache and didn't feel well and was going to bed. A few days later, when they finally got word to me, I realized he'd had a stroke about twelve hours after I tried telling him."

"Brix … his stroke wasn't your fault."

"I know that, *logically*, but I can't help wondering. What if I hadn't told him?" Would he still have had a stroke that day? Would it have happened another time? Would it have happened at all?

"He still would've had that stroke. I promise you it was poor timing. Strokes don't happen out of nowhere. It had probably been coming for a while."

"Maybe." I want to believe that. So bad. But I still have doubts.

"Gayness isn't that powerful. If it was, all those Westboro Baptist Church people would have strokes. Hashtag the real gay agenda."

I stare over at Harley, wondering if he's being serious right now. His stoic expression makes me laugh. "You did not throw a hashtag at me in conversation."

"But I cheered you up, didn't I? Hashtag winning."

"Oh God, make it stop."

I can't be more thankful for Harley making jokes right now. I didn't know what to expect. I've never told anyone about my dad even though, apparently, my entire team knows. I don't want pity … or help.

My dad is my responsibility. I just have to live with it. It was the way he raised me.

Harley squeezes my hand. "You don't have to introduce me if you're not ready. Knowing this part of you is enough for me."

"I want to take you in there, but I don't know how he'll take it. He, uh, can't speak. He's lost nearly all movement except for a little on his left side. He does these half-smiles."

"Can he communicate at all?"

"We figured out a system. He squeezes Morse code into my hand. I know he hates it, but just like I put on a happy face every time I see him, he always says everything is good when it's not. This place … it's not the best. The staff seem friendly and all, but it's …"

"Basic."

"It kills me knowing he can see everything and understand everything but he's stuck in those four walls day in and day out without anything to do. It's not like he can talk to the nurses to tell them if anything is wrong. He gets frustrated."

"I can see how that'd be frustrating."

"I want to do more for him. At least try to come see him more or something. The guilt eats at me."

"You can bring me up here anytime you want to see your dad. Even if I stay in the car and write."

My heart fills with more affection for Harley. "You'd do that for me?"

"I'd do a whole lot more if you'd let me, but I get the feeling that would be too much." Our dynamic is flipped when Harley reaches for me. He cups my face. "I will do anything for you. Just like you want to protect me, I want to give you everything you need."

I could ask for so many things right now, but I won't. I won't use him that way.

"I don't want you to ever think I'm only with you because of what you can do for me."

"I don't. I *won't*."

"There'll be no chance of doubt this way. But I will take you up on the offer to come up here with me. And ... and I want you to come in."

"R-really?" Hesitation etches its way onto Harley's face. "I mean, uh ... meeting the parents." He whistles. "Big step. That's like *relationship* stuff."

I press my mouth to his in a soft, chaste kiss. "Good thing we're in a relationship, then, am I right?"

Harley looks worried.

"Uh, right?" I press.

He hesitates. "I don't know if I'll be any good at it. I'm known to be a bit of a selfish boyfriend, you know. If my ex is anything to go by."

"You? A famous pop star is selfish? Call the tabloids about this revelation."

Harley shoves me. "You know what I mean."

"I do, but I'm new to this too. I've never been in one place long enough to have a relationship, and with Mike Bravo ... well, you saw Iris when his girl broke up with him. None of us are really relationship material."

"What if I'm too much?"

I want to take him in my arms and squeeze him so hard he believes me when I say, "I know being with you means the majority of my time will be spent dealing with *your* life. It's inescapable. But, Harley? Since working for you, I've realized I was born to be in the background. To be a protector. I was trained to stand in the darkness so the spotlight can shine on you."

"What if I want you next to me?"

I slink back into my seat. "You and I both know that can't happen while you're still recording and making music."

"What if I get out of my contract with the label and come out?"

I shake my head. "Won't change anything. If it became public that you and I were together, I'd become famous in my own right, and there's no way I could protect you if they're all trying to get to me too."

"I don't want you to ever think that I want to hide you. That's been a problem for me before."

"Never. It's the business you're in. Hell, for a long time, before I started working for Trav, I was in the same boat. Maybe not exactly, but close."

Harley glances out the windshield and back to me again. "I want to meet your dad."

My breath gets caught in my throat. "Then let's go." It comes out more of a nervous bumble than confident, and Harley picks up on that.

"But if you're not okay with it—"

"I am. I just … I don't know if I can tell him how close we really are?"

I hate the look of understanding on Harley's face because I wish I could give him this one thing. My dad is someone he could tell his secret to because there's no way he could tell it to anyone else.

"It's okay," Harley reassures me. "We can go in there and you can tell him I'm your assignment."

"Thank you. Umm …" I hand Harley sunglasses and a cap. "The nurses will recognize you, and I don't want another leak like at the hotel."

Harley puts the hat on and slides the glasses onto his face. "Can't even meet your dad the right way."

Even with the knowledge that Harley's cool not coming out to my dad, I'm still uneasy as we enter the building.

I don't like lying to my dad, but between that and risking his health, I'm okay with keeping my mouth shut.

We reach Dad's room, hopefully without Harley being recognized. After the elevator with the guy we suspect tipped off the tabloids, I can't be sure.

Dad's face lights up in the only way it can—his lips quirking on one side.

His gaze flicks behind me to Harley.

"Hey, Dad, this is Harley. He's my, uh …" *Assignment. Charge. I'm his bodyguard.* "Friend."

Now, *that* feels like a lie. Any of my other options still would have been the truth, but I hate putting that professional barrier between Harley and me when we're so much more.

"Nice to meet you, sir," Harley says.

Dad's fingers flex, indicating he wants to tell me something.

I take my seat next to his bed and grab hold of his hand.

He squeezes a sequence of dashes and dots, and immediately I'm pissed off, but I can't help laughing anyway.

"What?" Harley asks.

"I am never going to hear the end of this."

"What did he say?"

"He did two ones. *Eleven*."

Harley's smile is so fucking beautiful.

I hate him right now.

I hate even more I can't do anything about it.

"Your dad knows who I am? Your *dad*, Brix? Come on."

"Shut up," I mumble and turn to Dad. "First day I met this guy, I didn't know who he was, so I may have tackled him. Just a little. I thought he was a bad guy."

"A little. How can you tackle someone *a little*?" Harley exaggeratedly rolls his eyes.

Dad's lips twitch again.

"Thanks, Dad. No, really. Thanks. If I thought I got it bad enough already, it's nothing compared to what I'll get now."

His hand starts squeezing again.

Y-O-U-R-E W-E-L

Because it takes so much energy to get the letters out, I try to guess what he's going to say before he's finished. This one is fairly straightforward.

"Wow," I say dryly. "Really lovely."

"What did he say?" Harley asks.

"He said *You're welcome*."

Harley rubs his chin. "Who would've thought you could be sarcastic in Morse code?"

"Dad is an expert."

I know it's medically impossible, but I swear Dad is the brightest he's ever been since his stroke.

He grips my hand tight and squeezes a sequence into my hand that makes me stiffen. I know what he's trying to say long before he gets to the end, but I'm in too much shock to stop him. It's a long series of dashes and dots, but without a doubt, he *knows*.

B-O-Y-F-R-I-E-N-D?

My throat dries, and I stare at my dad with pleading eyes. I wish I could know exactly what he's thinking right now.

Y-E-S? Dad asks.

"What's he saying?" Harley asks.

"He, uh, he …" I glance between Dad and Harley. I swallow hard. "He asked if you were my boyfriend."

"*Oh.* I thought—"

"Have you always known?" I ask Dad.

D-U-H

I burst out laughing.

Harley looks at me expectantly.

"He said *Duh.*" I turn to Dad. "Since when?"

B-A-S-I-C

"Since I was eighteen?" I exclaim.

I can tell he wants to say more. He wants to explain but *can't.* Frustration mars the corner of his eye as he scrunches the few muscles in his face that work.

This is what I hate. He can only get single words or basic phrases out.

"Dad, it's okay. You don't have to explain."

W-A-N-T T-O

"Are you okay with it?" I hold my breath. "I tried to tell you, but I didn't know how, and you've always been so … military, I thought—"

Y-O-U H-A-P-P-Y?

"Very happy."

L-O-V-E Y-O-U

"I love you too."

There's a lot of reading between the lines with Dad. All he wants is for me to be happy. I'd be happier if I could do more for him.

CHAPTER 23
HARLEY

THE LAST SEED of doubt disappears as I watch Brix with his father. I've always known my badass with his hard body and soldier haircut was a big softy on the inside, but I might've underestimated how caring and amazing he is.

He sits by his dad's bed until my stomach grumbles for the breakfast we never ate, and now it's coming up on lunchtime. If I wasn't so hungry, I'd stay here all day and admire their father-son relationship.

I never had that growing up, but I also never thought I'd missed out on anything until I saw these two together.

Communication between them is really slow, but Brix never shows his frustration. He's patient and kind, and he never stops smiling at his dad.

I don't completely understand why he doesn't talk about his dad to any of the other guys on his team, but I do understand being trapped in a position or in a situation you feel you can't get out of. Asking for help isn't an option because pride, fear, and insecurity get in the way.

I want to take that all away for Brix. Just like he does for me.

He makes me feel safe. He makes me feel wanted. And not in the way my fans do.

He knows I'm a workaholic mess and doesn't care.

He gets it.

He gets *me*.

"We should go," Brix says to his dad. "I have to make sure my boyfriend gets fed and all." He stands. "I'll come back and visit again soon, okay?"

It breaks my heart the man in the bed can't respond.

We're still a good two hours away from the ranch, but with some drive-thru burgers we pick up from a place right near the care facility, we're silent for a good half hour of it.

"Cooper is going to kill me," I say around a bite of burger.

"Cardio points from the stairs this morning, remember? But speaking of which, we should cancel all upcoming appointments with your trainer. At least until we know how long we're gonna be at the ranch."

"I'll get Jamie on it." When I finish my food, I take out my phone and text her an update about what's happening and ask her to give both my personal trainer and vocal coach the week off.

When that's done, I shift in my seat and watch Brix as he expertly maneuvers the car through traffic while throwing some fries into his mouth.

The same mouth I plan to do sexy things to as soon as we get to the ranch.

This morning I was freaking out, but Brix has a way of making me forget the reality of my stalker situation and trust that he and his team have it covered. Billy Webber still scares the shit out of me, but when I'm with Brix, it's not a paralyzing fear.

Brix cocks his head in my direction. "What?"

"What, what?"

"You're looking at me weird."

"My turned-on look is weird? Good to know. Maybe that's why I haven't slept with many guys—they think my seductive face is creepy."

"You're turned on right now? Why?"

"Because I have a hot as fuck boyfriend who's a big teddy bear on the inside."

Brix scowls, and instead of seeing the hardass I met on day one who I thought was going to possibly kill me, the look is so damn adorable on him now. "Start spreading that shit around and I don't know how long you'll have a boyfriend."

"Aww, you're so tough."

"Aww, you're so condescending and mean."

I laugh. "Don't worry, your big bad secret is safe with me. Both of them. Though, I do think you should tell your teammates about your dad. You know they'll be supportive."

"It's not that …"

"Then what is it?"

Brix changes lanes again. "It's hard to explain, and I know saying it out loud will sound ridiculously … stupid."

"Stupid how?"

"Dad raised me with the *suck it up* mentality. Don't dwell on the shit you can't change. Deal with it. When I was in the military, people would get transferred, some wouldn't re-up, some … came home different than who they were when they left. People were always coming and going, and I realized quickly that long-lasting relationships in that environment weren't for me. Even friendships."

"I get it." It's sad, but I get it. "You've always been on your own, and you don't know how to let people in, but haven't you worked for Mike Bravo for four years now? Don't you want to let them in?"

"I want to let *you* in. But … it's hard. I've been this way my whole life. I don't know how to let those walls down."

I huff at the sudden realization. "The funny thing is, all I've ever wanted is for someone to see beyond the fake persona I was given. It's kind of ironic the guy who does is the one who doesn't let anyone see past his superficial stuff."

"I'm trying. I've never … I've never felt the way I do about you." He glances at me briefly but then looks back at the road.

I can tell he's trying, and I appreciate it. I just wish … I wish it were easier for him to let go. It's obvious he's getting uncomfortable with how much of himself he's admitting right now, so I give him a break.

"Drive faster."

"Uh, why?"

"The sooner we get to the ranch, the sooner I get to jump you."

Brix floors it and laughs but quickly slows back down to the speed limit. "As tempting as it is to risk crashing the car for sex, I think it'd be counterproductive when I'm supposed to be protecting you."

"Hmm, true. Uh, how far away are we?"

"A little over an hour?"

I groan. "That's too long."

"It's an hour of knowing that once we get to the ranch, my ass is all yours."

I throw my head back. "Oh my God, that's even worse."

"You're welcome."

"I can see you inherited the same dry wit your dad has."

Brix smiles. "I learned from the best."

That one hour feels like an eternity before I have Brix naked in the same room we stayed in last time. The same place where we first kissed.

Where I got my first taste.

His big muscular body is spread out for me on the bed, and after the adrenaline rush of today and meeting his dad, I'm aching for him in ways I didn't know existed.

I don't want to just fuck him.

It's about being close to him and showing him how much I want him. I want to prove we can make our relationship work.

I have to stroke my cock which is as hard as steel. It's tempting to jump on top of him right now, but there's a problem.

"Lube?" I ask, wondering which bag he put it in.

The distraught look on his face as it falls has me whimpering like a damn baby.

"It's back at the hotel," Brix complains.

"How could you forget the lube?"

"If you recall, we had to leave in a hurry. I've probably forgotten a hell of a lot worse." He winces. "Like our toothbrushes. But hey, I remembered the charger this time. Do I get points for that?"

"Trav would have some lube," I say, ignoring him about what else he left behind. There are more important things we need. *Sex things.*

"Any gay man with a healthy sex life would stash that shit every-where, right?"

Brix makes a derisive noise. "You say that as if Trav has a sex life. Also, I'm not going through my boss's things, so no."

"I'm guessing a grocery store trip is out of the question?"

"Right now?" he exclaims. "Yes, definitely out. But I can go later on my own. No one knows where this place is. It's safe for you to be by yourself …" He narrows his eyes. "Although, you do know where the guns are kept, and I don't know if I like leaving you alone with them."

I throw up my hands. "Lesson learned. That's all your department."

Brix sits up. "Well, if you can't fuck me, you can at least fuck my mouth. Give me something."

"You sucking me off gives me something, not the other way around."

"That's where you're wrong." Brix inches toward the edge of the bed, bringing that delectable mouth of his inches from my cock. "You know that high you get when you perform?"

"Oh, your blowjobs are performances now?" They totally could be because he's amazing at giving head, but I'm not going to let an opportunity to mock him go to waste.

"Award-winning. Or they would be if sex awards were a thing."

"Porn awards are a thing, but the label and Gideon would kill me if I ever leaked a gay sex tape."

Brix growls. "No one gets to see you like this but me. Got it?" His hand circles the tight velvety skin of my hard dick and moves in a downward motion in one slow, agonizing stroke.

I let out a shuddery breath and nod.

"As I was saying," Brix continues. "That high you always talk about? The high of thousands of fans screaming for you? Imagine how I feel when I make you scream my name. That I'm the one to bring this amazingly talented and loved pop star to his knees. That's all me."

I can't help but agree. My hands run over his short buzz cut. "All you."

With a flick of his tongue over my tip, he puts me out of my misery and shows me exactly what he means.

He sucks me down and makes my knees weak. I have to hold on to his shoulders to steady myself as I thrust over and over into his mouth.

I'm wound tight from the entire day, only getting more tense as my muscles crave the release of a whole-body orgasm.

Brix knows I'm close and works his own dick in his hand.

I want to stop him, but I'm jelly. If I let go of his shoulders now, I'd probably fall into his lap, and then the overwhelming sensation on my cock would stop.

So not going to do that.

Brix opens his throat and takes me deep.

I come hard and call out his name just like he wanted.

He continues to jerk himself off as I empty down his throat, but when I'm done shuddering and my grip becomes loose on him, he pulls off me and stares up into what I assume is my blissed-out expression.

"Need your mouth on me. I'm close," he grunts. "Really close."

I have no problem dropping to my knees and quickly covering his cock with my mouth. I suck hard and he explodes a second later.

By the time I've swallowed, my body no longer works. I think Brix is in a similar state.

I fall to my ass on the floor and use the bedframe as a backrest while he lies on the mattress with his legs still dangling off the side next to me.

All I can hear is his heavy breathing and the frantic beating of my heart in my ears.

As I stare around the fancy room in this six-bedroom mansion in the middle of nowhere, I'm reminded I don't really know much about Brix's job before he came to work for me.

"Brix?"

"Mm?"

"Random question is random, but who *is* Mike Bravo?"

CHAPTER 24
BRIX

I LAUGH SO HARD my stomach hurts. "I don't know if I should be offended or not. That's your first thought after I blew you?"

"I've always wondered, and for some reason I remembered I've been meaning to ask you. Clearly, I care a lot seeing as I keep forgetting."

"Clearly." I lean up on my elbows because Harley's still on the floor.

He stares over his shoulder at me with a sated smile. "So?"

I grab a pillow and flip around to lie on my stomach and prop myself up next to him. "Why was Eleven called Eleven when there were only five of you?"

"Whoa, we really are boyfriends now. Asking the hard questions."

"Really?"

"No. It's not a hard question. We were originally Eleven Ounces … like, the weight of a human heart."

"Aww, how cheesy."

"Right?" Harley exclaims. "Anyway, kind of like One Direction became 1D, it's like people were too lazy to always say Eleven Ounces, and eventually we ditched the Ounces part."

"Ah. That's a more boring answer than I was expecting."

"So? Who's Mike?"

"No one. It's the NATO phonetic alphabet."

Harley looks confused. "MB? Okay, so what does MB stand for?"

I lean over and kiss him. "I'll never tell."

"Asshole." He laughs.

I jump up before he can shove me, but he grabs my pillow and throws it at my head instead.

I swat it away before it can hit me. "Are you seriously trying to start a pillow fight right now?"

"Isn't that what boyfriends do?"

"I think you're confusing me with a twelve-year-old girl at a slumber party."

Harley eyes me from head to toe. "Yeah, I could see how someone could make that mistake."

I glare at him.

"Get it? Because you're, like, so big and the complete opposite? It's *funny*!"

"Hot tip. If you need to explain your jokes, they're probably not funny."

"Whatever," Harley mumbles. "I'm hilarious."

He's still sitting on the floor, so I go over to him and kiss the top of his head.

"At least you make someone laugh. I'm going to throw some clothes on and go to the store."

"O-okay." Harley bites his lip the way he does when he's nervous.

"You'll be safer here than coming with me, as much as I don't want to leave you."

"I know. I just wish I could do normal shit with you, like go to a fucking grocery store."

I slide down next to him to sit on the floor. "You know you could have a normal life if you wanted it. Truly wanted it. It'd take a few years to disappear from the spotlight, but it's a possibility."

"You want me to quit?"

"No! No, no, no. Let's get one thing out there. I will always support you, no matter what. I'm not with you because you're Harley Valentine. I'm with you because you're mine. Because ..." Those three little words are on the tip of my tongue, but something holds me back. It feels too soon or like we're not quite there even though I feel it in my gut. "Because I want to be where you are, no matter what you're doing. Even if you were to take away my contract when it's up, I'll still want to follow you."

"Y-you want to be my bodyguard after your contract is up?"

I reach over and cup his face. "Of course I do. I will be here as long as you need me to be."

Harley still looks like he has some doubt, but when I lean forward and press my lips to his, he melts. If he needs convincing that I'm not going anywhere, I'm more than willing to give it.

But right now, he needs a different kind of reassurance. I pull back. "If you want to give all this up, you can. Eventually, you'd be able to go grocery shopping and"—I gasp—"do your own laundry. Make your own bed. Doesn't that sound so fucking exciting?"

Harley laughs. "It sounds fascinatingly boring, but for now I'm good with music."

"I figured. Just trying to give you options." I kiss him again briefly. It's like I can't be near him and go five minutes without doing it. "Okay, I really am going to go now."

"Uh-huh." Harley kisses me this time, strong and hard, and then he throws his leg over my waist and climbs into my lap.

My dick perks up, trying to get ready for round two, but the poor thing is still spent. "Gatorade," I murmur against Harley's mouth.

He pulls back. "What?"

"If you're going to keep jumping me, I'm gonna need to stay hydrated." I smack his ass for him to climb off me.

He reluctantly does but doesn't look happy about it.

"Gatorade, lube, toothbrushes, and toothpaste. That'll be an interesting checkout. I can imagine the cashier's face right now. Anything else we need?"

"Uh, *food?*"

"Oh, right. Should probably pick up some of that too."

"And M&M's." He blinks at me innocently.

"I will never deny you anything you want, but I get to tell your trainer."

He slumps. "Fine. No M&M's. Just know I hate you."

"Be back in an hour."

Harley nods.

As I get dressed and kiss him goodbye, unease settles over me.

He's as safe here as he's ever going to be, so I have nothing to worry about, but it's still hard letting it go.

I possibly speed a little too much and shop a little too fast, but I want to get back to him as soon as I can.

I've loaded up the car with my bags, and I'm about to get back into the driver's seat when my phone rings.

I pause beside the car, and my gut twists when I see Trav's name. "Update?" I bark into the phone.

"It's him." Trav's tone is defeated.

"What?"

"Webber. The security footage at the hotel showed him in the hallway."

I lean against my car. "Where did he get the hotel cart and food?"

"He spoke to someone in the kitchen and said he wanted to surprise his girlfriend in the room. They put it together for him and sent him on his way. As far as the video surveillance goes, he took it straight up to the room and never touched the food."

"How did he know what room we were in? The only people who knew that were you, Gideon, and Harley's assistant."

"You know for sure the assistant isn't involved?"

"Why would she be?"

"Money?"

"She is well beyond compensated. Plus, she loves Harley. I doubt she'd put him in danger just for some cash."

"We'll figure it out," Trav assures me. "I'm gonna stay here a bit longer and go through all the footage from the minute you checked in."

"Keep me updated."

"Will do. Who would've thought this job would actually turn into something?"

"Of course you're excited about it." I would be too if it didn't put Harley at risk. "Might make the decision for me to stay on this assignment easier."

"Is that your way of saying you're not coming back?"

Now's not the time to have this conversation, but it's out there now. "Maybe? I mean … yes?"

"We'll talk soon. Right now, we're gonna track this guy down so you can keep your man safe."

"Thanks. Maybe he paid a guy at the hotel for the room number?" I run my hand over my hair, frustrated we don't have any real answers.

It can't be Gideon or Jamie. They would never do that to Harley.

A million different theories run through my head, but the only logical thing I can think is that one of the hotel staff knew it was Harley staying under that alias and told their friends. It would be a huge coincidence that they would know Webber.

My head hurts, but I don't stop thinking about it the whole way back. I can't.

It feels like the answer is right there, but I can't reach it.

I'm no closer to figuring it out when I pull into the ranch's long driveway, but the Gideon and Jamie thing still niggles at me.

I can almost certainly rule out Gideon. He's Trav's cousin, and if Trav thought something was up, he'd tell me.

Jamie is sweet and naïve. Maybe easy to manipulate.

I'm putting the groceries away in the kitchen when Harley comes to find me.

"Way to freak me out. Maybe call out that you're home?" He folds his arms across his chest. "I was sitting in the room wondering if someone had found me like they did at the hotel."

I force myself to play it off and make a joke. "Honey, I'm home." I must not pull it off because Harley's face drops.

"What's wrong?"

I continue unloading the bags. "I'm only going to ask this once, and if I'm completely off base, tell me to drop it, but"—I glance at him —"how much do you trust Jamie?"

"What the fuck?"

I put up my hands. "Okay. Sorry. I had to ask. I've been wondering how someone found out our room number. I'm grasping at straws."

"And you assumed Jamie?"

"The only other people who would've known were the hotel staff, Gideon, and Trav."

"It can't be Jamie." His words are firm, but I see a tiny bit of doubt in his eyes.

"Are you sure?"

The doubt is gone this time. "It's not her."

"Okay, I'll drop it."

"Did Trav look at the security footage?"

"He did."

Harley stares at me waiting for me to elaborate, but I don't know if I should. "It was Webber, wasn't it?"

I nod.

The large floor-to-ceiling windows let in the bright daylight, and as if in slow motion, I see the color drain from Harley's face.

I wrap him in my arms, wishing I could take it all away from him. He doesn't deserve this. No one does. "Trav is working it out, okay? And until then, you and I can hang out here where it's safe. You can write."

"It's annoying sitting back and doing *nothing*. It's like I'm just waiting for him to get me."

He said it, but I'm not going to agree with it. No matter how much I wish I was out there trying to find this guy, I'm where I need to be.

I hold Harley tighter. "Remember what I said outside of Denver's party that first week I worked for you?"

"It's okay to do nothing."

"This is one of those times. I trust Trav to find this guy."

He buries his head in my chest. "I know. I just—"

"Want to do more. I get it."

I have faith in the Mike Bravo team, but this has been a clusterfuck ever since Billy Webber sent that letter.

What I can't work out is how Webber found us.

The answer is right there, I know it.

What the fuck am I missing?

CHAPTER 25
HARLEY

I WISH I could say our next few days are filled with getting lost in each other and forgetting about the threat hanging over my head, but that's not what happens at all.

Not even close.

Brix doesn't come to bed when I do. He stays awake until there's an update from Trav.

He's preoccupied and barely listens when I talk.

I can tell he wants to be out there in the action instead of stuck inside with me all day.

He took me to the shooting range at the back of the property once as a distraction, but it wasn't like last time. We each took our own booth, and it was less fun than when he was teaching me.

Plus, I still suck at aiming.

I know Brix's attitude has nothing to do with me and everything to do with the situation in general, but I don't know what to do. Or say.

It's kind of awkward between us.

I walk into the formal dining room where a twenty-seat mahogany table sits. The crystal chandelier hanging from the ceiling shines under the bright light. A brick fireplace along one wall gives the room ambiance. It's without a doubt the fanciest room in the house. The décor in this place is definitely not something I'd pick for Trav.

Brix has turned the room into an office, claiming he didn't want to use Trav's office because it would be like invading the man's privacy.

"Maybe we should do something normal people do," I say. "Pretend this whole thing isn't happening."

Brix doesn't look up from the laptop he did feel comfortable enough to borrow from Trav. I mean, if Trav is going to hide embarrassing porn or something, the laptop is where it would be. "I need to figure this out. It's driving me crazy."

"You need to take a break … Whoa, crazy role reversal here."

Brix finally looks up from the screen to smile at me. It's the first smile I've seen in days. "Fine. What 'normal' activity do you want to do?" He eyes me from head to toe with heat burning in his gaze.

"Oh hell no. You don't get sex when you've been refusing to come to bed until I'm already passed out. Waiting for you to finish with"—I wave my hand at the table—"your work is tiring."

Brix pulls out his chair and pats his knee.

I wish I could say I was strong enough to resist, but I'm not. I sit sideways across his lap and wrap my arms around his neck.

His strong hands embrace me for the first time in days. Yeah, when he has eventually come to bed, he's cuddled into me and I've woken up wrapped around him, but this is different.

"I'm sorry I've been distracted." He kisses his way across my cheek and then down my neck.

"I want to watch a movie."

Brix pulls back, and his brow scrunches. "Like a porno? I'd be down for that." His hand makes his way under my shirt.

I snort. "No. Like, a movie movie. That's a normal-person thing to do, isn't it? It might distract us both. Does Trav subscribe to, like, Netflix or something out here?"

"You really want to watch TV?" Brix shifts underneath me.

"Yes, because you've been ignoring me for days."

"So this is my punishment?"

"Yes. No, wait, hanging out with me is *not* a punishment."

Brix laughs. "I'll watch whatever you want me to watch, and I promise I'll keep my groping hands to myself until you tell me I don't have to anymore."

"I kind of like the groping hands."

His lips touch mine nice and slow, and then he taps me to stand. "You go put something on the TV. I'll go find some popcorn. Trav should have some stashed somewhere."

"Confession …"

Brix's eyes widen. "What is it?"

"I hate popcorn."

He gasps. "You're a monster, and this will never work."

"It makes me so thirsty," I whine.

"There's this thing. They call it water. You might have heard of it."

"But then I need to piss during the movie. Popcorn is the worst movie snack ever."

"I don't think we can be together."

I pout.

"Okay, fine." Brix sighs dramatically. "I'll pretend this dark side of your soul doesn't exist, but you're asking a lot of me."

We move into the living room with the giant hundred-inch TV. Brix sits on the edge of the couch and leans back, lying half on and half off it, with his arm running along the top.

I fit next to him and lie with my head on his chest.

This. This is what I want.

"What are we watching?" Brix asks.

"Hmm, to continue to torture you or put you out of your misery …"

"I love chick flicks and rom-coms."

Something in his voice doesn't ring true. "Oh good, me too. They're my favorite."

Brix groans. "I was lying, hoping you'd pick the opposite."

I chuckle. "I know."

"How did you know?"

I lift my head. "You have a tell."

Brix's finger trails over my cheek, where my dimple supposedly appears when I'm lying. "You picked up on my tell?" he asks.

"Yep, but unlike mine, yours is in your voice."

Brix smiles at me weirdly. As if he never expected me to understand him the way he understands me.

Things might be strained right now because of my stupid stalker person, but there's no doubt this feels right.

Being with Brix is right.

I scroll through the options on the TV when one pops up on-screen. "Ooh, I haven't seen this yet. Blake invited me to the premiere, but I couldn't go."

Brix side-eyes me. "I'm starting to realize why you haven't heard from Blake."

"I was on tour!" Okay, that excuse is kind of shitty. "Fine, you have a point. But I'm going to watch it now, so that counts."

We settle in for the movie, and Blake is a surprisingly good actor. It's an action flick—all explosives and slow-motion scenes with lots of up-close shots of Blake's typical Hollywood face. It's a mindless plot, but Blake is really good in it. In seven years of performing with him, I had no idea acting was something he'd want to go into.

I should've known that. We were close once, and I can't help wondering what happened.

When did we become five selfish individuals instead of a team?

I can't pinpoint an exact time, but I know the last two years together, things were hard for all of us. We were over it.

"Isn't the sequel to this filming now?" Brix asks.

"Yeah. I heard it's going to be the next big series like *Die Hard*. If he plays it right, Blake could be Coby Godspeed until he's in his sixties like Bruce Willis."

Brix runs his hand down my arm. "You should give him a call."

"I don't know Bruce Willis," I joke.

"Funny. I mean Blake."

I nod. "I will when this ends."

"Spoiler: he kills the bad guy in the end."

I elbow him. "You did not just do that."

"I haven't seen it, but he has to get the bad guy. They always do. And then when the second one comes along, there'll be a new bad guy."

"What happens when they run out of bad guys?"

Brix squeezes me tight. "In my experience, more bad guys replace the old bad guys. Take out the leader of an extremist group, someone's waiting next in line to take their place."

"That's sad." And it reminds me that even if they catch the guy who's coming after me, there'll be another one at some point. Then again … "At least you'll always have a job with me if that theory is true."

We fall silent at that because it's a reminder we're not a normal couple watching a movie on a normal date night.

We get lost in explosions, car chases, and killing, and when the credits roll, I sit up.

I really should call Blake. I feel shitty about not keeping in touch with the guys. "I'll be right back."

But when I go to our bedroom and find my phone, I see three missed calls from Gideon.

He didn't call Brix, so it can't be that much of an emergency, but my heart pounds as I call him back.

"Is everything okay?" he answers.

"Shouldn't I be asking you that?"

"I figured you were either dead or out of hearing range."

"I'm really feeling the love here."

"It's nothing important, so I wasn't going to disrupt whatever you and your boyfriend were doing."

"We were doing nasty kinky shit all over your cousin's house."

"Don't need to know."

I laugh. "We were watching Blake's movie, actually."

"Nice. Well, I'm calling because you apparently promised Evah that if her fragrance launch was successful, you'd back it up with your own on her line?"

I bite my lip. "I might have said something along those lines. Does it still count now we're broken up?"

"Doing this could be a good career move, and it would solidify the friend angle you guys went with during the breakup. It'll dispel the rumors that claim shit is getting nasty."

"I'll do it."

"Great. I already have Jamie bringing you the contracts. She actually should be nearly there."

"Hey, Gideon? There's this cool new thing. You might not have heard of it because you're so old and everything, but it's called email. It's faster than making my assistant drive out to Palm Desert."

"They need to be signed in person, and they want the original copies."

I huff. "If you say so. Hey, any update from the label yet?"

Gideon goes silent for a beat. "Look, I'm going to be honest. I'm not sure there'll be a compromise on this. They know you're going through a lot right now, and they're sympathetic, but ..."

I hang my head. "They're flat-out refusing to produce an album with a new sound?"

"They're convinced it won't perform well. They said if you really want to go that route, that you can with your next album ... under a different label."

"They're threatening to drop me?"

"You're contracted for one more album. There are clauses in the touring section of your contract that say if your sales are below a certain level, you won't tour. But even with a shitty-selling album, I don't think Harley Valentine could ever sell below the threshold."

"So, let me get this straight. I have to record the songs they force me to, tour when they tell me to, and I get absolutely no creative control? Even after all these years of loyalty?"

"It all comes down to money," Gideon says.

"What will it take to get out of my contract for the second album? Is that an option?"

"Whoa-ho-ho, no. God no. You don't have that amount in net worth let alone liquid assets."

"Are you sure? Eleven still has royalties coming in, and my first solo album is still in the charts."

"Let me run the numbers, but you know how hard Mason had to fight to get out from under Joystar when Eleven broke up."

"Can you check Eleven's contract and let me know if I'd be stuck to the label through an exclusivity clause or not? Or did my new contract negate the old one?"

"Your new contract negates that one. The only time it would be a problem is if Eleven wanted to get back together, but that'll never happen, so that clause doesn't matter."

I purse my lips. "I'm not saying I want to get back together with the guys, but can you look at what it'd take to release Eleven as an act from the label?"

Gideon is silent.

"Gideon?"

"Has one of the other guys contacted you or something? Why would you want to look at getting back together when you have *everything*?"

It's not like I'm desperate to get back together with them or anything, but I'd be lying if I said I hadn't thought about it at all. I liked performing with them, and I didn't realize how much of a support system we had until it was gone. Ryder always jokes about doing it when we're forty, and if that does happen, I want to be able to do it on our own.

"If I'm preparing to leave, I want to cut all ties. Completely. They've fucked me and the other guys over so much already. I want to walk away with everything."

"Leave me with it."

"Thank you."

"Now, go back to your vacation."

I scoff. "You think hiding out is a vacation? Remind me to never go away with you."

"Trust Trav to do his thing. He knows what he's doing. It'll all be over soon."

Everyone keeps telling me that, and yet Webber is still evading him. My faith is wearing a little thin.

CHAPTER 26
BRIX

"EVERYTHING OKAY?" I ask when Harley reemerges from the bedroom.

He went in there to talk to Blake, but the conversation must not have gone well by the look on his face. I stand from the couch.

"With Blake?" I clarify.

"Oh. Yeah, I didn't call him. I was on the phone with Gideon. The label is still refusing to negotiate."

I hate his label with everything that I am. I hold out my arms for him. "I'm sorry they're dickheads."

Harley wraps himself around me. "They're so dickheads. Oh, also, Jamie's on her way out here. There are papers I need to sign for an Evah thing."

I stiffen, and Harley pulls back.

"What? What's wrong? You don't still think it's her, do you?"

"No. I mean, of course not." I might.

My phone starts ringing. "It's Trav."

The hope in Harley's eyes is heartbreaking because I don't think this is the call we've been waiting for. Gut feeling again.

I hit Answer and don't put it on speaker. "Update?"

"Get Harley into the safe room."

What the fuck?

I try to keep a passive expression, but Harley's face falls. Either he heard it or I'm not good at hiding my panic.

"What's happened?" I grab Harley's arm and drag him toward Trav's bedroom.

"We were watching the hotel footage when we got a hit on Webber's credit card."

"Where is he?" I growl.

"Gas station." He pauses. "In Rancho Mirage."

He knows where we are.

There's a knock at the front door, and Harley and I flinch.

I push Harley down the hallway. "Trav, get your asses here ASAP," I bark into the phone.

"On it. Don't kill him until we get there."

"Can't make any promises."

We disconnect the call.

"What's happening?" Harley asks.

"Well, I'm assuming that's Jamie at the door, but Trav tells me Webber's in town, so I'm not taking any chances. It can't be a coincidence."

"W-what?"

"I'm going to put you in Trav's room. It's the most secure. It has safety bars on the windows, a dead bolt on the door, provisions in the closet, and—"

"And Trav voluntarily has that in his bedroom?"

"It doubles as the panic room for this place. I guess it makes him feel safer, and he can sleep at night without worrying about someone coming to get him. Travis West has had a bounty on his head more times than I can count."

"*What do you guys actually do?*" Harley's freaking out, but I can't help finding it cute.

A laugh escapes. "Right now? I'm protecting you, so grab what you need and get your cute little ass into Trav's room."

"What about you? Everyone else won't get here in time, and—"

I place my hands on his shoulders. "I've got this. I can handle whatever is thrown at me."

Harley looks down at his feet. "Do you really think Jamie ..."

"I hope not, but we can't get into this right now."

Harley's phone starts ringing in his pocket, and he flinches. When he pulls it out, his thumb hovers over the green button.

"It's Jamie probably wondering why we're not answering the door."

"Leave it. I'll go get her when I know you're secure. You're my first priority."

"What if Webber is out there? You can't leave her out there on her own."

"Harley," I say, my voice stern. "I need you to promise me something. No matter what you hear, do not come out of that room, okay? Not if you hear gunshots, not if—"

"I can't lose you."

"You won't. Let's get you safe."

He glances around the uncluttered and very basic room, probably expecting something like the rest of the house, but this is Trav's space, and Trav is a necessities-only type of guy. No frills. Just what he needs to survive. I think it's the Ranger in him.

"And I'm supposed to stay in here for how long?" Harley asks.

I move toward the closet. "Until the threat is neutralized."

"N-neutralized?"

"Taken care of? Umm, arrested?" Let's go with that.

I pull down a bulletproof vest and some supplies I might need and then go to Trav's lockbox of weapons he keeps in here.

Harley watches me suit up with this wide-eyed panicked look on his face.

I walk over to the desk in the corner of Trav's room that has computer screens on top. I know they're connected to the house security system, but I don't want Harley watching if everything goes south, so I'm not going to let him in on that particular nugget of information. Instead, I open the drawer and pull out some stationery. I know the way to my man's heart. "To pass the time."

He takes the pens and paper but stares at them like they're foreign objects. "I won't be able to write right now."

"Whenever you're worried about me, write. Whenever you're thinking of even peeking out that door, write. Promise me."

Harley nods. "I promise."

I hug him and hold him close.

The Kevlar is thick between us, and I think it only serves to freak him out more.

He tucks his head under my chin. "It's hard for me not to order you to stay in here with me and pretend we're not even here."

"Kind of defeats the purpose of hiring a bodyguard."

"I know." He sighs.

"Would you ask the same of Iris?"

"No."

I kiss the top of his head. "Look on the bright side. After tonight, this will all be over."

"Until the next bad guy …"

"No. I think Webber is a once-in-a-lifetime kind of psycho. But even if he's not, I'll still be here. I'll protect you for as long as you want." I bring my lips down on his mouth and kiss him softly. "Forever, if you'll have me."

His eyes flutter, and then he's staring at me with love and awe in those shiny dark blue orbs. "Forever?"

"Forever."

Walking away from him and leaving him in that room is harder and more daunting than what I have to do now. No matter how secure the door is.

I crack my neck and stretch out my back, getting into focus mode.

With my gun cocked, I make my move toward the main foyer.

I have to compartmentalize and forget that Harley is in this building. I have to forget that he's in danger and look at his assistant like any other perp.

In any other job, I'd have no qualms about taking out the target and being done with it. They're a threat, end of story. But this isn't the world we usually work in. This is Harley's world.

I have to get my head in the right mindset. Interrogate first. Act later.

The knocking is more insistent now, but just before I open it, I take out my phone and check the security cameras. I've been watching them every night since we got here after Harley's gone to sleep just to be sure. It's why I've been climbing into bed later than usual. I haven't wanted him to worry.

Jamie's the only one out front, and she's frustrated by the look of it.

Still, I'm prepared in case Webber ambushes the place as soon as I open the door.

He doesn't.

Jamie lets herself in with a huff. "Finally. Shit, what were you guys doing that it took forever to—uh, you know what? I actually don't want to know. Here are the contracts Harley needs to sign."

I close the door and lock it, the sound echoing around the foyer.

That's when she looks up at me and notices my gear and my gun. Her eyes widen. "What ... why—"

I don't know if this is an act or not. I don't know if anyone can play dumb that well. "Put your hands on the wall."

"What?"

"I need to check you for weapons."

"What's—"

"Jamie. Hands. Wall. Now."

She does as I ask, and I go through her bag and check the folder of papers for Harley.

"I'm gonna pat you down."

"*Why?*" she exclaims.

"Where is he?" I ask.

"Who?"

"Webber."

She looks more confused. "W-Webber?"

Fuck it, I don't have time for *this*.

When I'm satisfied she's clean, I point my gun at her. "Walk."

"What the fuck is going on?" she hisses.

"Go down the hall on the right," I instruct as I kill all the lights in the entryway and living room. I'll put her in one of the other bedrooms while I find this asshole.

"Brix—"

"I don't know if you're involved or not, but I'm not taking any chances. If you're not involved, this is for your own safety. If you are, well, nothing could keep you safe from me."

"What is going on?" she asks again.

"Webber's here. Or, at least in the area. How did he know where to find us?"

"Wait, he's here? Where?"

Good question.

"Get in this room and stay there until I come get you," I tell Jamie.

"But—"

"You don't want to know what will happen if you leave this room. Got it?"

Her eyes well up.

"I mean it, Jamie."

She looks terrified, but I can't rule her out as being part of this just yet. She nods, and her chin wobbles.

Making my way into the formal dining room, I close the blinds, turn off the lights, and fire up Trav's laptop.

My ears are on alert for every sound.

From the computer, I can pull up more than one image around the house at a time. There are cameras covering every angle outside, but inside they're just in the hallways and main living areas.

My leg bounces because there's nothing here.

No one's here.

That's when a camera picks up movement. A figure, I'm pretty sure it's a guy, crouches as he runs toward the back of the house. The house is secure, so unless he's going to break shit and bring attention to himself, I don't see him breaking in until he's ready.

The figure hovers by the fuse box outside.

With only night vision available, it's hard to work out exactly what he's doing, or if it's even Webber, but I assume he's planning to cut the power to be like some villain in a scary movie.

Not the smartest move considering that will give me warning to be ready for him. It's not like he knows I'm already aware of his presence. Also, if cutting the power is his plan, he's gonna struggle. Not only could I kick his ass in the dark or light, Trav has a failsafe in place for shit like this. Trav's panic room and security system run on two completely separate power supplies.

Webber appears unarmed from what I can see, but I can't guarantee that.

He gives up trying to cut the power and makes his way around the side of the house. I watch as he approaches the front door.

I sit and wait, letting the adrenaline pump through me.

As much as I want to go out there, guns blazing, and take this fucker down the quickest way I know how, there are more tactical ways to handle this.

And, okay, maybe I'm finding this a little bit more exciting than I should, but I can't help it.

Years of training make me live for this shit.

When the click of the front door opening sounds through the quietness, I realize I'm not dealing with an amateur here.

That's what he must've been doing at the fuse box—disabling the electronic lock to the front door.

Smart man.

Smarter than I was anticipating. Had I not been expecting him, everything would appear as normal.

He's next to silent, and if Harley and I were in bed, I wouldn't be able to hear him.

If he was able to get in here that fast, it means I might have to take him out faster than planned.

He can't get anywhere near Harley. I can't let him.

I close the laptop to stop the screen glow from giving away my position and then take the gun and slink to the floor, crawling my way as silently as possible toward the living room.

Going in blind sucks, but that's better than being too late.

I manage to get behind the couch when his light footsteps reach the room.

They may be featherlight, but they're loud to my ears.

I control my breathing and try to calm the raging storm inside me waiting to unleash hell.

He's almost at the couch now, coming around the right-hand side.

I run the options through my head.

One, shoot out his ankle. Two, try to neutralize him by taking him by surprise and tackling him where he is now. Both will work if he's not armed.

But in what world would he come here unarmed?

He moves slowly and cautiously but gets closer with every second.

The third option is to sneak around the couch when he passes and come at him from behind.

Now to be able to do it without making a sound.

His foot appears in front of me.

Right. All plans are FUBAR now.

In the blink of an eye, I'm on my feet and launching myself at him.

He hadn't seen me yet, and he stumbles back but not far enough.

I take him down, but during the fall, my side slams into Trav's glass side table next to the couch, and I lose grip on my gun.

Motherfucker, that hurts.

Though Trav will be glad to know his furniture is fucking strong. It didn't even crack. I can't say the same for the ugly-ass vase that was on top of it, though.

Luckily, Webber breaks the fall, landing on shards of broken glass. He grunts in pain, but when I land on top of him, he throws a punch to my jaw.

The hit isn't solid, not even enough to throw me off-kilter, but pain shoots down my neck.

It's cute he thinks he can fight me.

I feel around for my gun because it's impossible to see in this light.

Webber squirms while pinned underneath me, but he ain't going anywhere.

That's when a glowing blue spark lights up in his hand. Shit, Taser.

I roll off him and scramble on my hands and knees to get away, but he extends his arm, swiping at me. The telltale tick-tick-tick sound of the Taser makes me realize the odds have shifted a little.

We both get to our feet, and I'm regretting not taking the time to stash more guns around the place.

Though, as much as I want to shoot this fucker, it'll be a lot less messy if we can take him in alive. Plus, Trav would never believe me if I said, "I had to shoot him. He was coming at me." I can hear it now. *You know about thirty different ways to take a man down with your bare hands. Try again.*

"Drop the Taser and I won't hurt you."

Webber scoffs. "Sure, okay."

"All right. I did try to be nice first."

I've taken down bigger guys who were holding much more powerful weapons.

Instead of facing me to fight, he turns on his heel and tries to run.

Seriously, so adorable.

It's a shame he's a fucking psychopath who wants to hurt my boyfriend or I'd want to keep him as a pet.

I'm even tempted to give him a head start, but Harley's safety is one thing I won't compromise just so I can have some fun.

I reach Webber right before he hits the wet bar at the back of the living room. "Thirsty?"

Grabbing the back of his shirt, I slam him into the bar so hard bottles and glass practically explode around him.

Trav will make me pay for that, but it was well worth it.

Webber's like a dead weight as I drop him to the floor. I stand on his shoulder blade, forcing him onto his stomach.

His hand with the Taser is still free, but no matter how he tries to get me with it, he can't while he's pinned beneath my foot.

I twist it in a little harder, and he calls out.

Kneeling, my knee digs into his back as I take the Taser out of his hand. He tries to hold on, but *bitch, please*. I wrestle it free and throw it on the couch.

He moans in pain, but I put more pressure on my knee just for good measure.

"Why are you here?"

"Fuck you," he spits out.

"You wish."

"I'm not talking."

"That's fine. We'll just call the cops, and they can make you talk. How many years were you looking at for stalking again?"

He doesn't reply.

Breathing heavy, I pull out some zip ties I grabbed from Trav's supplies and secure Webber's wrists behind his back.

Fuck, I love my job. Even if this will be a rarity when I work for Harley permanently.

Despite this fleeting moment, the sacrifice for him will be worth it.

CHAPTER 27
HARLEY

I FIGHT a nauseated feeling the whole time Brix is gone, but after what feels like a lifetime, I lose the contents of my stomach in Trav's bathroom.

Knowing Brix is handling it the only way he knows how, I don't know what I'm going to walk into when he inevitably comes to get me.

If he comes to get me.

That's what made me finally hurl—the thought of losing him.

I can't lose him. I just can't.

I use some of Trav's mouthwash and splash my face with cool water.

The keypad to the panic room beeps and the door opens. I tense because it could be anyone.

"Harley?"

Brix.

"Bathroom," I croak.

"Oh, fuck, what's wrong?" He appears beside me.

I throw my arms around him. "You're here. You're … What happened?"

He runs a hand through my sweaty hair. "Shh, I got you. Are you okay?"

I hold him tighter. "I am now."

"I have good news and bad news," he murmurs into my hair.

"Good news?"

"I got the guy."

I pull back and frown. "Bad news?"

"He refuses to talk … unless it's with you."

"No," I blurt but almost immediately want to take it back.

"Done. The cops can handle him."

"W-where is he?"

My boyfriend smiles. But it's not a normal smile. All the jokes about kill lists and neutralizing people seem like facts when he smiles like that. "He's … a little tied up at the moment."

"Tied … up."

Brix nods proudly.

"Do I really want to see this?" I ask.

"I don't know. Do you?"

"A little, yeah."

Brix holds my hand. "I've got you."

He leads me toward the living room, and there's my tormentor.

My stalker.

Bound with his hands and feet tied together with zip ties behind his back, his face is squashed against the floor. He struggles against his restraints, wiggling like a caterpillar on speed.

My memory of him from the night he broke in is hazy now. Has been ever since it happened. He appeared so dominating in my vision.

Then when I saw him at the courthouse, he looked like a remorseful college kid who made a mistake.

Now, he's almost unrecognizable with his bared teeth, his flushed face, and pure anger flowing from him.

"Let me go," he says.

"Hmm, nah," Brix replies breezily. "Here's Harley. Say what you want to him while you've got the chance."

"You ruined my life," Webber mutters.

"Uh, I did what now?" *Did he really just fucking say that to me?* "You break into my home, you terrorize me, and I'm the one who ruined your life?"

"My school found out about the conviction and took away my scholarship."

"How did you find us?" I ask.

"Why don't you ask your pretty little assistant."

My heart sinks. "J-Jamie?"

"Your bodyguards are so fucking dumb. They run circles around you and don't watch her."

Brix and I turn to each other.

"She's not blind," Brix says. "She would've noticed you following her for three hours. So, how did you know where we were?"

He huffs. "Can't give away all my secrets."

Brix narrows his eyes and storms out of the room, leaving me alone with the crazy person.

I don't know how smart that is, no matter how contained the psycho is.

I kinda feel like kicking Webber. I won't, but I want to. I can see those headlines now.

Harley Valentine Charged with Assault for Kicking Home Invader.

"It was an honest mistake, you know," he says quietly.

"Breaking into my home, threatening me with a pipe bomb, or following me up here?"

"The first one. The pipe bomb was fake. I didn't want to hurt you. I just wanted to *scare* you."

"*Why?*"

"You're famous. You're rich. You have everything, and yet you took my future from me. After you rejected me and had me arrested, I wanted to take something from you."

I grit my teeth. "Here's some advice. One, never think someone else has more than you just because their success is measurable." Brix taught me that. "And two, if you don't break into people's homes, you won't get arrested … Dumbass."

Brix reappears from the hall with Jamie. She looks so small next to him. Especially with his beefy hand gripping her arm tight.

"Jamie …" I want to go to her, but it's clear Brix doesn't want me to. He scowls at me and shakes his head.

He pulls her over to us so she can see Webber's face.

"You know him?" Brix growls.

"Yeah. He's Harley's stalker."

Webber smiles. "Hey, iPhone34QZXB1."

That triggers something. She pales and her mouth drops open.

"What?" Brix asks.

Her lip trembles. "He … he looks different. He had his hair different and wore glasses, but …"

"Who is he?" Brix asks.

"He fixed my phone a few months ago. Like, right before you went on tour. He's from Rent A Geek."

Webber laughs. "Okay, there goes the rest of my secrets."

"He's been in her phone," Brix says.

"Cloned it," Webber says. "It's amazing what information you can get from an iPhone. Places you've been. Touring schedules. You can record phone calls with a simple app. Find out the user's current location …"

"Wait, *before* the tour?" I realize something. "You didn't follow me home from the concert that night, did you? You weren't even there."

Webber laughs some more, and it's either me or it's starting to sound maniacal. "Oh, I was there."

"Honest mistake, my ass," I mumble.

"I asked about your precious Evah. I asked about your plans now the tour was done. I asked you a million questions in that VIP room, and yet you still didn't recognize me when I was in your kitchen. You don't give a shit about your fans."

That hurts more than anything he could've done if he'd have gotten to me tonight. I also know it's complete bullshit. I respect the hell out of my fans, and I've sacrificed a lot of myself over the years to give them what they want.

I glance at Brix. "I'm done here. I don't need to hear anymore. Are the cops on their way?"

The sound of whirring helicopter blades gets louder and louder.

"Is that them?" I ask.

"Uh, no. That will be Trav. One thing about him is he doesn't like cops snooping around his shit. So, uh, yeah, he'll take care of … this." He gestures to Webber.

I cock my head. "Is this another joke about burying bodies and shit?"

"Who says we're joking when we say stuff like that?"

Webber lets out a pained noise and fights against his restraints. Brix watches him like it's entertaining.

The ties break skin until Webber's wrists look angry and bloody.

"Ugh, don't bleed all over the rug," Brix tells him. "Trav will kill me."

Just as he says that, Trav, Iris, and Gideon appear from down the hallway, having come through the back of the house.

Iris and Trav are armed up to their eyeballs. Gideon looks like Gideon. Always put together.

"Who am I killing?" Trav asks.

Brix points to Webber. "Him. He's bleeding all over your dead zebra. He, uh, also smashed up some stuff. It was all him."

"Damn," Iris says. "Looks like you had fun."

"I don't even care about the mess. I'm more fixated on the fact you didn't kill him," Trav says. "My little boy is all grown up." He sniffs and wipes a fake tear away.

Gideon rolls his eyes. "Please, all you motherfucking badasses are like rottweilers. You all look scary but are just big puppy dogs." He reaches over to mess up Trav's hair.

"You promised your mom you wouldn't do that anymore," Trav grumbles.

"I will never stop giving you shit for naming your company—"

My eyes widen. "Wait … MB. Motherfucking badasses? That's what Mike Bravo stands for?"

Gideon laughs, and I can't help joining in.

"You know, considering the amount of weaponry in this room right now, you two are pretty cocky," Trav says.

"Brix will never let you hurt me."

Brix rubs his chin. "I dunno. Never get in between a man and—"

"His motherfucking badass friends?" I quip.

Brix pushes me toward his boss. "Trav, he's all yours."

"Traitor!" I exclaim.

Gideon approaches and looks at me sympathetically. "Are you okay?"

I let out a loud breath. "You … you came all this way to see if I'm okay?"

"Free helicopter ride." He smiles. "But seriously, are you okay?"

Am I even able to answer that right now? "I … think so? It's over, right? So I should be fine."

"I don't think that's how traumatic events work, but I'll let you have that for now."

Ugh. He's so going to bring up seeing a therapist. He mentioned it once or twice after the break-in, and I refused.

"Right. So …" Trav cuts in. "How are we handling this?"

"What do you mean, how are we handling this?" I ask. "With cops."

Trav winces. "Eww, fine. Play it that way. I have a DEA agent who owes me a favor."

Iris, behind him, makes a kissy noise and lets out an "Ooooh."

Trav levels him with a single look.

I wish I knew that trick.

"Let's clean this up," Trav says, and he and Iris cut Webber's legs free and lead him outside.

He struggles the whole way, throwing obscenities and more threats my way. "I'll be out in two years tops."

Yaaaay.

Brix steps behind me. "We'll make sure he gets more than that."

I lean back against him. "It's over?"

He nods. "It's all over."

Jamie's sobs echo around the room. "I didn't know … I promise you I didn't know. I should have. I saw Webber's mug shot and thought he looked familiar, but I couldn't … I didn't know where from."

I approach her and wrap her in a huge hug. "It's okay. I believe you."

"I'm so sorry."

Brix folds his arms. "How did he know you were Harley Valentine's assistant? He got a lot of information from your phone, but Harley's in there under another name."

She stiffens in my arms.

I pull back. "Jamie?"

"I-I don't know. I swear I didn't say anything."

"Could he have matched up venues and concert dates?" I ask. "I mean, it might not have my name, but it'd be obvious she's a PA to someone famous."

"Possibly," Brix says.

"Oh my God, it's all my fault." Jamie's uncontrollably sobbing now.

"It's okay." I hold her close. "You couldn't have known."

Brix rubs his chin. "It does bring up some new safety concerns. Her phone led him right to us. And it's not the first time a celebrity's phone's been hacked. Except this time, they went to the next available source."

"So, we don't get our shit fixed at Rent A Geek," I say. "Problem solved."

Brix grumbles something about it being far from solved, but he lets it go. For now.

"I can't lose this job," Jamie pleads.

"You're not going anywhere."

Both Brix and Gideon look at me like I just made an unkeepable promise, but she made a mistake. A simple mistake anyone could have made.

Of all people, Brix and Gideon know how easy it is to make a mistake, and theirs were conscious mistakes. Hers was an accident.

"Jamie, I'll drive you back to LA," Gideon says.

"The contracts you need to sign for Evah are in the room Brix put me in," she says solemnly.

Gideon turns to me. "You can bring them back signed tomorrow. Now this is done, it's business as usual."

I want to groan, but I think going straight back into work mode will be good for me.

They leave, Jamie with her head held low, and suddenly the night's events leave me drained.

Brix steps closer. "Let's go to bed."

We make our way to our room at the back of the property and strip down. I make a mental note to ask Brix to wear Kevlar next time we have sex because it's hot as he takes it all off.

Not tonight, though.

Tonight, I want to lie in his arms and convince myself it's all really over.

As soon as his strong arms surround me, I break down. Tears flow, and I don't even know why.

"It's okay, baby," Brix whispers. "It's over."

"I don't know why I'm crying."

"It's an adrenaline crash. It happens. I'm here."

"I thought I was going to lose you. I thought …" I shake my head.

He nudges me. "You need more faith in what I've been trained to do. I will never let anyone hurt you. Ever."

"I love you," I blurt like it's no big deal when it is. It's a bigger deal than a wardrobe malfunction on Grammy night.

It's monumental and something I never thought would happen again. Not to me. Not while I'm still living this life.

Brix doesn't do anything. He just lies next to me as still as he can.

When I pull back and look up into his eyes, he blinks at me.

And now I'm holding my breath, wondering why I chose right now to put that out there.

I had an hour and a half in a locked room to think of nothing else other than losing Brix. I could blame the adrenaline, the worry, or the life-or-death situation we were in. But that doesn't change the way I feel about him.

"I want us to be more than a pop star and his bodyguard. I want—"

Without warning, Brix's mouth is on mine.

He kisses me with everything he has. I feel it in the way he caresses my head and holds me close. And when he breaks it off, he doesn't go far.

His forehead stays on mine, and I breathe him in.

Spicy cologne with that badass scent that's all Brix.

My Brix.

"I love you too." Brix cups my cheek. "I've wanted to say it. Been wanting to for a while, but I'm kinda new to love, and I've been struggling with how to define what it was—the ache in my chest when I look at you. It's longing even though you're right in front of me."

"It could also be the tickling sensation of doubt. Or maybe you're having a heart attack. You should probably get that checked out." I have to joke because this is intense, and I don't know how to handle it.

I didn't think I'd ever find someone who'd put up with my bullshit. Who could see past it all.

Brix's thumb runs along my cheek. "Maybe that ache is for the uncertain future we have—the anticipation of losing the very thing in front of you because if that happens, your heart might very well implode with the pain."

My breath is stilted as I manage to get out, "That's how I've felt about you for a long time, but it wasn't until tonight when you walked out of that safe room and I didn't know what was to come that it all really hit me. I thought about losing you and how it would damn near kill me."

"You're not going to lose me. Ever."

"Promise?"

"We're a team."

"Pop star and bodyguard?" That's not enough for me.

"Partners, Harley. I want to be partners in every sense of the word."

"Partners," I murmur.

Brix seals his promise with a kiss that makes me forget the events of the past few weeks. He makes me forget that my contract with the label is in the toilet and that my life isn't exactly stable right now.

It all fades away as Brix's tongue teases mine. He moves his mouth over mine, slowly but confidently.

"Mm. You're doing it again."

He kisses his way over my jaw. "Doing what?"

"Making me think you and I are the only ones on the planet right now. No labels. No stalkers. Just us."

"For tonight, we can be. We'll face everything else tomorrow."

"Mm, tomorrow."

CHAPTER 28
BRIX

TRAV WAKES me up at stupid o'clock by knocking on our bedroom door. I heard him and Iris come back at some point during the night, and I was thankful they let us sleep.

Apparently, sleep time is over.

Luckily, Harley's too out of it to even stir, but as I throw on some clothes and follow Trav through the house into his room, I worry something went wrong with Webber's arrest.

He gestures for me to sit in the chair as he leans on his desk.

"What's wrong?" I ask. "What happened with Webber?"

He waves me off. "That went fine. We found the silver car he'd been driving a few miles down the road. It's registered to some kid at UCLA. Along with the stalking charges, we handed over his multiple laptops and shit we found in the car." His serious expression gives way to the faintest of smiles.

"What did you put on his laptop?"

Another small smile. "You really don't want to know. What Webber said last night is true. He'd be out in two years if we didn't provide the cops with *all* the information. At least this way he'll get a few more years added to his sentence."

"Seriously, what did you do?"

"Nothing!" He coughs and mutters something about cyber terrorism.

Best. Boss. Ever.

"Anyway, why I woke you up. I thought I should give you some warning."

"Warning?" Fuck, what now?

"Mike Bravo isn't going to renew the pop star's contract when it's up."

Okay, *that* I was not expecting.

"Too much work?" I joke, but on the inside, I'm trying like hell to work out a way for Trav to keep it.

"Well, we certainly saw more action than I was expecting. But the truth is, this was never a case we would've taken under normal circumstances. You know that."

"I do."

Trav crosses his legs at the ankle, and his intimidating stature is even bigger than usual. "So, here's the deal. You have a decision to make."

I suck in a sharp breath. My position with Mike Bravo or Harley. The words *I quit* are on the tip of my tongue, and I never thought it would be that easy a decision.

Harley will want to keep me as his bodyguard, and while I don't know the logistics of how it will work if I'm not with Mike Bravo, we'll find a way.

"I want you to take over the contract." Trav's words pull my thoughts up short. "Effective immediately if it works for Harley. I spoke to Gideon about it last night, and he's on board."

"What?"

"You said your future with Mike Bravo was unsure, and I can't afford to be a man down permanently. If you take the contract, you can pick your own team of guys for Harley's security detail."

"What about—"

He points at me. "Don't even think about poaching any of my men. Iris is mine, okay?"

I laugh. "Please, he'd be bored out of his skull."

"True. The thing is, I don't want to lose you, but I think I already have."

I don't answer him. I don't need to.

"And I know you can handle this assignment on your own with contractors working under you for those times when Harley's on the road and you need more hands on deck. The budget on this gig is hard to let go of, though. My cut alone is—" He hesitates but ultimately shakes it off. "No, this is what's best for everyone."

"So, what you're saying is …"

Trav grins, like honest to God *grins*. "It means, Brix, that you're fired."

"I think you got a little too much enjoyment out of that, boss."

He holds out his hand for me to shake, and when I take it, he pulls me into a hug. He slaps my back twice and then lets me go. "You'll be missed, but I'm confident this is the right thing for you."

"And if I ever need help like I did with Webber?"

"You handled that just fine, but if you do ever need us, I know how much you're going to get paid, so be prepared to pay through the nose for us to rescue your ass."

"What, no family-and-friends discount?"

Trav slaps my shoulder. "Go find your man and tell him the good news. Then get the fuck out of my house."

I go to leave when I remember the car. "Oh, umm, what about your car? Mine is—"

"Gone. I didn't want that piece of shit sitting in my driveway longer than it needed to be. Keep the Range Rover. Think of it as a parting gift."

My initial reaction is to say *no*. Of course it is. I didn't earn it, so I don't deserve it. But if being with Harley has taught me anything, it's that I need to accept help from others and let people in.

"Th-thank you," I stammer.

"Take this opportunity and look after that dad of yours, okay?"

My face must give away my shock. Harley said the guys knew—that Iris had said so. Hearing how much they know is jarring, but at the same time, a weight has been lifted. I'm not being held down by secrets anymore.

Trav's face takes on an expression that's part sympathy, part smugness, and part annoyance. "Did you know Samuel Reins was my commanding officer before I became a Ranger?"

My dad … was Trav's superior?

"You really think the timing on your Mike Bravo offer was a coincidence?"

At the time, while I was drowning in medical bills and trying to find a place for my dad to get treatment, I thought the offer to move to the private sector was a get out of jail free card. I didn't give it much more thought.

"You've known everything this whole time and you never said anything?"

"Doing something for someone you care about isn't about the glory or the thanks. Your dad is a good man, and so are you, Brix. I helped the only way I knew how."

"Thank you. So much. Like—"

"I just said I don't need a thanks." He disappears, leaving me stunned.

By the time I shake off my unease about the entire team knowing my situation—I know it shouldn't be there, but old habits die hard—and go back to our room, Harley's awake.

He sits up. The worry lines prominently across his forehead make me want to wrap him in my arms. "Where were you?"

I start packing without answering him.

"Brix? What happened?" he asks again.

I grin at him.

"Nolan Brixton Reins."

"I think that's the first time you've ever called me Nolan. Or full-named me."

"You're freaking me out. You deserve to be full-named."

I climb back into bed and pull Harley against me. He's shirtless, so I take advantage of his bare skin and run my hand down his back. "Hi. My name is Brix. As in dumb as bricks. And I'm your new head of security. Nice to meet you."

"What?"

I laugh. "Trav just told me he thinks I should take over your contract."

"You can't be fired? Like, ever?"

"You're stuck with me. I'm not going anywhere. Ever."

"Ever?"

"I will protect you with my life. For my entire life."

"Because you love me?"

"And because I was born to do it."

Harley pulls back. "You're lying, aren't you? You've actually been fired, and I'm never going to see you again."

"What makes you say that?"

"You … *Mr. I don't believe in fate or soul mates or destiny … You* believe you were born to protect me?"

"Well, shit. I guess I do."

"Your song isn't even going to make any sense now."

I laugh. "You can write me more songs. I expect them to be full of love and explosions. '*Explosions of Love and C4*.' Good title."

"Of course, Rambo … my motherfucking badass."

"Never going to live that down, am I? You call me a badass all the time."

"It's one thing for others to say it. It's totally not badass to self-proclaim it."

I lean in and bring my lips to his. "You're free to mock me whenever you want, Pop Star. I wouldn't love you any other way."

"Same goes for you … Badass."

Hmm, I have to wonder if that nickname is better or worse than Rambo.

We've been back in LA a week, and I've barely seen Harley.

He's no closer to coming to an exit agreement with the label, and he has no real plans for if he wins that battle. Or if he loses.

He's been keeping busy doing God knows what—writing new songs, I think—but I've basically only seen him when we've gone to bed each night.

In *our* bed.

That was the first thing we did when we got home. We moved my minimal belongings into his room and turned my bedroom into an office for me.

Which is why, when he appears by parking his ass on my desk with a wide smile on his face, I'm suspicious.

"What did you do?" I lean back in my seat and pretend to be exasperated.

"No. Nuh-uh. You can't go into this already hating the idea before I get to tell you the brilliantness of what it is."

"And now I'm scared."

"Come on, Badass. I swear it's a good idea."

"A good idea that I will like or hate?"

Harley hesitates. Averts his gaze. Flattens his lips.

"Right. That answers that question," I say. I'm totally gonna hate it.

"You might hate it, but once you get over yourself, you're going to love me for it. Or hate me. I haven't decided."

"I already love you, so is it worth risking that?"

Harley nods enthusiastically. "Absolutely." He takes my hand. "Come with me."

I'm totally confused until he leads me to a room he hardly uses. No, wait, I'm still confused.

The room is usually set up like a library with built-in bookshelves along the wall and comfy couches. Which have been pushed outside onto the patio leading to the backyard.

"An empty room? Uh, thank you?"

"I thought … well, I've been thinking … and planning. And doing all the research on how much it'll cost … Okay, well, if we want to get technical, Jamie's been doing most of the work. She's trying to get in your good graces because she's terrified you want to fire her."

I kinda do, but I keep telling myself she couldn't have known her iPhone fix-it guy was a psychopath.

"You want to turn this room into a studio or something?" I ask.

"No. I want to turn this into your father's room."

I blink at him. Then blink again.

"Hear me out. I want to do this for you. I want to hire two full-time nurses to trade off shifts with him. You'll get to see him daily unless we're on tour. But maybe we could arrange for you to fly back every other week or something. I don't know *all* the details yet, but I was thinking"—he goes to the middle of the room—"we could put the bed here. All the medical equipment should fit, and if he was propped up a little, he'd have a great view of the pool—"

"Harley, I can't … I can't accept this. I want to. Fuck, I really want to, but … you do know what kind of undertaking this is, don't you?"

Harley takes calculated steps toward me. "I knew this is how you'd react which is the only reason I didn't go ahead and already organize it behind your back. But, you said it yourself, we're a team now. You and I are in this, and I want to do this for you and your dad. Because I love you more than anything, and I want to give you every-thing you give me."

"What's that?"

"The kind of love I deserve. With all my shit, my baggage, and a career that tries to hold me back, you break through the fog of it all and give me hope. And you always give me a sense of normal. You make me feel loved. Please let me in. Please let me do this for you."

Tears prick my eyes. I'm not a crier. I didn't cry when my mom died. I never cried after Dad's stroke. But watching him wither away in that box I put him in … yeah, that I cry over.

"Okay."

Harley's face lights up. "Okay?"

I manage a small nod. "Just like your new security team, the nurses need to be vetted. You do know what you're doing here, don't you? You're inviting strangers into our home. They'll know we're together …"

Harley jumps up and down. "That's what NDAs are for. I hate NDAs, but for this, it's worth it."

"And what happens if the paparazzi or tabloids catch wind of you housing an old man who's the dad of one of your employees? That won't arouse suspicion?"

"You're my full-time bodyguard. You live with me. They'll think I'm an awesome and caring boss."

I don't buy that.

"Or they'll totally figure out we're together, but I'm so far past giving a shit what will happen if that can of worms is ever opened."

"You really don't care?"

"I'm not going to be shouting our relationship status from the rooftops or anything. I understand why this still needs to be kept under wraps, but I no longer fear the day my sales drop because of who I am. If it happens, it happens. I have the most important thing right here." He pulls me close. "I've learned from past mistakes, and I won't make them again."

I lean in to kiss him, but he pulls back and starts his excited jumping again.

"Ooh, I also didn't tell you the best part."

I love seeing this side of Harley. I love that he's excited about doing something for me and that the gesture is more than I ever could've asked for. I've been doing this on my own for far too long, and having someone there for me … it's hard to get used to, but I want to.

It's impossible to love this man more than I do right in this moment.

"What's the best part?"

"Do you know they have these computer programs for Morse code? If your dad can squeeze your hand, I'm guessing he can tap with his finger. They have this pad thing, and it's connected to a computer, and it can type out what he's saying. I know communication is hard, especially between your dad and his nurses, and—"

I can't take anymore. My heart feels full, but if he doesn't stop talking, I'm going to cry all over the place.

I close the gap between us and crush my mouth to his.

He grunts in surprise but then melts into the kiss and lets me take control. I try to own him with my lips the way his heart owns my soul.

"I love you so fucking much."

He pulls back and looks up at me with a smug expression. "I knew you'd love the idea eventually. I was prepared to convince you with a blowjob."

"Can I take it back? You can't do the nicest thing anyone has ever done for me. I won't let you!"

"No backsies," Harley sings. "I'm going to go and get the process started." He kisses my cheek and rushes off.

I can't even be disappointed about the blowjob.

CHAPTER 29
HARLEY

ONCE THE DETAILS for Brix's dad moving in fall into place, I move on to the next thing on my list.

I have a list.

A *life* list.

In order of priority, it goes: Brix, the label, and then the future of Harley Valentine.

Gideon couldn't find a loophole or an affordable exit strategy, so I've offered the label the next best thing.

I'll give them my last album. I'll even tour for them next year. But after that? I walk away with my name … and Eleven's.

I'm just awaiting their response.

Gideon is pitching it to them that I'm ready to cut all ties because of "creative differences." If they even suspect what I want, there's no way they'll hand over the rights to everything Eleven.

It's a long shot, but the more I've been thinking about it, the more I want to bring the guys back together and do another Eleven album. Maybe even a tour.

But I want to do it differently than the insane Joystar schedule they had us on when we were together. I don't want us to get burned out the way we did.

The plan is to make an album of all solo songs from each of us. Two solo songs each. Five new songs together.

Ryder can produce.

I can manage. Maybe create my own label.

We can have a redo and release an album in *our voice.*

All I have to do is get the guys to agree. That will be a feat in itself because we're so spread out and doing our own things now.

Ryder wanted out because of Kaylee. Mason is God knows where. Blake is in a completely different industry. And Denver has got his own crazy schedule going on.

But I'm getting ahead of myself. I need out of my current contract first. All the rest can come later.

When Gideon arrives and Brix brings him into the living room, my balls jump into my throat.

Gideon is stoic, not giving away anything. "I brought you something."

A voice I know well comes from the entryway. "Hurry up and tell him I'm here."

"She's so impatient." He says that, but you can hear the love in his voice.

"Get your butt in here, woman," I yell.

Evah turns the corner and basically crash-tackles me. I fall backward with her on top of me, and her knee lands suspiciously near my good bits.

"Whoa, there." I push her off me.

She hits the floor next to me with a thud, laughing hard. "Missed you too."

"You almost kicked me in the nuts."

"Yeah, don't hurt those," Brix says. "I kinda like them."

Evah gasps. "No! Really? You guys are together? I knew you had a crush." She shoves me.

I sit up. "You're so violent today."

God, I've missed her.

She looks at Gideon. "You never told me!"

"I think Harley's team has had enough NDA violations this year."

She gets off the floor and approaches him. I expect her to shove him too until she sinks into his arms. "You still could've told me."

"I'm loyal to my job."

"Aww, thanks, man, but I don't have secrets from her, so tell her whatever. For future reference."

They both have this happy glow about them.

"Okay, this is a little weird," I admit. "But good weird. You deserve the best, Evah … which is why I have no idea why you're with him."

"Hey," Gideon complains.

"I'm kidding. I'm happy for you. Both of you."

Gideon looks positively gleeful. "You're about to be happier."

"Really?"

"This will be your last album with Joystar."

"Yes!" I jump to my feet.

"Wait, there's more. I couldn't get you out of the tour—"

I shrug. "Figured."

"But I did get them to agree to a similar tour as the first album. Four months, tops."

"So, if I get this album finished as soon as I can, I could be free in …"

"A year. Max. Eight months if you push really hard. And then you can do whatever you want. Even release a new Eleven album."

That. That is what I want.

"With no cut going to Joystar?"

"Not on the new stuff. The old stuff will get a bump with a new release, and your royalties will be the same on that, but any new songs are all yours. Well … split between you and the other guys, but this is what you wanted."

I take a deep breath and slowly release it. "And coming out?"

Gideon winces. "You're free to do whatever you want, but you know my stance on that."

"You think I should still keep it on the DL." I agree to some extent, but maybe we don't have to be as uptight about trying to hide it.

I'll become looser with my vagueness. Maybe even hint, so when I do come out, no one is shocked.

"You okay?" Brix asks.

I look up into his eyes. "I'm free. I'm really free. I mean, well almost. But the sentiment is the same."

I don't care if the Eleven thing doesn't end up working out. I don't care if my future in music is uncertain without a big label behind my name.

I have what I want—what I need.

Future projects I can look forward to.

A life with a man I'm head over heels in love with.

And something I've never had since becoming famous.

I'm no longer searching for more. I will no longer be exhausting myself by throwing everything into proving my career and defending my accolades.

I have self-worth.

I have happiness.

I bury my head in my boyfriend's chest and know that while he's the one who has given me those things, I believe them in my heart.

As for Brix, I want to give him everything because he deserves it.

He gives me the best thing of all: something to look forward to outside of being famous.

I made him believe in fate.

He makes me believe in love.

THANK YOU

Thank you for reading *Pop Star*! Harley originally appeared as Jay's ex in *Hat Trick*, book five of my *Fake Boyfriend Series*, and while he was misunderstood by a lot of people and his actions were somewhat selfish, I always knew Harley had a good heart and deserved his own HEA.

Brix, Iris, Trav, and the Mike Bravo crew have been in my head for *years*, and while this is their debut, they will be getting a series of their own … eventually. My boy band hasn't had enough time in the spotlight yet.

Speaking of which, up next is Ryder's book titled *Spotlight*. All Ryder wants to do is slink away from fame and protect his daughter from the pitfalls of Hollywood. It's harder than he thought it'd be. Especially when Harley Valentine is trying to get the group back together.

I need to give special thanks to my readers for their suggestions.

Thank you to Jeannie Cooper for suggesting the name Eleven for my boy band. When I hear that name now, I can't help thinking of my boys.

And to Samantha Blundell for giving Harley, Ryder, Denver, Blake, and Mason their names.

Want to stay up to date on everything Eden Finley?
Join my reader group: https://www.facebook.com/groups/absolutelyeden/
Alternatively, you can join my mailing list: http://eepurl.com/bS1OFH

ALSO BY EDEN FINLEY

https://amzn.to/2zUlM16
https://www.edenfinley.com

FAKE BOYFRIEND SERIES

FAMOUS SERIES

MIKE BRAVO OPS

CU HOCKEY, co-written with Saxon James

PUCKBOYS, co-written with Saxon James

Up in Flames, co-written with Saxon James

STEELE BROTHERS

Headstrong

Football Royalty

Can't Say Goodbye

Unprincely (MMF)

ACKNOWLEDGMENTS

I want to thank my long list of betas, especially Leslie Copeland and Jill Wexler from Les Court Services, Susie Selva for development and line edits, and Sandra from One Love editing for copy-edits. Thanks to Lori Parks for one last read through for those ninja typos that have the ability to sneak through four rounds of editing. Lastly, a big thanks to Linda from Foreword PR & Marketing for helping get this book out.